# *Velvet Glove*

'If all you meant to do was torture me, why did you bother coming back?' said Tommy. 'Was it something I did? Was I lousy in bed? Too much of a slob?'

Audrey closed her eyes. 'I thought you were the only one who could save me.'

'Then why don't you let me?'

'Maybe I don't want to be saved after all.' As soon as she said it she knew it was true. She wanted to explore the mystery that had begun to open up inside her. There had to be a way to touch that fire again without getting burnt. It was simultaneously frightening and liberating, as if she were perched on the edge of a cliff with a pair of untried wings.

But none of this lessened Tommy's pain. 'If you walk out of here tonight,' he said, 'don't come back.'

# Velvet Glove

## EMMA HOLLY

Black Lace novels contain sexual fantasies.
In real life, make sure you practise safe sex.

First published in 1999 by
Black Lace
Thames Wharf Studios,
Rainville Road, London W6 9HA

Typeset by SetSystems Ltd, Saffron Walden, Essex
Printed and bound by Mackays of Chatham PLC

ISBN 0 352 33448 7

For Spencer, Jake and Elwood – good lads all.

With special thanks to Judy Theis, waitress no more,
but wise to the ways.

# Chapter One

Chains rattled on the rough stucco wall as Audrey stretched her arms. Hours must have passed since Sterling stripped her naked and cuffed her beneath the colonnade. When she rolled her head to work the kinks from her shoulders, her long dark hair tickled her waist. It was a small, sensual stimulation, one among a host. Florida's velvet night had long since swallowed the raging sun. Palms rustled in an orange-scented breeze. Insects creaked and chirped. Tiny lizards skittered across the springy grass as if it were skillet-hot. Fifty yards from where she stood, the pool cast a lurid glow across the lawn. Sterling had chained her here alone. He'd trusted she wouldn't scream. Not that it would matter if she did. Sterling's walled Coral Gables compound was huge. The nearest neighbours were his friends. They had screams of their own to worry about.

Sufficient time had passed to dry her tears, though now and then she refreshed them for the pleasure of wallowing in her misery. She was helpless, truly helpless. She could wallow as she wished. At the moment, she was savouring the delicious emptiness that follows a storm. She was an invisible being: no past, no future, no responsibility except to wait for her master's return. Unlike the rest of the human race, she was free.

She slid down the wall to rest her naked bottom on her heels. The chains caught her wrists, stretching her arms above her head and lifting her breasts. She had a strong, young body, a good offering for her master. Her hips and breasts were generous, her waist nicely curved. Her skin was brown from the sun and grown men had been known to blush at her teasing smile. That was before, though. Sterling never blushed. Sometimes, however, if pushed, anger would darken his aristocratic face. Audrey welcomed his anger. It was a reliable precursor to his lust.

Her breasts swayed as she squirmed on her heels, nipples tightening with the motion, their piercings still sore. Tiny surgical steel barbells traversed the tender peaks. Their ends dangled jewels: four smoky aquamarines. 'To match your eyes,' he'd said as he twisted the posts, each turn an escalating sting. At the memory, heat slithered through the folds of her sex. Her pulse beat softly against her clit and nipples: *pom, pom, pom*, like the batting of a kitten's paw.

She closed her eyes and thought of Tommy. He was the one who'd brought her to Florida in the first place. He was sweet and steady and had a face as open as the Minnesota sky under which they'd both been born. He'd been in love with her since high school, though he'd never said so, not once, because he knew she didn't feel the same. But they were friends – best friends. Nothing could change that. They'd attended the same university, worked in the same city, and when Tommy took his first vacation, he'd invited her along. 'We'll halve our expenses,' he'd said. 'That's what friends are for.' Audrey wasn't fooled. This trip was his last shot at making them

2

more than friends. If nothing happened on those sultry golden beaches, he'd give up on her, once and for all.

Something had happened, though, and on the very first night, but not what either of them expected. Excited by their tropical jaunt, they'd decided to treat themselves to dinner at the Restaurant St Michel. Its old world atmosphere was matched by new world prices, but why be a working stiff if you couldn't enjoy yourself? They waited for a table at the bar, ordered silly drinks with flowers in them, and toasted absent friends. They wore their nicest clothes, grown up clothes. Tommy had gulped at the sight of her slinky red sheath. Audrey had smoothed his conservative tie. The rum made her think: why not sleep with him? Make the poor guy happy. She did love him, after all, more than any of her ex- and very-ex boyfriends.

I will, she thought, watching him stride off, bouncy and slim, for a quick trip to the men's. She was looking forward to seducing him, melting a little as she imagined running her fingers through that carroty hair, above and below, picturing how excited he'd be to have her touch him after all these years.

But then Sterling had strolled over: Sterling in his creamy double-breasted suit; Sterling with his silver hair and smooth, tanned skin; Sterling with his eyes like chips of ice melting in a pool of absinthe. One look and everything Audrey knew about herself began to dissolve.

He was witty and urbane, charming even Tommy when he returned. He joined them for dinner, then clubbing. He seemed a friendly native showing the tourists around, an older man, avuncular, warming himself at the fires of youth. He could order drinks in three languages and paid for them with hundred-dollar bills. He could dance the merengue. He could

3

make Audrey's knees turn to jelly by blowing in her ear. She couldn't hide her attraction, though she tried to for Tommy's sake. Unfortunately, subterfuge was useless. One touch and her cunt swam into her eyes. Finally, with a sigh as old as the cavemen, Tommy ceded the field.

'Be careful,' he said as she kissed him goodbye. 'This guy seems nice enough, but there's something about him I don't trust.'

That, of course, was the attraction.

On the first night, Sterling tied her to his king-size bed and spanked her with the flat of his hand. She writhed on his black satin sheets, her skin throbbing with a pleasure so intense she thought he might have drugged her. But he was the drug: the pain he administered; the control he exerted; the sheer, fascinating force of his personality.

'How did you know?' she asked as he rocked her in his arms, her body shaking from too many bone-wrenching orgasms to count.

'I saw it in your eyes,' he said.

'What did you see? What?' Already she was fading from her own vision, existing only in his. He didn't answer. He shook his finger and smiled. That was part of the pattern, too: withholding answers, withholding tenderness. He grew colder by the day. He wasn't happy unless he drove her to tears, sometimes tears of fury. It didn't matter. He was her drug. She couldn't live without him.

He took her to parties and loaned her to his friends, made her grovel for them, accept their punishments. So long as he was there, she could bear it; could even take pride in her abasement. Life with Sterling was better than a stint in the marines. She had character to spare. Lately, though, he'd been threatening to send her to his cronies by herself.

'You need an iron hand,' he said, when she begged

4

him to stay with her, when she washed his feet with her tears. 'I've spoilt you.'

*Spoilt* me! she thought, but said nothing because in one dark part of her soul she knew what he meant. She needed to be forced beyond her limits, to do what she believed she could not. Only that fire would refine her. Then she would be – what? Something untouchable, she thought. Something hard and pure and perfect.

Something lost, Tommy would have said, but Tommy wasn't here. Tommy was back in Washington, doing his job, living his life.

Footsteps approached, the sort made by thin-soled Italian shoes. They rounded the corner of the colonnade, crunching lightly where sandy soil had blown across the marble paving. She leapt to her feet. He was here. He was back. Her heart thumped in her throat. The footfalls stopped and she strained against the chains. She could not see him clearly. He was a shadow between two pale columns.

'Audrey?' he said, half questioning, half stern.

She dropped to her knees and lowered her head. 'Yes, master.'

He walked to her with slow, deliberate strides. The dove grey linen of his trousers, barely rumpled, broke perfectly over his expensive shoes. Even his feet were elegant, their long, narrow shape hugged by the butter-soft leather. She trembled like a dog, willing him to touch her, to pet her kindly just this once.

Instead, he pulled a whip from behind his back. It had three leather tails and a polished mahogany grip, custom made to fit his hand. Dark droplets fell from the tails to the stone beneath their feet. He had oiled his favourite toy.

'Have you been good?' he said.

'Yes, master.'

He lifted her chin on the handle of the whip. She

5

knew better than to raise her eyes, though she wanted badly to see his expression.

'Has your wait humbled you?'

'Yes, master.'

'No impatience? No boredom?'

'I missed you,' she dared to say.

He slapped her across the cheek with his left hand, the crack of impact louder than the sting. 'I am with you always,' he said.

She knew what he was getting at. He wanted to send her alone to his friends, but did not trust her yet to mind her manners. 'I missed you,' she said again, plaintive and stubborn.

He yanked her to her feet using the chains. He caught her jaw in the vice of his hand and pulled her close. Their faces were inches apart, but still she did not meet his eyes. His nostrils flared above the whitened line of his mouth. His breath came quick and shallow. He smelled of coffee and Grand Marnier.

'I am always with you. Wherever you go, whatever you do, whatever you think, I am the source of it. I will it and it is done in my service.'

Audrey said nothing. His anger was palpable, a testosterone cloud buzzing in the air. Hot, silky fluid leaked from her core and trickled down her thigh. She stared at the crotch of his trousers, the cloth forced outward by the fullness of his erection. She wanted him to take her, between her legs, inside her mouth. She wanted to worship him, to destroy him with the violence of her desire.

Maybe he could read her thoughts. He cursed and slashed his mouth across her own, kissing her hard and wild. She reached for his tongue, trying to deepen the kiss, to make it more personal. As soon as she did, he shoved her away.

'Whore,' he said, his voice husky. 'Turn around and

assume the position. I'm going to whip the skin off your prideful bottom.'

'No,' she wailed, almost wishing she meant it. But they both knew she didn't.

'Turn around,' he said, his voice a low, dangerous growl.

Tears came as she obeyed, and tremors she could not control. The chains crossed to form an 'X' above her head. She flattened her hands against the wall and thrust her bottom outward. Perverse, as always, he made her wait.

He smacked the handle of the whip against his palm. 'You,' he said, 'are a stubborn, wilful slave. My desire should be your only concern. If I wish to leave you here all night, nothing in the world should give you greater pleasure.'

'I love you,' she sobbed. 'I only want to be with you.'

Part of her meant it. Part of her simply wished to drive him to a fury, to make him feel an emotion as intense as her own.

His breath rushed through his nose, a sound that could have been annoyance or excitement. He stepped back. She heard his jacket rustle as he lifted his arm, then the whistle of descent. The first blow licked fire across her buttock. The second made her moan. The third drove her to her knees. The leather tails sang through the air, flinging droplets of oil, curling around her body like amorous snakes. Her pain rose, then twisted, mingling with a deep, bone-warming hum of well-being. She began to drift on its swells as if she were stoned. He'd never struck her this hard before. She hadn't known she could take it. Then she wondered if she truly could. Was the pleasure an illusion? Was her mind losing its grip on what her body was telling it?

'Stop,' she pleaded. 'It's too much.'

But he did not stop until her backside and thighs

were a pulsing mass of heat. In the soft sub-tropical air, her body seemed to expand and contract, more vapour than solid flesh.

He dropped the whip. He tore off his jacket and threw it to the ground. He fell to his knees behind her. His hands hit the wall next to hers, his fingers kneading the flamingo pink stucco. He did not touch her, but his long, lean body arched close enough to blend his heat with hers. Waves of it beat at her, as if from an open oven door.

'Touch me,' she whispered.

He swallowed back a sound, a groan perhaps, or a growl. 'I say when I touch you, not you.' But his lips ghosted over her shoulders, gathering up her sweat. The feathery contact trailed down her spine and on to her buttock. He pressed his teeth into a throbbing, oily welt. She whimpered. He shuddered uncontrollably, then laughed. One hand slid up the front of her thigh and burrowed through her sex.

'So responsive,' he murmured, fondling those warm, slippery folds. 'Little Audrey, little whore. You'll be my masterwork, my finest creation. All the others –' he tweaked her aching clit '– were only practice for you.'

She shivered at the self-absorption in his voice. He had dragged her further than she'd dreamt already. Where would the journey end? What would satisfy his quest for perfection? And where were those others now?

I don't trust him, she thought, and a second later: I don't trust myself.

She moaned at the revelation, moaned and broke into tears. Where was the girl she'd been two months ago, the heedless, vibrant bundle of life? The girl who complained about her job, but was secretly proud to have it? The girl who thought the world was her oyster? How had she lost herself to this? She barely knew Sterling Foster, apart from the fact that he owned a bank and travelled around the world. Since that first night they hadn't had one ordinary conversation. She didn't know his favourite colour, much less the measure of his soul. How had she come to kneel for him, her pride in ribbons, her vanity fed only by the odd, and assuredly manipulative, word of praise?

Tommy would be so ashamed of her.

Recalling her old friend, her sobs grew fiercer, requiring all her strength to squeeze from her body.

'Hush,' said Sterling, but he was drinking in her despair, dropping kisses across her back and reaching beneath her body to fondle her dangling breasts. His longest finger circled one piercing, moving it just enough to hurt. A cry of pain cut through her tears and he began to pant. She knew this sound; knew he could scarcely wait to take her. Once again, she had driven him to the brink of losing control. Shame fought with exultation. She loved this so much, this dark victory over her master. She feared her life would be nothing without it.

His zip rasped down, a soft scream of metal teeth. She felt him fumble to free his cock. He breathed hard against her nape, his crisp, smooth shirt brushing her back. He was trying to pull himself together, to force her to wait. She knew he would fail. A moan caught in his throat, torn from him against his will.

'You don't love me,' she said, goading him to do his worst. 'You only love my misery.'

The burning satin of his cock pressed the burning stripes on her thighs.

'You are your misery,' he said, and thrust into her from behind.

Afterwards, he carried her to her small, simple room, as tender as he'd been in their early days. He kissed

9

the side of her face and said she was his pride and joy. She snuggled closer even as she told herself his praise meant nothing. He didn't love her. He loved the creature he thought he could mould her into.

He laid her on her stomach on the cool cotton sheets. He spread a menthol salve across her welts, tutting like a nurse at her occasional jerk of pain – which didn't preclude his relishing every flinch. Then he slid his hand between her legs. Curving his palm over and around her bottom, he eased two fingers inside her sheath. The intrusion made her moan. He hadn't brought her to climax, not even when he snarled out his pleasure and burst. His angle of entry had been wrong. Maybe he'd meant it to be, as punishment for making him lose control, or maybe just for the hell of it.

Now he worked his second hand under her body. Curling it over her mound, he lightly rubbed her clit. She couldn't suppress a squirm.

He nosed a lock of hair from her cheek. 'Need it bad, don't you, Audrey?'

She bit her lower lip. She did need it bad, but she wasn't sure what answer would make him give it to her. One elegant finger circled her swollen shaft, its pad slick with her juices and the sticky remains of the salve. Abruptly, she realised her pussy was tingling where it hugged his probing fingers. In fact, it was almost cold.

'Oh, God,' she said. 'The salve is numbing me.'

'Is it?' His tone was amused. He shifted his body over hers. 'Let's see how it feels.'

He removed his fingers and slid inside her, hard and thick again, though not as hard as before. His strokes were filling, steady, as was the hand that rubbed her clit, pressing it firmly against the bone, massaging it up and down. He knew how to crank her up as well as she did. She climbed. She teetered. But she did not go over. Then again, neither did he.

He laughed: a little shakily, she thought.

'Yes,' he said. 'This is frustrating.'

He pumped harder, pounding her depths with the smooth, round hammer of his cock. His breathing changed and hers joined it. Then an orgasm like a ring of steel tightened on her cunt. The ache was so piercing that, if it had had a sound, it would have been a bell ringing through a temple. She clamped hard on his pumping cock, drawing the sensation out.

'Jesus,' he said, clearly taken by surprise. He could not hold back his climax. His body jerked, hips jack-knifing in as he gave himself to the spasm.

For a brace of heartbeats he lay on top of her, his clothes damp and warm, his bones hard. Then he pushed up on his arms and pulled free. Suction tugged at her, then released. She was empty again. 'Sleep,' he said, both permission and order.

She didn't turn over until the door closed behind him. Her bottom protested but she ignored it. One of her nipples was bleeding. She'd torn a scrap of healing flesh. Would Sterling say he loved her if he saw it? Or would that miracle require a larger sacrifice than blood? She pushed her tangled hair from her face. I've got to get out of here, she thought, before I lose myself completely.

She sat up and opened the bedside table, removing a calfskin pouch from the wicker drawer. The pack contained her wallet and five thousand dollars in twenty-dollar bills. Sterling had given it to her the morning after her first spanking.

'Your ticket out,' he'd said. 'Because I'll never keep you here against your will.'

She counted the money, bill by bill, then opened her wallet. She stared at her driver's licence. Audrey Popkin, that was her. She pulled out the picture she'd taken of Tommy, Cynthia and crazy Axel Corman. She'd shot them before the Gothic arches of Healy Hall. Axel had his arm around Cynthia and was licking her cheek. Cynthia was trying to squirm away. Tommy was blowing the camera a kiss. A typical college moment. They'd all been students at Georgetown, residents of the same dorm. For four years, this lot were the only people in the world who'd mattered to her; never mind how many boyfriends came and went. Had she lost them as she'd lost her job and her flat? Could she go back? Would they forgive her?

Simply running away from Sterling wouldn't work. His pull was too strong. She had to run *to* someone, someone who would hang on tight and keep her sane. She touched Tommy's puckered mouth. It wasn't fair to make him her saviour, but she didn't think another soul could do it.

'I love you,' she said, and transferred a kiss from the tip of her finger to his face.

She left at dawn, her belongings crammed into a leather tote. To her relief, Sterling slept through her departure. She didn't think he'd force her to stay, but she feared he could persuade her. She walked for miles down the quiet, palm-lined avenue, past Mediterranean villas and walled compounds as grand as Sterling's own. She tried not to imagine what secrets they might hide. If she did, she might turn around. At last she reached a small plaza with a fountain and a pay phone. She called a cab and sat on the kerb to wait.

Despite the bright, warm day, her teeth were chattering. She felt like the survivor of an illness or a fast. Her legs were barely strong enough to hold her. She nudged her dark sunglasses further up her nose and clasped her hands between her knees, squeezing a little to keep them snug. Her long flowered sundress covered the whip marks but didn't make sitting any easier.

She told herself she didn't wish Sterling were here to make it worse.

The cab arrived before a quarter hour had passed. The driver was an older man, spry and cheerful. He jumped out and held the back door for her. If he noticed the bruising on her face and wrists, it didn't dim his smile.

'Airport?' he said, confirming what she'd told the dispatcher. She nodded. He adjusted the mirror and winked at her. 'Looking forward to going home?'

Such a normal question to ask; such an impossible question to answer. But, 'Yes,' she said. 'I am.'

Sterling Foster was disappointed.

He smoothed his hands along the edge of his curving glass-and-steel desk. Plainly, he had been too soft; had allowed Audrey too much independence. Alas, her independence was part of her charm, along with her wonderfully emotional nature. He could play her like a violin: make her laugh, make her cry, and none of her responses were feigned. What she felt, she expressed; not only with her face, but with her body. Her sex was an open book.

He gazed out the picture window at his lush, private compound, his world away from the bank, his tame jungle.

One day, with his help, little Audrey might achieve something rare; might, in truth, become the ideal submissive. He wasn't overly concerned with her crisis of courage. His fault, really. He'd let passion get the best of him. He'd let her tempt him into displaying his humanity. But this would not happen again.

A sleek, black speaker phone sat on his spotless desk. He pressed the silver button that dialled his personal security consultant. The call was answered. 'The bird has flown,' he said.

'Ah,' said the man Sterling only knew as Jake. 'Thought so. The transmitter has been moving all morning.'

'You're tracking her?'

'I can pinpoint her location within a thousand feet. You want my team to bring her back?'

Sterling blinked at the phone. He'd known the man was good, but not that he was too service-oriented to quibble at kidnapping. 'No,' he said. 'No need for that. For the time being, I want her watched and kept safe. When we see where she comes to roost, I'll give you further instructions.'

'Will do,' said the man called Jake.

Sterling settled back in his chair and smiled. Little Audrey was proving quite the source of entertainment.

# Chapter Two

$S$everal hours later, Audrey landed at National Airport, just across the Potomac River from Washington, DC. As always, she found the old terminal depressing, more so today because no one was here to meet her. Brown, beige and grey was not her idea of a cheery colour scheme.

Holdall in hand, she trudged through a concrete-sided tunnel that displayed more grime than architectural flair. Miraculously, she'd made it through the flight without crying. Now she wanted to let go in the worst way. Even Sterling's questionable comfort would have been welcome.

She dropped her bag in front of a pay phone and fed it a quarter with a trembling hand. More than emotion lay behind her shakes. She'd choked down some peanuts on the plane but, other than that, she hadn't eaten since the day before.

Stupid, she told herself. Do you want Tommy to think you're pitiful?

His line rang four times, during which her heart began to pump with a semblance of enthusiasm. Soon, she thought, soon.

His machine picked up.

Shit. She almost rang off, then stopped herself. She could handle this. She'd leave a message and take a cab to a hotel. She had money. Sterling's money. Resolved to act like a grown up, she gripped the earpiece more firmly.

'Hey, Tommy,' she said at the beep. 'It's Audrey. I'm in town again and I thought we could get together.' That was good, she thought. She almost sounded normal. 'I'll be staying at the Latham Hotel on M Street. You can call the desk if you want to –'

'Christ. Audrey.' Tommy's breathless voice interrupted her monologue. A clatter and more curses told her he'd dropped the phone. 'Are you there? Are you all right? Where are you calling from?'

'I'm fine,' she said, smiling through her tears. She pinched the bridge of her nose to bring them under control. 'I'm at the airport.'

'I'll pick you up,' he said without a moment's hesitation. 'I've got to cancel some plans but I'll be there soon. Don't move, OK? I mean, you can move as far as the passenger pick-up point, but do not go anywhere without me.'

'I won't.' She stroked the side of the phone, waited through a brief silence, then heard a low, grateful sigh.

'I can't wait to see you, Aud.'

'Me, too,' she said, and quietly replaced the phone.


Tommy must have flown through the Saturday tourist traffic. The humidity had barely begun to wilt her spirits before he pulled up in front of the blockish concrete edifice. A plywood barrier, the mark of some doomed beautification project, hemmed in the roadway. Despite the queue of cars behind him, he hopped out of his chocolate-brown Volvo and ran around the front to hug her. He was short for a man, just a few inches taller than she was. Hugging him had always

16

been easier than hugging other men. As they held the cosy embrace, his orange hair tickled her cheek. From the way it stuck out, he obviously hadn't taken time to comb it.

'Thanks for coming,' she said.

With a groan, he squeezed her tighter. Their bodies pressed together so closely she could feel how happy he was to see her. Her eyebrows rose at the warm hard ridge that prodded her through his wrinkled walking shorts. It hit her right above the crotch. The sensation was surprisingly pleasant.

Embarrassed, she pulled back and ruffled his hair. 'You need a trim, Mr Black.'

'I know,' he said, trying to smooth the unruly waves. 'You can cut it tonight at my place.' Her startled expression hardened his. 'You are staying with me. You know I've got the room.' He opened her door, then stalked to the driver's side. She watched his dear, mulish face as she fastened her shoulder harness. She didn't tell him she was perfectly happy to stay with him. That would have spoilt his triumph.

He didn't notice the bruises until they'd pulled beyond the shadow of the airport. When he did, fury darkened his lean, freckled cheeks. 'He hit you? He *hit* you?'

Distraction made him swerve in the lane. Audrey steadied the wheel before he could strafe the next car over. 'Watch it, Tommy.'

He didn't look at her again but he ground his teeth together. 'I can't believe that bastard hit you.'

'It's not that simple.'

His glance darted sideways, then back to the road. 'What do you mean?'

'I mean he didn't hurt me without permission.'

'You wanted him to hurt you?' A white Mercedes cut unexpectedly in front of them. Tommy jammed on the brakes by pure instinct. His attention was all on her. 'Answer me, Audrey. Did you want him to hurt you?'

She unclenched her hand from the arm rest. 'Most of the time I enjoyed it.'

She knew Tommy had heard because he gnawed his lower lip. They turned on to GW Parkway, following the broad, silvered river towards Georgetown. The Washington Monument rose above the grassy mall, a marble needle encased in scaffolding. Waiting for Tommy to speak, she felt as much in need of shoring up as the country's most famous phallic symbol. Finally, he cleared his throat. 'So this, uh, this pain thing started right from the beginning?'

'Yes.' She shook her skirt straight. 'Believe me, it took me by surprise as well. I didn't expect to like it.'

His knuckles whitened on the steering wheel. 'If you liked it so fucking much, why aren't you still there?'

For a second, Audrey couldn't breathe. Tommy had never used that tone with her. Never. Of course, she'd never ditched him at the start of a long-awaited vacation, either. When her lungs recovered, she answered as calmly as she could. 'I got in over my head. I realised I didn't trust him. Or myself.'

Tommy digested that, then released a shaky breath. 'Sorry. I didn't mean to yell at you.'

'You weren't yelling. You never yell. I know you were worried about me. Hell, I was worried about myself.'

'But you're OK?' All anger gone, he brushed a lock of hair from her cheek. 'He's not going to come after you, is he?'

'No. Sterling gave me the money I needed to leave. My escape hatch. Though he probably didn't expect me to use it. When he finds me gone, I'm sure he'll write me off as a failed experiment.'

'The only failure is doing shit like that with people you can't trust.'

Audrey bit the side of her thumb. 'Yeah, well. I screwed up.'

'Hey.' Tommy patted her knee. 'All's well that ends well. You'll be back to your old self in no time.'

'Right,' Audrey drawled. She knew wishful thinking when she heard it.

Tommy's house was just as she'd remembered, though what she'd expected to change in two months she didn't know. He lived in Georgetown with the doctors and the diplomats on N Street. Worn red brick and tall black shutters distinguished his narrow, three-storey house. Built in the simple Federal style of 1817, it didn't have a proper garden, just a hedge and some ivy surrounded by a cast iron railing. Garden or no, the house had been pricey. Much to everyone's surprise, Tommy was raking it in, designing websites for corporations around the country. His basement was crammed with computer equipment Audrey didn't have names for.

Inside, the house was deliciously cool but as cluttered as ever. Tommy tossed her bag on a porridge-coloured sofa whose cushions overflowed with computer catalogues. He rubbed his slender hands together. 'Hungry?'

'As a bear.'

'Pizza?' he suggested, nodding towards the phone that hung outside the kitchen. She agreed and he went to arrange delivery.

She wandered through the living room while he ordered their usual large with extra cheese and sausage. 'Onions,' she reminded, and he gave her a thumbs-up. She and Tommy weren't dating, after all; they could eat all the onions they wanted. The chance this evening would end with a kiss was minuscule.

She pawed through a bowl of computer innards, odds and ends he couldn't bear to throw away. Dust coated his two-hundred-year-old Duncan Phyfe end tables. Her favourite chair, a leather monstrosity with a tendency to swallow its inhabitants, was buried in last Sunday's paper. The comics were on top. Tommy always saved the best for last. She lifted the stack in preparation for sinking in. As she did, she found something unexpected: a pink cashmere cardigan with seed pearls embroidered around the edges.

She held her discovery in front of the window, letting the light shine through the delicate knit. A woman's sweater. In Tommy's house.

She was so distracted she didn't hear Tommy return. He snatched the sweater from her and rolled it into a ball. 'That's Cynthia's. She must have forgotten it. She, uh, dropped by last week.'

If he hadn't been beet red, she wouldn't have read anything into his explanation. Cynthia had been part of their gang for ages. So far as Audrey knew, she and Tommy had never so much as held hands. Cynthia had slept with Axel once while under the influence of a controlled substance the scruffy biology major had grown in his bathroom. To that day, Cynthia swore it hadn't happened. Audrey would have doubted it herself, if she hadn't walked in on them. Axel had been grunting like a pig at a picnic and Cynthia had been far from comatose. But that was old news. She needed to focus on the present.

'Tommy,' she said, 'are you and Cynthia dating?'

Tommy blanched. 'No! I mean, not exactly. Just recently, sort of, we've been hanging out together. But it's not serious. Not like a romance.'

His eagerness to deny the relationship amused her. 'I see. You just share a friendly fuck when either of you is feeling horny.' Tommy's face turned scolding, but she saw she'd guessed correctly. She lifted her hands. 'Sorry. Don't mind me and my crude mouth.' She stroked the top of his leather chair, not sure she wanted to know, but felt compelled to ask. 'You were on your way to meet her when I called, weren't you?'

'Yes.' He looked at his feet. 'Does my seeing her bother you?'

Audrey snorted. 'Now there's a trick question.'

He didn't repeat it; he simply waited, letting the silence draw out. Patience was Tommy's secret weapon, patience and expecting everyone to be as decent as himself.

'I guess I mind,' she admitted. 'A little. I'm used to being your best friend.'

He cupped her face. 'You still are. That won't ever change.'

But it had. If he was fucking Cynthia, it surely had.

'Won't she mind my staying with you?'

'I told you, it's not serious. It's like you said: a friendly fuck. Only twice, in fact. Almost accidentally.'

Audrey rolled her eyes. Cynthia Will was not the type to sleep with someone out of friendship, or by accident. Apparently, despite his oversized brain, when it came to women Tommy Black was as clueless as any other male.

Some time later, Audrey sat in his bright, messy kitchen, sipping her way through a pot of black espresso. Sterling hadn't let her drink it. He'd claimed caffeine wasn't good for her. Audrey begged to differ; this jolt of liquid energy was just what the doctor ordered. She propped her feet on the maple table next to an open box of cereal. Kellogg's Frosted Flakes. Tommy's favourite. She was home. She had coffee. It was almost as good as a nice, brisk spanking.

She was savouring her buzz when Tommy padded in, damp from his shower. Like her, he wore sloppy grey trackpants. Unlike her, his chest was bare. It wasn't a bad chest: skinny, but his shoulders were broad and his stomach had definition. Maybe twelve red hairs curled between his small pink nipples. His physique wasn't the sort to make girls swoon, but only the pickiest would kick it out of bed. Audrey wondered if he were trying to show her what she'd been missing.

She hid a smile behind her cup. Tommy was getting his own eyeful. His gaze had locked on the cling of her strappy white undershirt. Actually, it was his undershirt; all the clothes she'd taken to Florida were in his washing machine. She wore a bra beneath the cotton, a filmy Victoria's Secret number. It provided coverage, but not enough for Tommy. He'd been fascinated by her breasts since they grew in. His ogle inspired a familiar glow of satisfaction.

Shaking himself like a dog, he laid a brown zippered case on the table. Audrey swung her feet to the floor. It was her old hair-cutting kit. As a teenager, she'd helped at her mother's salon, washing and pinning Minnesota's twittering blue-haired biddies. She'd assumed she'd lost the kit along with everything else in her flat. She pulled it closer. 'Where did you get this?'

'When you didn't come back, I put your stuff in storage.'

'That was so sweet of you.'

He shrugged. 'It wasn't a big deal. I hired a couple of movers to do the heavy lifting.'

'It was a big deal.' She stood and hugged him, then pushed him into her chair. 'You sit. I'll get you tidied right up.'

He wriggled in anticipation as she draped a towel around his shoulders. Tommy's idea of heaven was a two-hour haircut. When she started a slow scalp massage, his spine appeared to melt. 'You're just a big old tabby cat,' she teased, and worked around his ears.

22

Too blissful to speak, he sighed and folded his arms across his belly. She massaged his scalp until his eyes closed, then gently combed him out. The batteries in her clippers still worked, so she trimmed the back close, the way he liked it. Thick locks of shiny red-gold fell to the towel. In the bright kitchen light, his hair was the colour of a tangerine. Cheerful hair. Tommy's hair. Nostalgia stung her eyes. She'd been cutting his hair for half her life. Would she ever be as innocent as she'd been before she tasted Sterling's whip?

'Asleep yet?' she murmured. He shook his head, but did not open his eyes. She set down the clippers and picked up her shears. This was her favourite part: comb and snip, comb and snip, the rhythm hypnotic and peaceful. She took her time, knowing how much Tommy liked the attention and the touching. Finally, though, there was no more to cut unless she wanted to clip him bald. Rather than stop altogether, she laid the scissors down and ran her fingers through his newly shorn waves. Almost dry now, they slipped like thick, cool silk against her skin.

Tommy shifted in the chair. 'I can feel that between my legs. It's as if your fingers were running up and down my cock.'

Audrey froze. She looked down his chest, past where his hands laced over his navel. An unmistakeable bulge lifted the front of the baggy cotton fleece. He was hard. Her friend, Tommy, was hard. Even more shocking, he wanted her to know it.

Muscles twitched between her legs and heat flooded her face. She started to reach for her brush to whisk the hair from his neck, anything to break the tension, but Tommy caught her hand and held it to his mouth. As if he were breathing her in, he dragged his nose back and forth across her palm.

'You never . . .' she said, then lost her words as he licked up the arch of her thumb.

'I know. I've never said I wanted you, not straight out. But you know I do. We seem to have this rule that I'm not allowed to tell you but –' he curled her hand into a fist and pressed it over his heart '– following the rules hasn't got me anywhere.'

'I don't know what to say, Tommy.'

He turned in his chair and looked up at her, his pale green eyes as clear as a child's. 'Say there's a part of you that wonders what it would be like between us.'

'There is, but –'

A lapful of hair fell to the floor as he rose. He covered her lips with his fingers. 'No buts,' he said and clasped her head between his hands. They were bigger than she remembered and they kneaded the back of her skull in strong, drugging circles. 'I'm going to kiss you now, Audrey, and you're not going to stop me.'

She didn't. She let him kiss her. His lips brushed hers, thin and satin-soft. The sensations startled her. How strange that she could know him so well for so long and not know how he kissed! Her eyes drifted shut as the tip of his tongue teased the seam between, then slid gently inside her mouth. His body sidled closer. His arms circled her back, fingers playing lightly along her spine. She shivered. He held her close, but not tightly. She found herself leaning into him, hugging him back. He was so warm and comfortable. She didn't have to tiptoe to reach him and, really, the kiss was very nice: surprisingly practised. She'd expected a boy's kiss, but his technique was deceptively simple. This kiss did things to her, low and deep. It stirred up a longing to go further. When a sound broke in his throat, tight and hungry, it arrowed straight to her groin.

He was the first to pull back. She wondered if her

eyes looked as dazed as his did. He lifted his hands to forestall a protest she hadn't the strength to make.

'Don't worry,' he said. 'I won't push you tonight. I know you've been through a lot lately. I just want you to think about how good it could be if we gave us a try.'

She touched her mouth. An unsteady pulse beat beneath her fingertips. Her lips felt swollen. He smiled at the gesture and swept his thumb across her cheek.

'Promise me you'll think about it,' he said.

As if she had a choice.

Audrey thought about it as she lay in his guest room on the lumpy double bed. The shell of a computer sat on a table by the window, covered by a plastic sheet, its innards waiting to be cannibalised by its mates in the basement. Tommy had apologised for the mess and the mattress, and told her she could have a spot in his bed any time. 'It's a Serta Perfect Sleeper,' he'd said, sly and hopeful. Audrey had pinched his grinning cheek, but she hadn't said yes or no.

I'm a tease, she thought, a heartless, horrible cocktease. It was time to put out. More than time.

But maybe putting out would ruin everything. Lots of friendships ended when the people involved started swapping sweat. Sleeping together set up all new expectations, expectations Audrey doubted she could meet. She loved Tommy. But she didn't love-love him.

With a tired exhalation, she curled on her side and pressed her hands between her knees. Her body didn't give a damn about her scruples. Her body remembered the nice firm rod between good old Tommy's legs and said: go jump the boy's bones. After two months of spending every waking hour either anticipating sex or engaging in it, she was primed for more of the same. Despite the air conditioning, her skin was moist, her pussy dewed with cream. She wanted to be fucked hard and long and soon. She was sure Tommy would oblige her. She was also sure that, when the steam cleared from the windows, Tommy would want something more.

Damn, she thought, sliding her fingers to the source of her discomfort. Why couldn't life be simple?

Masturbating didn't help. Audrey rolled on to her belly and groaned. She didn't just want release. She wanted the pleasures Sterling had offered, plus the ones he hadn't. She wanted someone else's sweat hitting her skin, someone else's pants gusting in her ear. She wanted warm, human, sex-to-sex contact.

Grumbling under her breath, she rolled out of bed and stared at the guest room door. Tommy's room was right down the hall. Don't think, she told herself. Just do it. But she didn't get halfway there before she turned on her heel and headed for the stairs instead. She was not going to ruin a ten-year friendship just to scratch an itch. If she knew Tommy, and she did, he'd have sweets in his kitchen. God willing, some of them would be chocolate.

But she never reached the kitchen. Tommy sat in the darkened living room at the foot of the stairs. He sprawled on the couch in his boxers, a cold beer wedged between wiry thighs. She winced to think what he must be trying to chill.

'You, too?' he said, and lifted the long-necked bottle to his mouth.

'I, uh, had a yen for chocolate.'

A streetlamp shone through the window, the light catching fire in his hair. 'I know you, Audrey. There are only two reasons for you to be scrounging for chocolate in the middle of the night. Either you're on the rag, or you've got an itch for someone you haven't been able to scratch. Since you haven't been bitchy enough to have your period, my money's on horse number two.'

'Tommy,' she sighed, exasperated by his persistence.

'Audrey,' he sighed back, a perfect mimic.

'I don't want to ruin our friendship.'

'What if I double-triple promise sleeping together won't ruin anything?'

She crossed the worn Turkish carpet and sat on the magazine-littered coffee table. Her legs brushed the couch. She reached out to squeeze his knee. 'You can't promise that. Sex changes everything. And having your heart broken can bring out the worst in a person.'

'I would never, never hurt you.'

'Maybe you'd hurt yourself. Maybe you'd hurt Cynthia.'

He turned the bottle in his hands, his nails shredding the label, his face turned down and shadowed. 'I want you, Audrey. I've wanted you for so long it's making me crazy. I'm not saying that because I want a pity fuck. I'm saying it because I'm afraid if things keep on like this, our friendship will be ruined anyway.'

'Oh, Tommy.' She cupped his cheek. 'Talk about emotional blackmail.'

'I'm not trying to blackmail you. At least, I don't think I am. Oh, hell, is it working?'

She laughed. 'Tommy, Tommy, Tommy.'

He set his beer on the end table and sat up. His thighs warmed either side of hers, their soft hair surprising her. She said his name again in warning. Ignoring her, he put his hands on her waist, then slid them up her ribs. His thumbs grazed her breasts, and not by accident. As she gasped, he pressed inwards over her nipples. He rubbed their centres until they sharpened. A second later, her panties grew wet. She

27

wished they hadn't, but her body had a mind of its own.

'Don't fight it,' he said, lips whispering over hers. 'Let me give you what you need.'

He pushed her back on the coffee table, turning her sideways until they both lay full length across the magazines. She wore his thin T-shirt and a pair of cotton panties, neither of which blunted the feel of his erection, or the way his heart was thudding against her breast. Desire seemed to hum through his muscle and bone, striking answering sparks in hers. He rubbed his weight over her, up and down, restless and hard, using each motion to perfect their fit. The pressure was very, very welcome, a gift to the ache between her legs. He kissed her. It was soft and deep and more intense than she'd dreamt. Ten years of longing were in that kiss. It was incredibly hard to resist.

She moaned against his mouth, still trying to fight the pull. Before she could, he worked his fingers under her panties and drenched them in a welcome another man had trained her to provide. 'You should be wet when I look at you,' Sterling would say. 'You should be wet when I even think of whipping you.' The memory made her gush against Tommy's hand. His breath sighed out in appreciation. Two fingers slid inside her while his thumb stretched upward for her clit. He massaged her as if he meant the digits to meet through her flesh. The pressure caught something sensitive behind her pubic bone, something that made her arch towards his crotch as unthinking as an animal.

'More,' she said, writhing on his hand. He deepened his grip. A second later, she came, crying out at the hard, necessary force of it.

'God, Audrey,' he breathed. 'Do it again.'

She tried to sit up, sanity fluttering across her brain

28

like a ribbon in the wind. Tommy wouldn't let her rise. Too excited to register her distress, he yanked her panties down her legs and buried his face in her pussy. She meant to push him away but found herself clutching his ears instead. Sterling had never gone down on her, not once, and no one had ever done it this well. She could tell Tommy enjoyed this. His mouth was avid, forceful. He licked her all over, then centred on the tiny pulsing rod above her core. She could feel the wetness of his mouth, the subtle texture of his tongue, its strength as it pressed and flicked her clit. The sensations were pure nirvana. She whimpered with a pleasure she could not contain.

His hands slipped under her T-shirt to squeeze her breasts. That was welcome, too. He fondled her with a boy's enthusiasm, a man's skill. His fingers found the piercings. He stiffened, surprised, then stroked the skin beside the silver rods. Audrey's body tightened. What he was doing hurt just a lovely little. He must have read her arousal; maybe tasted it. His respiration increased. He paused for breath, then resumed his oral efforts with even greater fervour. Under the lashing of his tongue, her excitement built quickly to another peak. She went over with a hip-quaking shudder.

With a muttered prayer, he shifted swiftly up her body. Magazines spilt to the floor. His boxers were gone. He was naked. The hot, sweaty thrum of his erection pressed the hair of her mons, insistent, demanding. This was it. If Audrey didn't stop him, two seconds from now, her dearest friend would be shoved inside her cunt. Worse, in two seconds, she'd be grateful.

'No,' she said, loud and sharp. He groaned in disappoint, in reluctance to obey. Ignoring both, she spread her hand across his belly and pushed. 'We are not making love.'

'But you want this.' His voice was rough. He was

stronger than she'd expected. Despite her efforts, the tip of him strained deeper along her cleft, its swollen rim brushing the entrance to her sex. 'You need this.'

'I need to be fucked,' she said bluntly. 'It doesn't particularly matter who's attached to the dick that does it. For you, Tommy-boy, it ought to matter.'

With a huff of disgust, he rolled off her. He dropped back on the couch, his legs gaping, his wrist pressed to his forehead. 'I don't care,' he said. 'I don't fucking care.'

'You do.' She knelt between his feet and ran her hands up his legs. His buttocks rolled against the cushions, taut with unreleased energy. She kissed the soft skin of his inner thigh. 'Why don't I return the favour instead?'

'I don't want favours,' he complained, but he squirmed when she licked a bit higher.

'I'm sure making love to me isn't the only fantasy you've entertained.'

'Well, no. But I wanted –'

'No buts, Tommy.' Remembering his words to her, she lapped the curve of one plump, tight testicle. 'I'm going to kiss you now and you're not going to stop me.'

'But I'd rather –'

She silenced him by taking the crown of his cock in her mouth.

A sound of startled pleasure met her ear. His fingers dug into her scalp. 'Oh, boy. Oh, Audrey.'

She didn't give him time for second thoughts. Her tongue worked the nerves of his glans while her hands wanked his shaft, not fast, but firm, moving the skin over the hardness inside. Lick by lick, rub by rub, she learnt his shape, his textures, the limit to which his crown could swell. When his hips lifted in silent plea, she took him deeper. Half his length pulsed against her palate, then three-quarters. Creating a gentle suction with her cheeks, she licked him like warm, sweet

30

chocolate. This hard, vital flesh belonged to her dearest friend. It demanded her best. She used everything Sterling had taught her: every flick of the tongue, every finger press and stroke.

Tommy was no match for such tricks. Soon he sighed and gasped, fighting not to lose the pleasure before he'd drunk his fill. His thighs trembled with the effort of holding back. Desperate for distraction, he spread her hair across her shoulders, petting it, letting it lift and fall. Then, as if he couldn't help himself, his palms settled on either side of her head, guiding gently, so gently. He said her name as if it were a poem. Audrey. Au-drey. She smiled around his heated flesh. Giving this way was healing. She felt human again, clean. She cupped his scrotum, her thumb rolling, her fingers rubbing.

His breath hitched sharply at the new caress. He must like it, she thought. He must want more. Happy to please, she steadied the rhythm of her mouth to match her hands. With the flat of her tongue pressed firmly to the folds beneath his glans, she worked his most sensitive nerves, loving them, teasing them, making them work their fiery magic. Tommy's thigh muscles clenched. His hands tightened on her head. An odd keening squeezed from his chest. She increased the pressure one fraction more.

He lost the battle.

'Audrey,' he gasped and pulsed down her throat in jets of living heat. His hips jerked wildly. His belly ran with sweat. He was sweet. He was warm. He was limp with a surfeit of bliss. Touching her cheek, he sagged against the cushions. 'Audrey. My God.'

She caught his penis as it slipped from her mouth and petted him across her palm. 'Better?'

'Yes.' The word was drowsy and slow. 'But I still wish –'

'Hush,' she said, and kissed his sleeping shaft.

31

# Chapter Three

Patrick Dugan had grown up in the house in McLean. The wooded lot had been his playground, the two-storey mansion his refuge from the world. The walls held memories, good and bad, which wrapped him like his own skin.

The study, where he stood now, was a symphony of dark wood, Asian carpets and the sweet, heavy scent of pipe smoke. The furniture was old and solid, the books redolent of leather and time. Located in a tower on the eastern end of the house, the study was a man's room, well-suited for grunted conversations over the paper or companionable digestion after a meal. Most importantly, it provided a haven from the fairer sex. This evening, however, none of their number were present. Patrick and his father, the honourable senator from Virginia, had the russet-walled womb to themselves.

As befitted a dutiful son, Patrick was fixing drinks: a brandy for himself and a whiskey, neat and Irish, for his father. The bottles occupied an 1840s side table, a glossy mahogany monster with lion heads and four-toed claws carved into the legs. Its grain swirled like liquid satin beneath the finish and its back curved to hug the tower wall. Patrick had coveted the piece since he was fifteen, when this father–son drinking ritual began.

Not coincidentally, that was also the year his mother ran off to join a commune in Colorado. 'Silly flake almost cost me the election,' his father said whenever the topic arose. Patrick knew he wasn't as flippant as he sounded. He'd stood witness to the senator's silent agony. Thankfully, the fallout hadn't all been bad. When Eva left, the senator realised he couldn't take his only son for granted. Despite his schedule and his natural reserve, he made time for weekly walks around the grounds, and for yachting in Chesapeake Bay. Their awkwardness eased with the work of trimming sails, with the warmth of the sun and the briny sting of the spray. For the first time, Andrew Dugan really talked to his son and, for the first time, his son really talked back. The depth of Patrick's thoughts surprised the senator. Here, unsuspected, was a mind that would, some day, match his own. They debated the issues of the day, rarely agreeing, but never bored. Their outings became more pleasure than duty. Senator Dugan might have lost a wife, but in the process he'd gained a son. Patrick took comfort in the fact that his father did not seem to regret the trade.

He smiled as he set the Jameson's on the small, round table between their chairs. The senator filled the wing-backed leather like a bear in a burrow. He was a big man, with a shock of white hair, twinkling blue eyes and the high colour of a hard-drinking Irishman. Fortunately, he had the constitution of an ox.

He'll live to be a hundred, Patrick thought, relaxing into his own seat. He did not fill the chair as completely as his father. Though he shared the senator's height, and his eyes, and his fondness for fine drink, the rest of him resembled his mother's side of the family: athletic, but elegant, the sort of man who was born to wear good clothes. Since Patrick loved good clothes, that was fine with him. He had a tailor in London who made his wardrobe to order. Tonight he wore a close-cut tweed jacket with high lapels. His father called him a peacock when he saw it; told him he shouldn't waste such finery on his old Da. Patrick assured him he was the most distinguished company he'd had all week. His father's eyes had sparkled with pleasure even as he called him a shameless flatterer.

Now the old bear took a contemplative swallow of whiskey, set the cut-glass tumbler down, and patted the arms of his chair. 'I suppose you're wondering why I asked you to dinner tonight.'

Patrick swirled his brandy around the snifter. 'It occurred to me you might have something on your mind.'

'Need a favour,' said his father.

Patrick's brow lifted. That was a change. Usually his father was trying to do him a favour. 'Name it,' he said.

His father shook his silver head. 'Don't agree until you hear what it is.'

'All right. I'm all ears.'

Rather than answer at once, his father rubbed the brass studs on the arms of his chair. Patrick's interest was seriously piqued then. His father was never slow to speak his mind, at least in private.

'I've been asked to do a favour myself,' he said, 'by a man who once got me out of a bind. I don't know if you recall – I doubt you were more than ten – but back when I ran for governor, the press raised some questions about a real estate venture I'd participated in. I didn't, and still don't, believe my involvement was illegal, but it was open to interpretation. This

34

man loaned me the money I needed to make my share of reparations to those who thought they'd been cheated. I've since paid back the loan, with interest, but this man seems to think I owe him more for keeping the details of our transaction quiet.'

'Could the truth hurt you if it came out?'

His father considered this. 'Perhaps. But not badly. I've made too many allies since those days. I'd say my political future is as secure as anyone's on the Hill.'

'Then turn him down. I can weather a scandal if you can.'

Patrick's father squeezed his wrist in a big, weathered paw. 'You do my heart good, but that's not why I called you here. I've decided I want to do the favour – to do it so well, in fact, that he'll be sorry he ever asked for it. I do not like blackmailers.'

'Neither do I, Da, but what does this have to do with me?'

His father leant forward, forearms to knees, the same pose he used whenever negotiations got tough, whether those negotiations concerned Patrick's future career goals or the latest anti-tobacco bill. 'There's a young woman this man wants befriended and kept safe until she, as he puts it, "regains her senses and returns to his care".'

'And?' Patrick said, unconsciously leaning forward himself.

'And she happens to have come to light three streets north of your bar. Her name is Audrey Popkin. She's twenty-two years old and, apparently, quite the little submissive.' The Senator chuckled at Patrick's sudden start. 'Yes, I thought that might interest you.'

Patrick got to his feet. He buttoned his snug tweed jacket, then unbuttoned it and smoothed his fitted vest. 'I guess this means you know about my ... extracurricular activities.'

35

Leather creaked as his father settled deeper in his chair. His voice was its quietest, and its most gentle. 'I probably know more about your private life than any father should, but in my position, I have to. Unfortunately, my opponents don't restrict themselves to digging up dirt on me. I need to know everything I might have to defend myself against.'

Patrick rubbed the sides of his face, his five o'clock shadow rasping his palms. 'I ought to be furious.'

'I've never interfered,' said his father. 'You have to give me that.'

'Yes, I'll give you that, though at the moment I'm wondering why you restrained yourself.' Patrick turned to face him. To his surprise, his father's expression was fond.

'I saw you were discreet and responsible,' he explained, 'and your partners seemed the same. Frankly, Patrick, I was grateful you'd turned out to have more sense than your mother. A halfwit son could do me more damage than one whose sexual habits are somewhat beyond the norm.'

Patrick didn't know about that, but he wasn't going to argue. He returned to his seat and downed a swallow of brandy. 'What exactly do you expect me to do with this girl, this Audrey Poppins?'

'It's Popkin, and I expect you to do what Sterling Foster couldn't.' His blue eyes glowed with anticipated vengeance. 'I want you to master her, Patrick, if that's the appropriate term.'

'Why do you think I'll have any more success than he did?'

'Patrick, Patrick.' As always when he was pleased with himself, his father put the Irish in his speech. 'You have your Da's brains and your mother's charm. My faith in you is boundless. Besides which, Sterling Foster is an arrogant, cold-hearted son of a bitch. I'm thinking a lassie that young might want a bit of warmth with her whipping.'

Patrick slung one foot over his knee and gripped the ankle. This had to be the strangest conversation he and his father had ever had. Stranger still were the prickles of interest that swept him from scalp to toe. He wanted to do as his father asked. He wanted to master this mysterious Audrey Popkin who'd run from her icy lover. But that wasn't how he chose his partners. He loved a challenge, yes; his pride demanded one, but not at an innocent's expense.

'What about her?' he said.

'Her?'

'The girl. What about her feelings? Suppose she forms a genuine attachment to me?'

'All the better.'

'Maybe from your point of view.'

'From hers, too,' said his father. 'Believe me, son, any man who pries that girl away from Sterling Foster will have done her a lifelong boon.'

'I don't know, Da. Domination and submission isn't a game.'

'Just take a look at the lass,' said the senator. 'Then tell me she isn't worth rescuing.'

With a quiet sigh, Patrick followed him to his Empire-style desk. A fat brown folder marked PRIVATE sat on the green marble top. The senator removed a set of black and white pictures and spread them across the desk. They were obviously surveillance photos; the subject betrayed no awareness that she was being observed. In one, the photographer had caught her coming down the six curving front steps of an elegant Georgetown home. Patrick recognised the address. He'd considered buying it when it came on the market a year earlier, but it hadn't offered as much privacy as his penthouse. A man of Patrick's interests was better off not sharing walls with his neighbours.

He focused on the girl. She was young, so young it hurt his chest to look at her. She had long wavy hair, dark brown or black, and a soft, oval face. Her eyes seemed huge, startled, as if life were taking her by surprise. Her jaw hinted at stubbornness, as did the way she held her hands slightly clenched. Did she fist them out of anger or determination? The latter, he decided. Her mouth was too generous and too relaxed to suggest a habitually bad temper. A pair of baggy khaki trousers sagged below the slash of her navel. Her shirt was a cropped pocket T. Ironically, her body seemed all the more alluring for being so unflatteringly clothed. Her breasts were high and full. Her belly possessed a curve that cried out for admiring hands. Her bottom was aggressively pert. What a joy those cheeks would be to punish! He studied her face again, at the big, lost eyes. How had a woman with eyes like that found the strength to run from anyone?

'She is pretty,' his father said, dry and amused.

Patrick bristled that his father read his interest so easily. 'That's really not the point.'

'And young,' his father continued, tossing another picture out. This one showed Audrey with a friend in front of an ice cream parlour: Thomas Sweet's, he thought, up on Wisconsin. She was laughing full out, her head thrown back, her throat exposed, her eyes slitted with pleasure. The cone was dripping down her hand. 'She's fresh out of college, Pat. Still wet behind the ears. At the very least, you could set her on the right path; teach her what she ought to look for in a master.'

'You're not going to give up until I say "yes", are you?'

'Have I ever?'

Patrick met his father's grin with a grimace. 'No, Da. You haven't.'

His father gathered up the pictures and slid them back into the folder. He handed it to Patrick. 'The pictures are from Sterling's investigator. The report is from mine. Read it over tonight and give me your decision tomorrow.'

Patrick took the packet and nodded. He appreciated his father's diplomacy, but they both knew his decision was made. For better or worse, Audrey Popkin had a new dom.

Audrey spent Sunday morning reading the classifieds and growing increasingly disgusted with the dearth of interesting jobs for which she was qualified. A degree in English Literature simply didn't prepare one for much. Before she'd tossed her life into the sewer, she'd been an assistant manager at a trendy boutique on Wisconsin Avenue. She'd worked her way up from a clerk's position and, while the pay wasn't astounding, she'd loved the job. She had a light, friendly manner the customers appreciated. She made them enjoy shopping at Regina's, whether they bought anything or not. Her boss had taught her every visitor should leave happy. That way they'd come back. Regina had been both friend and mentor to her. Recalling the way she'd let the woman down, Audrey dropped the paper and sighed.

Tommy looked up from the business section. He lay on the floor in a ragged T-shirt and jeans. 'You don't have to worry about finding a job right this second,' he said. 'I don't mind putting you up for a few weeks.'

'I don't know how to break this to you, Mr Entrepreneur, but if I start job hunting tomorrow, it will probably take more than a few weeks.'

Tommy shrugged and went back to reading. 'Why not ask Regina to give you your old job back?'

'Right.'

'She might do it. You always said she liked you.'

'Which is why she won't take me back. Not that I blame her. If I'd cut and run on me without notice, I wouldn't forgive me, either.'

'Hey, none of that.' Tommy pushed to his knees and scooted across the rug to her chair. Once there, he clasped her calves and put his head in her lap. 'It'll work out. You'll see.'

Audrey smiled and stroked his hair, though she suspected he'd been waiting all morning for an excuse to touch her. 'I'm going for a walk,' she said. 'Do you want anything from the grocery?'

'A box of condoms,' he mumbled into her thigh.

'Dream on,' she laughed.

'Believe me, I will.'

Ten minutes later, she was skipping down the front steps, her hand trailing down the curved black railing. A couple standing at the end of the street caught her eye, but when she turned her head, they were gone.

On Monday, Audrey swallowed her pride and returned to the boutique. The meeting with her former boss went as she'd expected. With her mouth pursed primly, Regina said she appreciated the apology but, in all honesty, she didn't want to hire a manager she couldn't trust. Audrey considered grovelling, then discarded the idea and left.

No grovelling except for fun, she decided with a flash of humour that surprised her. She shrugged to herself. The interview could have been worse. Regina had agreed to give her a reference, though Audrey doubted it would glow.

Resigned to finding a job the hard way, she ducked into a stationer to buy a notebook and pen. She had a

CV to write, spotty as it was. When she emerged, she noticed a tall, gangly man in a black T-shirt and jeans. He was peering into a shop window across the street. An expensive camera hung around his neck.

The hair on Audrey's arms stood up. She was certain she'd seen this man outside Tommy's the night before. He'd been with a woman and he'd worn a different shirt, but the left back pocket of his jeans was ripped in exactly the same place.

He'd been wearing a camera then, too.

Immediately she looked away and turned on to M Street, her heart pounding frantically in her chest. Was Sterling having her watched? Was he crazier than she'd thought? She clutched her parcel to her side. What should she do? She didn't have enough cash on her to hail a cab. Of course, it might not matter if she did. If her watcher knew where she was staying – and it seemed likely he did – he'd simply find her again at Tommy's. She walked faster, beginning to sweat as her nervousness combined with DC's end-of-summer heat. She could call a cop but she'd have to explain why she thought someone was following her. If she didn't explain, she'd sound paranoid.

But maybe she was paranoid. Maybe her experience with Sterling had spooked her so badly she was jumping at shadows.

Unable to bear the suspense, she ducked into the next doorway and looked back the way she'd come. The man with the camera had stopped to chat with a woman who held a straining puppy on a leash.

See, she told herself. He's out for a walk. You're imagining things. But she couldn't help seeing how his eyes scanned the street, as if searching for something he'd lost.

Shit, she thought. She looked at the door behind her. DUGAN'S said the curly, gold-leaf lettering, obviously denoting the entrance to a bar. She pushed through it. It was too early to be drinking, but what the hell. Any port in a storm.

The bartender looked as surprised to see her as if she'd walked in naked. He was tall and had short dark hair, so short she thought he might be trying to hide a curl. A pair of red braces stretched over his blinding white shirt. His sleeves were rolled to his elbows. He was washing beer mugs and setting them to dry on a long checked towel. By the fine lines around his eyes, Audrey judged him somewhere short of forty.

'Hey there,' he said, arms in the sink. 'I'd tell you we weren't open yet, but you look in dire need of a cool libation.'

'I'm in dire need of something,' she muttered. She glanced back over her shoulder. Surely the man wouldn't follow her in here, if he *was* following her. With a shudder of unease, she slid on to the nearest stool.

'Name your poison,' he said.

He had a lilt, but not an accent, as if the Irish in him were a few generations removed. He also had a big Roman nose and twinkly blue eyes, really nice twinkly blue eyes. Audrey told herself to ignore them. She had enough on her plate right now. She stared in confusion at the array of bottles on the mirrored shelves behind him, many of which had foreign labels. Blue curaçao, what was that? Then a familiar logo caught her eye. 'I'll have a Killian's Irish Honey.'

The bartender put on a brogue. 'Lassie, with taste like that you can have it on the house.' He set the beer before her and popped the cap with a flourish. 'Hard day?' he added, all broad-shouldered, twinkling charm.

She could have resisted the charm, but not the

shoulders. They looked perfect for leaning on and she was feeling vulnerable. 'I think a man is following me,' she said.

The bartender's countenance changed so swiftly it startled her. His twinkle turned hot and his face went hard. To her amazement, he vaulted over the bar without overturning a single glass. Before she could catch her breath, he gripped her upper arm and pulled her towards the door. 'Let's see who's out there,' he said in a tone as dangerous as any she'd heard from Sterling. Despite the situation, a thrill slithered from her ear to her groin.

At the entrance, he shouldered her behind him and pushed the yellowed lace curtain an inch from the edge of the window. 'That man across the street? With the telephoto lens?'

'Yes.' Her limbs were trembling, and not merely from the presence of her watcher. The bartender reached determinedly for the doorknob. Sanity pinched her conscience. 'Wait!' she said. 'What are you going to do?'

He stopped to smile at her. 'Don't worry. I'm just going to talk to him. You stay here.'

He loped through the midday traffic as if he were used to dodging cars, and to running. As he'd promised, he began by talking to her watcher, but the conversation quickly turned heated. After a few exchanges, the watcher shoved the bartender's chest. The bartender's right hook was almost too quick to see. The man stumbled to his knees. When he regained his feet, blood dripped from his nose. He stared at the bartender as if he were crazy, then took off at a run.

The bartender's return to the bar was as sprightly as his exit.

'There,' he said, wiping bloody knuckles on the

cloth that hung from his waist. 'Now you can enjoy your beer in peace.'

'Thanks,' she said, grateful for his lack of questions. 'I owe you one.'

He smiled as if he liked the sound of that. The calculating gleam in his eyes reminded her of Sterling. She shivered, but the gleam was gone almost as soon as it had appeared. 'Always happy to do a favour for a pretty girl.'

I'll bet, she thought.

He didn't vault the bar this time, but strolled to the end where a section of counter flipped up for entry. Audrey watched him walk. He had a pair of legs on him, he did, and a beautifully high butt. Warmth swelled in her groin, a brightening ember of interest. Her nipples were always a little hard, since the piercing, but now they pulsed with tiny shards of fire. She doubted her bra could hide them and she wasn't counting on the dim light, either. If the bartender noticed her arousal, she feared she'd melt on the spot. Get a hold of yourself, she ordered, but her gaze devoured the muscular symmetry of his back. He had the build of a well-fed model, the grace of an athlete, and a smile that boded trouble.

Looking as if he were amused by her inner struggle, he extended his bruised hand across the bar. 'I should introduce myself. I'm Patrick Dugan.'

She allowed her clammy hand to be swallowed by his warm one. 'You own this place?'

'Lock, stock and wine barrel.'

She swivelled backwards on her stool to peruse the dark interior, and to give herself a chance to calm down. This was definitely a watering hole for grown ups. No sports pennants hung on the panelled walls. No graffiti scratched the heavy wooden tables. Brass lamps lit the walls above the booths. The leather upholstery was a rich shamrock green.

'It's very nice,' she said.

He pointed past her shoulder at the wall. 'That's ebony-black bog oak. Shipped all the way from Ireland.'

'It's wonderful,' she said, though she had no idea if it was. She turned back to her beer. She'd better finish it quickly, she thought, and remove herself from temptation's twinkly eyes.

As blithe as ever, Patrick resumed washing glassware. 'You know,' he said. 'I didn't take you seriously when you said you owed me one, but there is something you could do for me.' Audrey tensed. He set a wine glass on the drying cloth. 'I'm short two waitresses, you see, and I'm that close to desperate. I thought, perhaps, since it's one in the afternoon and you're having a beer, you might be available for a job.'

'Maybe I'm just a lush.'

Patrick skated the tip of his index finger down her nose. As light as the touch was, it sent a tingle down her spine. 'I know a lush when I see one, lassie.'

The way he said 'lassie' put more than butterflies in her stomach.

'My name is Audrey,' she said.

'Audrey,' he agreed, but that wasn't much better. He set his elbows on the bar and leant close enough for her to smell the soap he washed in. 'Got any experience, Audrey?'

The tickle of his breath turned her brains to mush. 'I did wait tables at school.'

'You see.' He swept his dangerous finger around the shell of her ear. 'It's fate.'

She jerked back with a shaky snort. 'It's convenient, anyway.' He looked at her with innocent eyes and a ridiculous pout. *A big, bad wolf: who, me?* She shoved her hair from her face and shook it down her back. Sterling never would have pouted. In a way, though,

45

that was a point in the bartender's favour. Maybe he wasn't a Sterling clone. She did need a job. And he had bloodied his knuckles on her behalf. 'Oh, all right,' she surrendered. 'But it's only temporary, just until you can hire someone for real.'

His smile was pure devilry. 'Ah, lassie, you're going to enjoy working for me.'

But Audrey wasn't as gullible as she used to be. 'That,' she said, 'remains to be seen.'

# Chapter Four

$A$udrey was not what Patrick had imagined. Beauty he'd expected, and youth, both of which she had in uncomfortable plenty. Her intelligence, however, was a surprise. Sterling Foster's detective hadn't believed he'd been spotted by a bimbo barely out of her teens. He'd insisted someone else must have blown the game.

Patrick smiled to himself as he buffed the antique bar. The private dick had been – well, a dick, but it was nice of him to chase Audrey into his arms, however inadvertently. Too bad she was as skittish as a cat with a can on her tail. Something would have to be done about that.

He was carefully weighing options when his hired entertainment breezed in. Slim and elegant, Basil Arch had a dry cleaning bag draped over his shoulder. Within the plastic, sequins sparkled in a long, clinking flow. The dress was undoubtedly his. Basil became Basha when he performed, though he was more than a female impersonator. As far as the audience was concerned, Basha was not a man pretending to be a woman; Basha was a skilled jazz stylist with an intriguing, androgenous face. She performed at Dugan's Thursday through Saturday night, her disguise so convincing few patrons dreamt she wasn't female. Now the singer grabbed the stool nearest to Patrick.

'Hot as hell out there,' he said in his husky contralto. 'Isn't summer over yet?'

Patrick tossed him a frosty Perrier, which he caught one-handed. 'You're not due in tonight. What happened? Your air-conditioning go out again?'

'Yes, and it's the third time this month.' Basil threw his plastic-wrapped gown over the bar and ran the cold green bottle around his face. 'If you paid me more, I'd move into your building. I bet your landlord bows when you walk in.'

'Only at Christmas bonus time. Here, give me that.' He took the bottle from Basil and unscrewed the top. Basil had long, lily white hands, his only overtly feminine feature. When he performed, he covered his plain brown hair with a Harlow-blonde wig. His face didn't look like a woman's until he painted it. At the moment, it simply looked tired. Patrick didn't know much about Basil's private life except that, lately, it hadn't been going well. A long-time lover had died in an accident, he thought, though he wasn't certain of the details.

Basil chugged the mineral water and 'ah'ed with satisfaction. He wiped his mouth on the back of his hand. 'I really could use a rise,' he said.

Patrick started to say 'no', then stopped himself. 'All right. I'll pay you an extra fifty a night.'

Basil clunked the bottle down. 'All right? No arguments, just all right?'

'I need a favour.'

Basil narrowed his coffee brown eyes. 'What sort of favour?'

'I need a beard.'

'Then you should grow one.'

48

'I need the kind of beard a man uses to protect his reputation, a human beard.'

Basil scratched his temple. 'Unless I'm sadly – or perhaps happily – mistaken, you, Patrick Dugan, are a flaming heterosexual.'

'I know. I need someone to think I'm gay. Not permanently. Just until I've snuck past her defences.' Patrick rubbed his chin, remembering the private investigator with the telephoto lens. 'Actually, I wouldn't mind if two someones thought I was gay. I think you'll have to move in with me. It won't be convincing unless you do.'

Basil began to laugh. He laughed until tears appeared in the corners of his eyes, until Patrick had to slap him on the back for fear he'd choke. 'If you think this is ridiculous, Basil, just say so.'

'No, no.' Basil waved the suggestion away. 'I'd be honoured to serve as your beard.'

'You'd have your own room,' Patrick said, to ensure Basil understood he didn't want more than a pretence.

'Yes, yes. I'm sure everything will be lovely.' He stood, wiped his eyes and slung his cleaning over his shoulder. 'You don't have a problem with cats, do you?'

'No-o,' Patrick said, immediately picturing a horde of caterwauling beasties.

'Just one small, fluffy kitten,' Basil assured him. 'You won't even know he's there.' He was still chuckling as he plunged back into the heat. It was a sniggering sort of chuckle, as if Basil knew some joke that Patrick didn't.

What am I getting into? he wondered, but it was too late to turn back. At any rate, this wasn't the worst idea he'd ever had. Women fell for gay men all the time. He had no reason to think Audrey would be different.

* * *

Audrey tucked the celebratory Merlot beneath her arm and slid her key into Tommy's door. The trip to the wine shop had been a defiant little thrill. Like coffee, alcohol was a vice Sterling had forbidden her. Today, she could almost thank him. Her panties were sticky by the time she'd finished browsing the shelves, her arousal intensified by memories of her afternoon with the big twinkly wolf. That bartender, that Patrick Dugan, had radiated sex appeal. If she closed her eyes, she could see the dark hair on his forearms; could smell his soapy-musky scent. Her tongue curled over her upper lip as she imagined how he'd taste. That mouth of his . . .

She shook herself. Enjoying her thrill was one thing. Wallowing in a dangerous attraction was quite another. She could only hope Tommy wouldn't guess how vulnerable to seduction she was. In fact, she hoped she wasn't being foolish by adding wine to the mix. She needed to hang on to her inhibitions, not cast them to the wind.

She swung the door shut behind her and kicked off her shoes. To hell with worrying. She had a job, however modest, and a friend, however infatuated, and the slippery, pulsing heat between her legs proved she was thoroughly alive. With or without Sterling, her zest for adventure remained. She loosened the cork, grabbed a pair of wineglasses from the kitchen, then tiptoed down the basement stairs to surprise her hard-working chum.

The basement was musty and cool and dark, like the den of some futuristic animal. The walls were brick, the floor covered with plastic mats to cut down on static. Beneath the mats, snarls of electrical cord snaked from one bank of equipment to the next. She counted six monitors, three modems and God knew what the rest of the stuff was. Tommy sat before the largest monitor, a twenty-one inch, high definition screen. He was scrolling through a website with so much concentration he didn't hear her come up behind him. As she watched over his shoulder, a woman with big naked breasts flashed into an animated box. 'Come see our XXX beauties,' the caption said.

'What *are* you working on?' she asked.

Tommy jumped, but didn't turn around. In the light from the screen, she saw he was blushing. 'I'm making sure my last update downloaded correctly.'

'This is your site? You designed this?'

'Actually, I own it. Here. Take a look.' He rolled a second chair next to his and returned the display to the top of the page. Tommy might have been embarrassed by her intrusion but, evidently, he had no intention of acting ashamed.

She slid into the chair and poured them each a glass of wine. Tommy took his without comment; no surprise, considering how lost he tended to get in his work. Maybe later he'd think to ask what the occasion was. She swallowed her amusement in a rich, red sip, grabbed the mouse and began to explore. The site was called Private Pleasures and, for a fee, it offered visitors a collection of pornographic stories and pictures. Sampling them, Audrey experienced a warmth the Merlot could not account for. 'Tommy,' she said, somewhat bemused. 'These stories are all about masturbation.'

His response was bland. 'Yes, they are,' he agreed.

Audrey giggled at a reference to a towering fountain of come. 'Well, my English professors wouldn't be impressed, but these stories do, um, have a certain energy. And people pay to read them?'

'Lots of people. The sponsors pay, too.'

'Ah, the triple-X, boob-flashing fellows.'

He covered her hand before she could click to another story. 'You're in no position to judge me.'

51

'I'm not judging, I'm teasing. OK, maybe I'm judging a little, but you took me by surprise.'

Tommy released his grip. 'I have had one or two thoughts I haven't shared with you.'

'That I can believe.' Curious, she clicked on a button marked EXTRA. After a few seconds' load time, she found herself on a page called Spanker's Heaven. A woman in a French maid's uniform was baring her big pink bottom to the world. Audrey covered her mouth with both hands.

'If you laugh,' Tommy warned, 'so help me, I'll kill you.'

Audrey shook with the effort but managed to hold her hilarity inside. Was this the same man who'd sputtered with outrage over a few consensual bruises? It was too rich. She was never, never letting him live this down.

'My customers asked for it,' he said, bristling with defensiveness, though she hadn't said a word. 'Spanking stories are very popular. For God sake, Audrey, it's not the same as doing it.'

'Of course not,' she soothed, oozing insincerity and enjoying every drop. 'It's not remotely the same as doing it. I'm sure you, for instance, wouldn't consider raising your hand to a woman's poor, defenceless bum.'

'I wouldn't!'

'But you enjoy reading about it, don't you?'

He ran his thumbs across the edge of the keyboard. 'Sometimes. The better stories.'

'And which are the better stories?' With teasing fingers, she crawled up his knee. 'The ones where the boy gets what's coming to him or the girl?'

He smacked her hand away. 'I am not spanking you and that's final. And stop grinning like that.'

But she couldn't straighten her mouth. For all his protests, her friend was breathing as if he'd run up a flight of stairs. He finished his wine in one angry swallow and thunked the glass on to his desk. Silly boy. Alcohol wouldn't cool him off. Her gaze slid down his chest. The bulge in his jeans was big enough to brag about, a real handful. One of the faded spots in the denim was threatening to split. Oh, his hypocrisy made her feel so naughty. She ran her tongue around the rim of her glass, savouring the smoky taste.

'I was just thinking,' she said with an exaggerated pout. 'It's too bad we didn't meet when we were young enough to play doctor.'

'I'm not playing doctor with you, either! The next time we do anything, we'll be doing the real thing. Slot A, Tab B. Humping up and down. Sweat on the sheets.'

'Actually –' she dragged her hand down his T-shirt until it covered his twitching diaphragm '– I was thinking of exploring a fantasy from your other site, the Private Pleasures one. You could watch me and I could watch you. We wouldn't even have to touch.'

'And that makes it better?'

Though Tommy sounded appalled, she noticed he was rubbing his hands along his thighs. She fanned her fingers across his tight little belly, then drew them up like spider's legs. He shivered at the light scratching so close to the swell of his cock. 'Come on, Tommy,' she purred. 'You must have thought about it. I know I have. I've never seen a man get himself off.'

'What about Sterling?'

'Sterling didn't relish the idea of losing control in front of me.' She moved the heel of her hand until it rubbed the hummock at the top of his zip.

Tommy's hips rolled sharply upward. 'So you've never . . .?'

'Never. And I've never done it in front of anyone,

either.' She finished her wine, swallowing slowly, knowing his eyes followed the motions of her throat. Her inebriation was slight but it joined with her arousal to deepen her voice. 'Imagine, Tommy, watching a woman pleasure herself. No distractions, no pressure, close enough to smell the cream dripping from her sex. You can't really watch the way you'd like when you're participating, can you?'

His face was the colour of rust. 'Damn you, Audrey.'

She took his curse as acceptance and mentally rubbed her hands. Good, good, good. Right or wrong, she wanted to play with Tommy in the worst way. Last night's taste had been very sweet. She stood and tugged him from his chair. 'Let's go upstairs and get to it. I trust you've got a supply of baby oil?'

'Yes,' he said, glumly. Despite his tone, the hand that held hers was hot.

Audrey had been in Tommy's bedroom twice: once when he moved in and once to help him pick a tie. It was very navy: the walls, the rumpled coverlet, the thick wool carpet. Thankfully, he'd left the trim white, otherwise she'd have thought she was trapped inside a blueberry. The furniture was a clear-finished knotty pine, 1800s farm-style. Everything was attractive, but Tommy hadn't really stamped the room with his personality, unless you counted the mess.

As she set the wine on the bureau, he dashed ahead to yank the bedcovers straight and snatch some dirty clothes off the floor. Laundry clutched to his chest, he looked around as if he couldn't think what to do next. Audrey nodded at an empty wicker basket in the corner. 'Right,' he said, tossing his armload in. His shoulders sagged. 'I don't know, Audrey. Maybe this isn't such a good idea.'

Rather than argue, she crossed the room and kissed

him. His mouth responded at once, opening, reaching. He moaned at the tangling of their tongues and wrapped her in a breast-flattening, groin-grinding embrace. The friction was heaven. She crooked her knee around his hip and crushed her mons over his bulging zip. That was even better. God bless being the same height. Tommy liked the pressure, too. His fingers dug into her buttocks so hard they hurt.

He broke free with a gasp. 'I want the whole thing, Audrey. I want us to make love.'

She let her foot slide back to the floor. 'I'm not ready for that.'

He muttered something she didn't catch, then shook himself. 'OK. You're not ready. I can handle that. I can do this one step at a time. Shit.' He turned halfway around as if lost. 'Where's that baby oil?'

She caught his wrist before he went in search of it. 'The oil is for you, not me. And I thought you might want me to go first.'

'It's in the bathroom,' he said, pointing vaguely, a funny edge of panic in his voice. He waved towards the bed. 'You make yourself comfortable. I'll be right back.'

He was gone long enough for her to get naked and arrange herself across the mattress, a process that required the removal of a dog-eared Ludlum novel and a box of unopened floppy disks. She glanced at the bedside clock. He'd been gone ten minutes. Perhaps he was giving himself a pep talk. She pictured him before the mirror. 'You can jack off in front of Audrey. You're hard enough, and you're brave enough and, by golly, you know she'll like it.' She was biting her lip to control her smile when he returned. He'd brushed his teeth and hair. He might have shaved, too, though his beard was so light it was hard to tell. Wrapped in a terry cloth robe, he carried a bottle of baby oil and a box of condoms. He dropped the condoms on the bedside table.

Audrey raised her brows at them.

'Just in case,' he said, then let his breath gust out at the sight of her. As if he'd gone weak-kneed, he dropped to the edge of the mattress. 'You are so beautiful.' He touched the sparkly aquamarines that dangled like counterweights around her nipples. 'These are ... These make me so hot, Audrey, even if they must have hurt like hell.'

She laughed and made them jiggle for him.

Tommy shook his head. 'Aren't you the least bit uncomfortable with this?'

'How can I be, when you look at me like that? I feel wonderful.'

He plucked at his robe. 'Well, I'm uncomfortable. You've never seen me naked in the daylight. I'm short and skinny and as white as a corpse.'

'Tommy.' She kissed his forehead. 'You are lean and wiry and as pale as fresh buttermilk. You're a pocket Adonis. Now take off that robe. If I'm naked, you should be naked.' She lowered her voice. 'I want to watch you watching. I want to see what it does to you.'

He hemmed and hawed, but finally shrugged off the robe. He'd lost his erection but, other than that, he was everything she'd claimed. His fair, freckled skin flowed smooth as cream over slender, perfectly formed limbs. He was sleek and lightly muscled, and the red-gold thatch between his legs made her want to bury her fingers and play. Being so slight made his penis look larger, or maybe it wasn't entirely soft. She let herself stare at it; let herself smile. The head twitched and began to swell. She pressed her tongue between her teeth. The shaft thickened; wavered towards horizontal. Her pussy pulsed with excitement. This had to be one of the best shows God had ever invented. 'Woo-woo,' she said, fanning her face.

With a bashful grin, Tommy held out the baby oil. 'I want you to use this. I want you to rub it on your breasts.'

'Well,' she drawled, 'since you inspired this game, I suppose I could take requests.'

Wide-eyed and wider-mouthed, he watched her smooth the oil around the tanned, silky globes. Then, knowing his attention was hers, she dripped some on her nipples. Tommy wet his lips and swallowed. Laughing to herself, she pinched the reddened peaks. They lengthened beneath the plucking; grew tender and glistening. Completely rapt, he scooted closer, his hip brushing hers. Audrey looked down. His erection had recovered with a vengeance, bobbing in his lap as if it were set on springs. It was a lovely cock: smooth, lightly veined, with a crown so full and round it cried to be touched. Only her memory of the rules she'd set kept her from reaching out to stroke it.

Settling lower on the pillows, she dragged one slippery hand down her belly. His eyes followed the motion as if her fingers were hooks. She lifted her knees; let them fall slowly to the side. The leg nearest Tommy came to rest on his flank. His skin was wonderfully warm. Moving even closer, he propped one hand beside her waist.

'Spread yourself,' he said. 'I want to see all of you.'

The tension in his voice sent a surge of heat through her sex. She slid fingers from both hands between her labia and pulled them wide. A draught brushed her pussy, a taunting ghost of a touch. Her clit felt huge and ripe, pulsing helplessly in the open air. He bent closer yet, his forehead beaded with sweat. 'Ah,' he said, the sound admiring and pained. 'You're so – you're red, Aud. I can see you, the tip of you. It's shining and dark like a little berry.' His hand fisted on his thigh. 'It's so pretty.'

His admiration unravelled the last of her patience. She couldn't wait. She had to touch herself. She began to rub her clit, two fingers working the hood, palm pressing her mons. Her free hand rose to her breast where she flicked her thumb across her nipple, light and quick, each twinge magnified by Tommy's eyes. Her need coiled tighter. What had started as a show turned into something necessary. She rubbed the pliant flesh of her sex, deeply, strongly, pinching the hood against the little rod. She wanted to come so badly, she didn't worry how she looked. The peak was all that mattered, the pleasure of the rise. She tensed her buttocks. Her hips rolled with the rhythm of approaching climax. Tommy dried his hands on his thighs.

'Oh, God,' he said. 'I want to – can I put my finger inside you? I want to feel you come.'

'Two,' she gasped, and groaned when he complied.

He didn't move his fingers; just pushed them deep and held them tight against her upper wall. The position was perfect, the pressure divine. She tightened around him, her fingers flying. Sensation gathered. Sweat trickled, and cream. Her fingers began to slip on her skin. She lost track of him, all of him except the place he touched; except the hot rush of his breath. 'Yes,' he urged. 'Yes. Come.'

His fingers lifted upward on her pubic bone. Feeling blazed through her. He gripped her shoulder, she arched her back, and she came: deep, aching pulses, citrus bright, honey sweet. Again, she thought, one more just like that. Gyrating against his hand, she coaxed her orgasm to a second peak, then sagged with a happy hum. 'Mm.' She stretched her arms over her head. 'That was nice.'

Tommy shook himself from his trance. His fingers

were still inside her. Gently, he pulled them free, blinking as if he'd seen a marvel too bright to bear. He turned his hand back and forth, watching her cream shine in the light. He brought it to his mouth and licked one finger. His expression changed, transformed by wonder.

'Like that?' she asked, thinking no man had ever been as sweet as he.

He nodded, still licking. A grin flashed across his face, wide enough to split it.

She sat up and handed him the baby oil. 'Your turn.'

His grin faded. 'Um,' he said and wriggled on the coverlet.

'Now, now,' she said. 'You've been a good playmate so far. Don't spoil it by chickening out.'

She patted the mattress in encouragement until he clambered on to the bed. He sat back on his heels and looked down at his erection, so stiff and high the head was threatening to glue itself to his belly. A tear of clear fluid balanced at the centre of the distended crimson bulb. 'I'm not sure I can last very long.'

'But you'll try,' she said. 'For me.'

The moment hung. Audrey's will curled through her body like dark, warm satin. Do it, she thought. Do it for me.

He rolled his lips together. 'I guess I do owe you a show. You know, though, I never use oil when I, uh, get myself off.'

The admission that he did get himself off heated Audrey's sex. 'How do you usually do it?'

She'd never seen a man's face turn so red. 'I, uh, like to lay face down and rub myself against the mattress. Sometimes I put my hand under my hips and, you know . . .'

'Make a sleeve of it?' she suggested. He nodded, miserable, but deliciously aroused. She could picture

59

him just as he'd described, humping the mattress, pretending his hand was her. The image was both poignant and provocative. She touched his shoulder and he flinched. His nerves were wound as tight as hers.

'You couldn't watch me that way, could you?' he said.

'Not very well.'

'I could do it any way you like.'

She kissed him, gently, pressing her lips to his heated cheek. If only courage were as easy to convey. 'Any way I can see will be fine. Here. I'll get you started.' She tipped the oil and squeezed the plastic bottle. The flow arched down, hitting his bright thatch first and then, as she adjusted her aim, the upper slope of his penis. It dripped down his shaft in shiny streams, rich and fragrant. His cock jerked. She stopped squeezing and put the oil aside. 'Rub it in,' she said, her voice as thick as his cock.

He shuddered at this evidence of her excitement. Slowly, shyly, he gripped his shaft at the base. He adjusted his hold, then used his middle finger and thumb to move the oil-sheened flesh, dragging it up the rigid core until his veins stretched out of line. He used much more pressure than she'd expected, really squeezing the shaft, though he was careful not to hit his testicles on the downstroke. She took note of that, storing the information away almost without realising she had; there was so much else to occupy her attention. The way his skin flushed enchanted her, the way his knuckles whitened, the way his chest moved in and out. Each rib lifted against his skin, each muscle bunched and released. His eyelids fluttered as his fist squeezed over his glans. Unfamiliar or not, this road to pleasure could quickly overwhelm him.

'Slower,' she said, not wanting it to end.

'The oil,' he said, gasping between the words. 'It

60

makes everything more sensitive. It makes everything slip.'

'You have to,' she whispered. 'You have to make it last for me.'

His jaw clenched with tension. 'I'll try,' he said, and she could barely hear the words.

She went on all fours, watching him as closely as he'd watched her. If she didn't have much time, she'd make every second count. He'd stopped squeezing the crown with his fist, she saw. His index finger swept it instead, at the top of every pull, as if he feared the stimulation but couldn't stand to forego it. His erection had grown even more intense since he'd begun to masturbate. His veins stood out sharply from his skin, fatter and bluer. She wanted to touch one; wanted to lick the tiny drops that oozed from his slit. How wet it was, how angry and red. It contracted once and the fattest drop yet, this one silvery and thick, pushed from the secret mouth. She could smell his musky juice. The scent dizzied her, driving her lust even higher. But she wouldn't do anything to ease it. No. She had to watch him, had to pay attention to him.

Determined to catch every nuance, she hovered so close her hair brushed the front of his thighs. He gasped at the gossamer caress and spread his legs even more. He was totally exposed, his penis, his balls, the tendons at his groin. Had she been like this: so trusting, so abandoned?

'Touch me,' he begged. 'Just touch my balls.'

It was what she wanted, to touch him, to take part in what he was doing. She sat back on her heels, then scooted her knees between his. When they nudged the swell of his taut, uplifted sac, she cradled it on her palm. Tommy sighed, but she wasn't finished yet. Behind the joggling weight, her fingers found the root of his cock, a firm ridge stretching from his scrotum to his anus. His head fell back as she began to rub it, her longest finger teasing the crinkled skin of his sphincter. She didn't have to ask if he liked the stimulation. A quiver of pleasure rolled up his body. The motion of his arm intensified. Against his shaft the oil made a clicking noise, audible above both their heavy breathing. The skin of his glans was a shiny, cherry red. She knew she had seconds to do what she wished.

With her free hand, she reached around his cock and speared her fingers through his slick tangerine curls. She combed them, tugged them, stretching the delicate skin in which they rooted, tightening the base of his cock. The stretching of his skin would increase the pressure on his nerves. It must have felt as good as she'd intended. He ground out a curse, his fist pumping so frantically it seemed to blur. His balls tightened in her palm.

'Squeeze,' he gasped. 'Now!'

She squeezed his balls, not hard, but deeply. He cried out, a sharp, penetrating sound, and then he came. A ribbon of seed spurted through his fist. A towering fountain of come! she thought, as it shot repeatedly into the air. Amusement, however, could not dull her pleasure. The force of his ejaculation, the sounds and the smells, were an incredible turn-on. If he'd been capable of taking her, he could have had her then and there. Instead, exhausted by his climax, he fell forward on to his hands. Audrey pulled his head to her shoulder and let him rest. He remained there, panting and nuzzling in turn.

Her body pulsed in reaction, from heart to skin and back. She was so aroused she could only pray the feelings ebbed before he noticed.

'Phew,' he finally said. 'I don't know about you, but I could use another glass of that wine.'

Grateful for the distraction, she twisted the cork and broke the news about her job.

On Thursday, she returned to Dugan's. Patrick wanted her to take a tour, then spend the evening training alongside a waitress who was due to go on maternity leave. As before, the bar was empty of customers when Audrey arrived. According to the sign, business hours began at five. Also as before, Patrick stood behind the bar. He looked up and smiled as the door jingled shut behind her. His grin wasn't as infectious as Tommy's, but it certainly lit his handsome face. He was shaking an ice-filled drink between two canisters, one glass, one metal. Condensation misted the metal. 'Just in time,' he said, releasing the seal between the two containers. 'I need a guinea pig.'

He strained the contents into a short, flaring tumbler. When the creamy golden fluid was half an inch short of the rim, he added a dollop of whipped cream. On to this he dropped a single chocolate-covered coffee bean. A small red-and-white straw completed the creation. 'Taste this,' he said. 'I'm creating a signature drink for Dugan's. It's called a Velvet Glove.'

A frisson of dark sensation shivered between her shoulder blades. Lord. Would everything this man said make her think of sex? She sipped, swallowed and promptly closed her eyes. There was chocolate in here.

'Well?' said Patrick, his voice as smooth as the drink.

'It's delicious. What's in it?'

'An ounce of Crème de Cacao and Kahlua, a half ounce of Irish whiskey and an ounce and a half of cream.'

Audrey slid the drink back, fearful of its effect on

her self-control. Tommy she could halfway resist while under the influence. Her attraction to this man was made of sterner stuff. She tried to respond in a bantering tone. 'Anything with coffee and chocolate is fine by me, but I'm surprised an Irishman would put good whiskey in a mixed drink.'

Patrick winked and tapped the end of her nose. 'The good whiskey's for you, Audrey. The tourists get the Canadian stuff.'

He had crowded towards her to speak and didn't back off once he'd finished. The air between them seemed to thicken, to tug her even closer. Feeling like a fly caught in a web, her gaze wandered over the blue-black sheen of his eyelashes, the devilish arch of his brows, the height of his expressive forehead. Here was a face one could never tire of watching. He had a beard shadow, like steel beneath his shaven skin, flagrantly male. In contrast, his mouth was smooth and sensitively shaped. Its top lip was thin, the points sharp. Its bottom had a slight, kissable cushion that flattened when he smiled. He was smiling now and his big nose hooked over his mouth in a manner she found inexplicably appealing. From what she could tell, that nose was his only imperfection. Audrey really liked that nose.

With an effort, she pushed herself away. 'You wanted to take me on a tour?'

His eyes smouldered. He wet his lips as if he had an entirely different tour in mind. 'That I did,' he said, and she shivered at the heat in his words.

He pointed out the waitress station, a wheeled trolley parked at one end of the bar. Along with piles of cocktail napkins, its top held garnishes like lime wedges and cherries. The bottom shelf bore round green trays with Dugan's logo. 'You dress your own drinks,' he said. 'I'll give you a recipe list so you know what decorates what. Here's your cheat sheet.'

He indicated a list of liquors taped to the front of the trolley. 'Gin, vodka, rye, bourbon, brandy, Irish whiskey, rum, vermouth, tequila. That's how I've got my bottles arranged behind the bar. If you tell me the drinks you need in that order, it halves the brainpower I need to make them. So get it straight or I'll give you hell.'

Audrey glanced up to see if he was serious. His eyes twinkled, but he didn't say he wasn't. 'I have some time to memorise this, don't I?'

'Of course,' he said. 'You have till Monday. Then I'll give you hell.'

He issued the threat in a mock growl that, to her, sounded suspiciously like a promise. She found herself imagining how hell might feel if the big Irishman were administering it. He had beautiful hands but, by God, they were not small nor soft.

Get a grip, she ordered herself, and crossed her arms over the telltale tips of her breasts. Her nipples felt like stones. 'Do you serve food?'

'Snacks,' he said, all business again. 'Chicken fingers and chips.'

To Audrey's relief, he walked ahead of her into the kitchen. There she met the taciturn Asian cook and Eric, the busboy. Eric was a skinny college kid, all elbows and knees. He looked about twelve years old until she noticed the muscles in his arms. Patrick slapped the boy's shoulder. 'Eric is in charge of bringing up supplies from the basement. We've got a walk-in cooler down there and extra kegs. He also busses tables when it gets busy, restocks the waitress station, and tends bar when I need a break. Eric is training to bartend, himself.'

'Busy man,' said Audrey.

Eric saluted in agreement, but did not speak. Apparently, he and the cook were men of few words.

Next, Patrick led her up a set of narrow stairs, their

walls half-panelled with the same rich, dark wood that lined the lower floor. She tried not to stare at her boss's butt, but the glimpses she caught were pretty mouth-watering. When they reached the top, four doors opened off the smoke-stained hall, all leading to the right.

He laid his big hand behind her shoulder. 'Up here we have three private rooms and a lounge. The employee bathroom is in the lounge, along with Basil's dressing room.'

Audrey struggled not to melt at his casual touch. 'Basil?'

'We offer live jazz Thursday through Saturday night. Basil sings.'

'So I'll hear him tonight?'

For some reason, this question made him smile. 'You will, indeed.' He opened the nearest door. Above the dark wainscotting, the walls were mustard gold. An iron chandelier hung over a large round table. Draped with a white cloth, it was set for ten. 'This room is used for private parties. Groups of business-men reserve it; lobbyists; other political types. We have a deal with a few local restaurants to bring meals in. Meg, my senior waitress, takes care of this floor, but you might be asked to help out. If you are, you should know that Dugan's has an iron-clad con-fidentiality policy. People discuss sensitive infor-mation here. Privacy is the number one value we offer.' His face grew stern. 'Nothing you hear between these walls gets repeated. To anyone. If I find you've broken that rule, however innocently, I'll dismiss you without notice.'

He snapped his fingers to prove how quickly he'd do it. Suddenly, he seemed to loom a foot taller. Audrey took an involuntary step back, then forced herself to hold her ground. Dismiss her without notice

– as if that would be the end of the world! 'What if I overhear someone plotting a crime?'

'Then you bring what you've heard to me and I'll decide what to do about it.'

He was serious. His eyes did not hold a glint of humour. Audrey's spine stiffened. 'That's fine,' she snapped. 'So long as I'm convinced *you're* trustworthy.'

They glared at each other, neither willing to back off. His brows were saturnine wings, his eyes fiery blue slits. The energy he gave off made the hair stand up on her arms. It wasn't precisely sexual, but sex was a big part of it. Finally, a smile spread across his face, arrogance incarnate. In that moment, he reminded her so strongly of Sterling she shuddered. He looked as if he'd enjoy squashing her little rebellion. Warmth rushed from her core: inevitable, helpless. God willing, the bastard didn't know what his dominant stance was doing to her, but if he did ... She gritted her teeth. I won't give in again, she swore. I won't.

Perversely, the vow made her sex contract with longing.

'I'll show you your uniform,' he said, his gloating grin in place.

Fighting an involuntary tremor, she followed him to the door marked EMPLOYEE LOUNGE. Battered rummage sale furniture filled the room: a velveteen couch, a coffee table, a trio of big cushioned chairs, none of which matched. Here the walls were chocolate brown and, oddly enough, decorated with posters of Bruce and Peggy Lee. A martial artist and a sixties songstress. What a combination.

Patrick nodded his head at the pictures. 'Basil,' he said. She supposed this meant his employee was a fan of both celebrities. While she pondered this, he opened a small closet and removed a garment bag.

Unzipped, it revealed a white dinner shirt, black trousers, and a pair of bright red braces. Black lace-up brogues, well-shined, completed the ensemble. 'This is your uniform. You will wear it, without fail, every night you work, from shoes to braces. No component is optional. Nor are you permitted to add anything to it. At the end of the night, you take it off and leave it in the closet for the cleaning crew to collect. I don't care how tired you are, under no circumstances do these clothes go home with you.'

'Y-yes, sir,' she said, and was instantly sorry. A knowing smile tugged his lips.

'I like the way you say that,' he crooned. 'It makes me feel terribly important.'

'Yes, *Patrick*,' she corrected, her face hot to the roots of her hair.

He pursed his lips in dismissal, a subtle motion, an aborted kiss. He patted her shoulder and spoke softly. 'Try everything on, Audrey. I'll be back in a while to check the fit.'

She stood a full minute after he left, staring at the closed door. Sir. She'd called him *sir*. She could have kicked herself. Then again, perhaps she should have been glad she hadn't called him master.

Back downstairs, behind the bar, Patrick halved a lemon and sliced it in sections. He knew he was grinning like a mooncalf but he couldn't help himself. She was so damned susceptible. 'Y-yes, sir,' she'd said, the little stutter ruffling the skin of his cock. He hardened again recalling it, a deep, throbbing rise that made him glad to be alive.

The only blot on his mood was that Audrey wasn't enjoying her seduction quite as much as he was. He'd spooked her. He'd seen it in the sudden dilation of her pupils before she'd backed away. He didn't mind consensual fear, but this pricked his conscience. A submissive ought to take as much pleasure as her dom in being brought to heel, if not more. That a sensitive creature like Audrey should waste a moment of her subjugation wishing it were not happening was an awful shame.

He frowned at the neatly sliced lemon, gleaming wetly on the cutting board. He liked this girl. He liked the way she listened so intently to his instructions. He liked the way she smiled at the homely busboy, and stood up to him when she thought he'd demanded too much. He had a feeling she was going to be a good waitress, and he liked that about her, too. But liking her could be awkward.

He set the knife down and pondered the nicked mahogany rim of the bar. What if she discovered he was acting at the behest of the man from whom she'd run away? Would she care that Patrick's purpose directly contradicted Sterling's? Probably not. But so what? Even if she did discover his duplicity, Audrey wouldn't return to Sterling Foster. She'd never forgive either of them such a trick. The problem was he didn't merely want to foil Sterling's plan. He wanted Audrey for himself. That meant allaying her suspicions and those of her watcher. If Sterling caught wind of Patrick's intent to seduce his runaway pet, he'd stop him in his tracks. Worse, he'd expose his father's secret to the press.

Angered by that possibility, Patrick swept the lemon into a bowl and shoved it in the little refrigerator.

Clearly, he and Basil would have to play a careful game.

# Chapter Five

*A*udrey shook her head at her lack of control and carried the uniform to the adjoining bathroom. A gold star decorated the next door over. Someone had drawn a smiley face on it in lipstick, perhaps the mysterious Basil. Too engrossed in her own concerns to spare much curiosity, Audrey locked the bathroom door. She had no desire to be caught, half-naked, by her new employer.

'Liar,' she mocked the small, cracked mirror. She could picture a few scenarios where a surprise appearance might be welcome. Of course, her crumbling defences were all the more reason to use the lock.

To her surprise, the uniform fitted, even the shoes. That Patrick had observed her so closely after a single meeting unnerved her. True, some men were skilled at guessing dress sizes, but shoes? Audrey hadn't noticed him looking at her feet. Obviously, his perceptions were acute.

The braces presented her only challenge. Designed to clip to rings on the front and back of the trousers, they cut directly across her healing nipples. Within certain contexts, Audrey enjoyed a bit of pain. Hoisting drinks around for strangers wasn't one of them. The blasted things chafed every time she moved her arms. By the end of the night, she'd be in agony. She wished Patrick hadn't insisted they were mandatory.

She returned to the lounge grumbling to herself. Did she dare explain her predicament to her boss? As she debated, a melodious voice called out from the room with the star. 'Hello, out there. Can someone lend me a hand?'

She opened the door and leant in. The individual who met her eyes inspired a moment of complete gender confusion. She could have sworn the voice was female. The body from which it issued *was* clothed in a sequinned blue gown. But there her certainty ended. An unzipped bodice lay around a narrow waist, and from that waist rose a lean and very masculine chest. Its skin was hairless, but the configuration of its muscles, the flatness of its breasts, proclaimed it male. Audrey looked down. Beneath the dress, shapely, stocking-clad legs led to a pair of elegant navy heels. Those were a woman's legs, but that chest ... Its pale pink nipples were as sharp as pencil rubbers. Still lost, her gaze trailed up a graceful neck with a small Adam's apple. She encountered a gaunt but interesting face, its skin-tone smoothed by ivory pancake. Above the face, straight ash-brown hair was pinned tightly back.

The face creased upward as its owner laughed. 'Oh, dear. You must be Audrey. I'm Basil Arch. I'd offer to shake, but as you can see –' he displayed a hand swathed in a white bandage '– my shaker's out of commission.'

Head spinning, she stepped into the brightly lit dressing room. 'What did you do to it?'

'Had an accident warming formula on an unfamiliar stove.'

'You have a kid?'

He chuckled. 'I see you're no prisoner to your preconceptions. No, I don't have a child, just an orphaned kitten too young for solid food.' A mischief that was almost manic glittered in his eyes. He leant forward, a man about to share a confidence. 'My new flatmate found the bugger in the rubbish and took him home. Don't tell anyone, but Patrick Dugan is a big old sweetie-pie.'

For the second time that night, Audrey was speechless. Her boss was a big old sweetie-pie? Her boss lived with this less than manly man? Her mind revolted. No way could that testosterone factory be gay. Except, what reason did this man have to imply they were lovers, if they weren't? And since when, come to think of it, did being gay rely on a lack of testosterone?

'What, uh, what did you need help with?' she asked, amazed that her brain was functioning well enough to do so.

Basil gestured to a tackle box of make-up that sat on the vanity. 'I'm hopeless with my left hand. If you could put my lips and eyes on straight, I'd be eternally grateful.'

His manner wasn't campy, but it wasn't strictly male, either. Fighting an urge to scratch her head, Audrey scooted on to the table in front of him. 'No problem. I used to do make-overs at my mother's beauty salon. One or two of our clients must have been under fifty.'

Basil grinned at her. He had wise, old-soul eyes, their chocolate irises shining with bittersweet humour. 'I'll have you know I'm a long way from fifty, so go easy on the Hungarian blue.'

Audrey returned his smile and pulled a few items from the tackle box. He was the perfect palette: good bones, clear, fine-pored skin. He sat very still as she

72

smoothed blush over his cheeks and painted a fuller line around his lips. His skin, even where he'd shaved it, was oddly soft. It wasn't the same as a woman's, though. It had a hardness, a tightness, that made it alien. The difference intrigued her. She'd never put make-up on a man before. His gender changed the natural intimacy of the act, enhancing its sensuality. Possibilities existed that usually didn't with a woman, unless Basil only liked men? But her body wasn't taking his preference into account. Her body was thinking: nice pecs, nice arms. A dark, spicy perfume rose from his chest and neck. Opium, she thought. But it could have been a man's cologne as well. Whatever it was, it tickled her nose.

With a tiny frown, she reached for a container of earth-coloured shadows. Basil closed his eyes as she brushed the powder over his lids, her movements careful and slow. Here his skin betrayed his age, but he obviously took care of himself. He had thick, sandy-brown eyelashes. She couldn't wait to see how they looked darkened by mascara. Already, he was prettier than she'd imagined, film star pretty.

'Mm,' he said, squirming slightly in the seat. 'This is more relaxing than a massage.' His movements suggested he might be aroused. Then, with a salaciousness that seemed to settle the matter, he wound her hair around his fist and rubbed it across his cheek. 'This is the glossiest, most gorgeous hair. Promise you'll sell it to me if you ever decide to cut it.'

Audrey's tension came out on a laugh. He didn't want her, he wanted her hair. Her confusion, her – truth be told – disappointment, threw her off balance. When he smoothed her hair back over her breasts, she forgot to protect their tender peaks.

He sat straighter at her jerk of pain, suddenly alert. Easing her hair aside, he stared at the braces as if he had X-ray vision. Carefully, he stretched the red elastic to the side. 'You're pierced.' His voice dropped an octave. 'Does he know?'

Audrey didn't have to ask who 'he' was. She shook her head. 'He said I had to wear them. I didn't dare disobey.'

Basil choked on a husky laugh. '"Didn't dare disobey?" No wonder Patrick –' But he bit his lip against whatever he'd intended to say. His palms hovered over her breasts, close enough to warm their pulsing tips. Then he moved. Before she guessed what he meant to do, he had three of her buttons undone.

'Hey!' She caught his hands. They were surprisingly smooth and small.

He smiled like a basilisk staring out from a fire, inscrutably amused. 'You need a reason to enjoy this pain. I can give you one if you let me.'

'You're crazy,' she said, but he'd come too close to guessing her thoughts to put much outrage in the claim.

Shaking off her grip, he undid another button. 'Everyone who cares about Patrick goes crazy in the end.'

She wanted to ask what he meant, but his actions cast a spell that precluded rational speech. With infinite care, he pulled the starched edges of her shirt around her shoulders. She wore a lacy white bra beneath. He popped the front clasp as if he'd been doing it all his life, then peeled away the cups. Had he been practising on himself, she wondered, or on other women? She couldn't reason it out. Her eyes threatened to close with the languor he stirred. His thumbs were tracing the outer edge of her areolae, barely brushing the dangling gems. The rose-coloured circles wrinkled in response, their centres pushing out even more dramatically. Slowly, hypnotically, he petted her breasts with a peculiar mingling of avarice and admiration.

'Beautiful,' he said, the word a hushed, warm breath. Then he took her in his mouth.

The brush she'd been holding clattered to the floor. Audrey swallowed a moan and clasped his head. He had the softest, gentlest mouth she'd ever felt. It wrapped her in liquid warmth, his tongue circling her sore nipple with the most exquisite delicacy. At once the soreness melted into something wild and sweet. Enchanted, she stroked the nape of his neck. His shoulders rolled in response and he hummed his pleasure against her breast. Fingers kneading, he switched sides. His gentle suction pulled the second steel bar within her nipple. Emptiness swelled inside her even as her breast delighted to the pain. She wanted more. She wanted to be filled. As if sensing her need, he pulled her off the vanity into his lap. She'd spread her legs to do his make-up. Now the softness between them met an unmistakeable bulge. Beneath the sequins and the silk, Basil Arch was hard.

This time, she couldn't hold her moan inside. He chuckled and began a slow rotation of his hips, one that pressed his sequinned cock into the split of her labia. She could come, she realised, with no more stimulation than his mouth on her breast and this lush circling pressure at her groin. The muscles of her pussy tightened on themselves, her clit tugged by each lubricious contraction. A whimper of longing squeezed through her throat.

'Do it,' he said, his tongue flicking the very tip of her nipple. 'Go over for me. I want to feel you shake.'

She groaned and gripped his shoulders. She wanted to feel him shake, too. With that intent, she slid her hands down his chest and pinched his nipples. His sharp intake of breath speared through her as if a cock had breached her womb. He growled and pressed the edge of his teeth to her breast, a tense, but careful bite. 'Again,' he demanded. 'Pinch me again.'

As soon as she did, their hips began to move in unison, in strong, grinding rolls. Their drive for pleasure was earnest now. She was all body, all tingling, needy flesh. She wanted. She craved. She could not wait a minute longer. Caught by the same urgency, he gripped her buttocks and crushed her close. The ridge of his erection grew beneath her. It dug between her swollen lips. Their tension rose, sighs lengthening, hips jerking, until they shared the tight convulsion of release. His groan was not a woman's or a man's, but it was sexy. The sound made her shiver. Wetness spread across the cloth where their bodies were crammed together: her wetness and his.

She could not bring herself to care. Her body was limp with satiation, and the arms that held her were warm. He nuzzled her ear and whispered something sweet.

The door swung open. 'What the hell?'

With those words, her contentment shattered. Patrick had returned.

Audrey scrambled to her feet. Basil merely smiled. He waved one languid hand towards her reddened nipples. 'She was in pain, darling. I couldn't leave her like that.'

'You –' said Patrick. He couldn't seem to force anything else out. Jaw twitching, he stared at Audrey's piercings until she jerked and covered them with her arms. He was so angry his face looked boiled.

'I know,' Basil soothed, 'but you did say we could see other people.'

Patrick pointed towards the lounge, his finger stiff and shaking. 'Out here right now.'

When Basil obeyed, he slammed the door behind

his flatmate. Audrey was left to stutter her apology to a blank stretch of wood. She covered her face. Her cheeks throbbed with heat. First night at work and her boss caught her lap-dancing with his boyfriend. What a way to make a good impression!

Patrick had never been so angry in his life. Basil's actions had caught him completely off guard. Before tonight, he'd have bet his right arm the singer wasn't capable of such perfidy. Too enraged to speak, he glared as Basil lowered himself to the sofa, his long curvy legs crossed calf to calf. He'd pulled up the bodice of his dress. The neckline cut straight across his collar bones. Basil was skilled at applying cosmetics, but apparently Audrey was an artist. Even without his stuffed brassiere or wig, he could have passed for female. With a delicate moue of distaste, the singer fingered the wet spot on the front of his dress. Patrick's hands fisted at his sides.

'I told you to convince her I was gay,' he said. 'Not that you weren't.'

Basil smoothed indigo sequins over his knee. 'You should have made yourself clearer, dearest. Many transvestites like women. As it happens, I swing both ways.' His lips, the same cherry red Patrick had seen smeared on Audrey's breasts, curved faintly in amusement. He offered his wrists like a prisoner awaiting handcuffs. 'Perhaps you'd like to punish me for my sins.' His amusement increased at the sudden narrowing of Patrick's eyes. 'Yes, I know about the games you play. Believe it or not, you and I share mutual acquaintances.'

'You're not part of the scene,' Patrick said, almost sure this was true. He knew nearly everyone in the capital's upscale S&M community.

'No,' Basil admitted. 'But I do get around.'

Something in his half-mocking, half-seductive

expression triggered a few neurons in Patrick's brain. He crossed his arms over his chest. 'You're attracted to me, aren't you?'

Basil touched the tip of his tongue to his upper lip. 'Only since the day I met you.'

'Damn it, Basil.' Patrick fumed at this unexpected development. No wonder the singer had laughed his head off when Patrick asked him to be his beard. This complicated everything. 'You could have told me.'

Basil rolled his eyes. 'No, dearest, I couldn't.'

A short while later, the singer rejoined Audrey in the dressing room. He proceeded to don his padded bra and reassure her that Patrick wouldn't fire her.

'Although, if he did –' he paused in the act of pulling on a fluffy, platinum wig '– I have friends who'd pay you to do what you did for me. The make-over part, of course.' He winked. 'I don't imagine the rest of your service was standard.'

She groaned at the reminder. 'I am so sorry for making trouble between you and Patrick.'

'Nonsense.' He bent towards the mirror and brushed a wave to fall more fetchingly over his eye. 'What happened was more my doing than yours. You fulfilled a long-time fantasy of mine. I've always wanted to have a woman effect my transformation.' He gave his chest, no more than an A cup, a satisfied pat, then squeezed Audrey's shoulder. 'Don't worry. Patrick's bark is worse than his bite.'

His wolfish grin suggested his bite was not to be dreaded, either.

With that as an introduction to her work environment, meeting Glenda, the pregnant waitress for whom she'd be filling in, was anticlimactic. The older woman was tired, but friendly, and experienced enough to teach Audrey a great deal of what she needed to know.

'Patrick's a doll to work for,' she gushed as they ferried loaded trays between the tables. 'He hardly ever gets mad about anything.'

'Really?' Audrey recalled his vein-popping rage. 'He seems a little stern to me.'

'Not Patrick.' Glenda nodded at the money-stuffed glass on her tray. 'He even pools his tips with everyone else's. "We're a team here", he says. "Not a slavering band of mercenaries." He fired a girl once for complaining that the busboy got a cut. Of course, he gave her two weeks' redundancy after that. Trust me, Patrick is a pussycat.'

A pussycat, a doll and a sweetie-pie. Clearly, her new employer had shown Audrey a side of himself the rest of the world didn't see: the dark side. Too bad she didn't have the common sense to mind.

Basil's appearance on the tiny stage promised to distract her from her thoughts, though the promise was somewhat misleading. To the accompaniment of cello, keyboard and drums, he sang a seductive assortment of torch songs, each more knee-melting than the last. When he launched into Peggy Lee's 'Fever', Audrey lost her grip on her fantasies. She couldn't help picturing Patrick as the hero of the song, the one who lit her up when he called her name, the one she would be treating right.

Dolt, she thought. She had no business mooning over her boss. Even if he weren't taken, she was done with those games, done, done, done. She was going vanilla, at least for now, at least until she got clear on what she wanted out of life.

Jaw firmed with decision, she set two pitchers on the centre of a crowded table. When she straightened, she noticed Tommy and Cynthia had just been seated. They waved as she caught their eye.

'Friends?' said Glenda, manoeuvring her prow-like belly between a pair of chairs. Audrey nodded. 'Take a break and say "hi", then. This lot is set for a bit and you look done in.'

Audrey didn't refuse. She'd only been working an hour, but her feet were whining and her tray arm wasn't much better. Shamed though she was that a pregnant woman had more stamina, she slid into the booth with a grateful sigh.

'You look snazzy,' Cynthia said, nodding at her crisp new uniform. Basil had found a pair of band-aids to blunt the chafing of the braces, so she was indeed wearing full regalia.

Tommy, who sat next to Audrey, squeezed her thigh in agreement. 'You look great.'

She tried to ignore the lover-like touch. Cynthia looked pretty snazzy herself, in a simple black sheath dress. Her melon-pink cardigan, a bulwark against the air conditioning, was decorated with tiny jet beads. She looked like a blonde Jackie O. A real lady. Audrey fought a twinge of jealousy. 'I didn't expect you to drop by so soon, but it's really nice you're here.'

Cynthia smiled at Tommy as if he'd founded the UN. 'Tom and I couldn't let you spend your first night on the job without seeing a friendly face.'

'No, we couldn't,' Tommy agreed.

He wasn't looking at either of them. Suddenly Audrey knew this visit was Cynthia's idea, and Tommy hadn't been able to find a graceful way out. Worse, he hadn't told Cynthia he and Audrey were fooling around. Tommy, Tommy, Tommy, she thought. If you're 'just friends' with her, why are you acting like a guilty spouse?

Seemingly oblivious to the undercurrents, Cynthia burbled on about how nice the bar was and what a good location it had. 'I saw a commentator from one of the news stations going upstairs as we arrived. You're going to meet lots of interesting people here.'

'Yeah,' said Audrey. 'Waiting tables is a great career move.'

'You never know.'

The funny thing was, Audrey knew the other woman meant it. One of the bigger mysteries in her life was why Cynthia Will liked her. Of their gang of four, only Cynthia came from money. Though she didn't flaunt it, now and then she'd mention skiing in Aspen or clothes shopping in Paris. Her more modestly situated friends would exchange disgusted glances, but she wasn't trying to lord it over them. She simply forgot the majority of the world didn't live the way she did.

Cynthia, God bless her, was a genuinely nice girl. She'd clung to her virginity until her final year at Georgetown, when she'd given it to a polite fraternity boy of whom her parents approved. She had the largest collection of twin sets Audrey had ever seen, all in soft, feminine shades.

Everything about her was designed to set Audrey on edge: her sweet oval face, her discreetly highlighted hair, her perfect wardrobe that would never go out of style because everything in it was a classic. In the beginning, she'd only been civil to Cynthia because her friend, Axel, had insisted. 'She's a good egg,' he'd say whenever Audrey complained about her tagging along. Audrey had concluded he was thinking with his dick, and he was. But he was also right. No matter how Audrey tried to brush her off, Cynthia remained unfailingly kind. Cynthia was the one who held Audrey's head over the toilet the night she drank three kamikazes in quick succession. Cynthia was the one who coached her through her required maths courses. Cynthia was the one who listened wide-eyed to her amorous adventures, without once judging her. Axel and Tommy were inclined to tease, but Cynthia never did.

Then, one evening, as Cynthia sipped the single glass of Sauvignon blanc she allowed herself per week, she told Audrey something amazing. She, who had everything – good manners, good looks, good family – said she idolised Audrey; said she wished she had half her lust for life. Audrey, who'd had considerably more than one glass of Cynthia's expensive wine, returned the favour by confessing she'd hated her on sight.

'I know,' Cynthia said with a funny, pursed smile. 'But you're starting to feel guilty about it, aren't you?'

The two had laughed until they'd cried, then hugged and laughed some more. Then, in the way women do, they became friends: not close friends, but friends. Now and then, though, when Audrey screwed up and Cynthia stayed perfect, Audrey wished she hadn't given up despising her. Tonight was one of those times. She really hated knowing Tommy had slept with Cynthia and that she, by fooling around with him, was probably in the wrong. Again.

One look at Cynthia's radiant face told Audrey the other woman didn't consider him a friend. If Tommy couldn't see that, he was blind. 'Why don't you scare us up a drink?' Cynthia said to him now, ignoring the fact that the woman at his side was a duly appointed cocktail waitress. He hopped up and headed for the bar like a man whose death sentence had been revoked. No surprise there. The odds that Tommy had two-timed a woman before were slim to none.

'So,' said Cynthia. She twirled her coaster as Audrey resumed her seat. She was wearing that funny downcast smile she had. 'You and Tommy are finally doing it.'

'Shit,' said Audrey. 'He didn't tell you that. I know he didn't.'

'No, he didn't, but when a man gets something he's

82

been wanting half his life, it tends to show on his face.'

'Shit,' Audrey said again. 'I am so sorry, Cynthia. He told me you were just friends, but I knew you wouldn't have slept with him unless you felt a good deal more.' She squeezed Cynthia's hand. 'If it makes you feel any better, we didn't go all the way.'

'I hope you do,' she said.

Audrey's jaw dropped. 'Excuse me?'

'I hope you do,' she repeated. She lifted her eyes. They glittered with unshed tears, but their expression was fierce. 'For as long as I've known him, Tom has been in love with you. I would never, never stand in the way of something he wanted so badly.' One of the tears spilt over and she dashed it away. 'I know you love him, too.'

'More than anyone I know, but obviously not the way you do.' Audrey covered her mouth, astonished by what she was hearing. 'God, Cynthia, you're a frigging saint. I don't think even Tommy is good enough for you.'

The other woman shook her head. 'I can't really blame him. You have no idea what a crush I had on you that first year at school.'

'Jesus.' Audrey's heart slid towards her stomach. She pressed her hand over it. 'I ought to be locked up. I'm a menace.'

Cynthia giggled, a sound Audrey hadn't heard in years. 'You're not a menace. You're just full of life. And you act as if there's nothing you wouldn't dare. That appeals to a person like me.'

'Hm, well, your courage seems to be increasing by leaps and bounds.'

Cynthia smiled, her face glowing like a Renaissance madonna. She wrapped her fingers around Audrey's wrist. 'Don't disappoint him.'

Audrey was still trying to formulate a response

when Tommy returned with a mug of beer and a glass of white wine. His eyes smiled into Audrey's. 'Don't expect a tip,' he said. He looked as if joy was bubbling up inside him, simply because she was here. Had he always looked at her that way, or had her games made it worse? Audrey dug her nails into her palms and slid out to let him in.

'Speaking of tips,' she said, feigning a light tone, 'I'd better get back to work before someone else gets mine.'

Tommy gave her hand a squeeze before she left. Hurry back, said the hidden gesture. Make me as happy as I am right now. Audrey dared not look at him. Cynthia didn't know what she was risking. Cynthia didn't see how close Tommy was to never falling out of love again.

Except for Patrick and the busboy, who were doing a last cleanup, the bar was empty. Too tired to move, Audrey sat at the top of the narrow stairs. She'd put her uniform away like a good little waitress, exchanging it for a pair of hip-hugging jeans and a loose T-shirt. Her breasts were sore, but not unbearably; nothing compared to the arm she'd used to carry her drink tray. Muscles ached from her wrist to her shoulder and there was not one fun thing about it.

She put her head in her hands. She ought to go home; get a good soak in the bath. No doubt Tommy could be coaxed into rubbing her weary feet, or anything else that needed soothing.

Hell. What was she going to do about Tommy?

'Hey, lassie,' Patrick called from the bottom of the stairs. He waved a white envelope. 'You forgot to collect your share of the tips.' Audrey started to rise but he motioned her back. 'Stay where you are. My legs need the stretch.'

He sat next to her, the tread so narrow Audrey had

to lean into the wall to keep their sides from pressing together. The fact that he was gay or – at the very least – taken really irked her. Wasn't that always the way? You wanted to run until you discovered you didn't have to.

He patted her knee. His male, soapy smell was overlaid with tobacco smoke and liquor. It didn't matter. Her blood simmered to be sitting this close to him. Ignoring the nagging heat, she took the envelope and rifled through the bills.

'We had a good night,' he said. 'You ought to be smiling.'

Her head clunked against the wall. 'Too tired.'

He laughed, a warm, pleasant sound. He was being so nice. In fact, he'd been nice all night. She guessed his employees were right about him. He didn't hold a grudge. Or maybe Basil had convinced him she wasn't worth worrying about.

'You'll get used to being on your feet,' he said. 'Got a ride home?'

'It's a five-minute walk.'

'It's late. You should call your friend.'

She shook her head. 'I don't think so.'

'You don't think he's your friend, or you don't think you should call him?'

'He's got a crush on me.'

Patrick resettled his weight, his hipbone rubbing hers. 'And that's bad because . . .?'

'Sorry. I didn't mean to bring that up. You must get tired of people telling you their troubles.'

He stretched his arms between his knees and laced his fingers together. 'I don't have to tend bar. I own this place. I could sit home and count my money.'

Audrey wrinkled her nose. 'It's not important enough to bother you with.'

'It's important to you.' He was looking at her like a big brother, without a shadow of the domineering man who'd nearly scared the literal pants off her. He was still handsome as sin, but the pull he exerted was different. She wanted to tell him her troubles. She wanted to lay her cheek on that big strong shoulder and let her worries fade away.

'I'm afraid I'll disappoint him,' she said.

'Because he likes you more than you like him.'

'And because Cynthia, my other friend, really, really likes him. Tommy won't give her a chance as long as I'm staying with him.'

Patrick pursed his mouth. The kissable cushion on his lower lip plumped out. So much for thinking of him as a big brother. 'Do you have to stay with him?'

She tore her eyes away. 'I sort of have to stay with someone.'

'Because of the man who followed you the other day?'

She nodded, her lip caught between her teeth. 'It's a long story. This guy I broke up with didn't like me leaving him, I guess, and I think he's having me watched. He hasn't hurt me or anything, but it's kind of creepy.'

Patrick's chest expanded on a slow inhalation, his gaze on the knot of his hands. 'You could stay with me and Basil.'

'You and Basil?' She turned to gape at him. He could offer that, after the scene he'd broken up in Basil's dressing room? Those two must have an unusual relationship.

He shrugged. 'Why not? I took in the damn cat. What's one stray more?'

Audrey rubbed the back of her wrist across her furrowed brow. One stray more could cause a lot of trouble if your boyfriend was attracted to her. Not that Audrey considered herself much competition for Mr Twinkly here. Of course – she fought a grin – if she were going to compete, it wouldn't be for Basil's attention. 'I don't get it,' she said. 'You hardly know me.'

His eyes lifted to hers, blue fire burning in a frame of black. 'Did you ever meet someone and know they were destined to be important to you?'

Audrey had to catch her breath before she could answer. Was he serious? He certainly looked it. 'As a matter of fact, I have,' she said. 'But the last time it happened, it didn't turn out so well.'

'It will turn out well with me,' he said. His smile held secrets and promises, surprisingly carnal promises. Whatever game he and Basil were playing, it wasn't a simple one. When, however, had Audrey chosen the simple route?

She rubbed her aching temple. 'I should have my head examined.'

They both took that as a 'yes'.

# Chapter Six

*T*ommy walked in on Audrey while she was packing the leather satchel she'd taken on their ill-fated trip to Florida. Her sundresses were spread across the guest room bed and she was folding them carefully, one by one, so they wouldn't wrinkle on the way to Patrick's. Audrey hated ironing.

'What are you doing?' he asked.

She smoothed the wrinkles from a red, lily-splashed skirt. Her chest felt tight enough to crack. 'I'm moving out. My boss invited me to stay at his place.'

'Are you nuts?' Tommy grabbed her shoulder and pulled her around to face him. 'You just met him.'

'All the waitresses swear he's a pussycat. I'll be perfectly safe. Anyway, he's gay.'

'That bartender is not gay.'

She wished he didn't sound so certain. Was Tommy a better judge of character than she was? She tucked a folded sundress into the bag's open maw. 'He's living with that singer. And she's a he. I put his make-up on myself.'

Tommy chewed on that, then sat on the bed, squashing a pile of unsorted socks. The glance she

88

snuck at his face told her the news was not going down well. 'They might just be flatmates,' he said, 'trying to save on rent.'

'Trust me, they're a couple.' That, at least, she was sure of. People didn't fight that well unless they were sleeping together. Of course, since at least one of them was bisexual, Tommy might not find their romantic status reassuring. Shaking off that worry, she tucked in a last sundress and began folding T-shirts.

The mattress creaked as Tommy shifted closer and put his hand on her arm. 'Audrey, if you want your own place, I can loan you the money. You don't have to move in with strangers.'

Audrey wasn't about to explain why she couldn't live alone. The knowledge that Sterling was having her watched would only make Tommy more determined to keep her close. Nor would he care that his scrawny, five foot five-inch self wasn't well suited to bodyguard duty. Basil Arch looked more imposing than he did, in drag or out. Rather than say this aloud, she covered the hand he'd laid on her arm. 'They both seem very nice. I'm sure I'll enjoy the company.'

'Was it something I did?' he asked. 'Am I too much of a slob? Was I lousy in bed?'

Audrey dropped the shirt she was folding to bracket his face in her hands. His clear green eyes swam with misery. 'Don't even think it,' she said. 'What we did was really fun. It was special.'

'Special.' He spat out the word.

She tipped his face back up. 'I'm not saying that to be nice. I mean it.'

'Did Cynthia say something? Maybe imply that things were more serious between us than they are?'

'She wouldn't do that.' Audrey stroked his tousled hair, willing him to see the truth she told, rather than the one she withheld. Tommy wasn't likely to appreciate Cynthia's interference, even if she'd meant it to have the opposite effect. 'Cynthia knows how you feel about me.'

'Then why are you leaving? This is crazy!'

'I let things go too far.'

'Damn it, that is not a reason to –'

'Hush.' She petted the flushed contour of his cheeks. 'You know I love you, but not the way you need me to.'

Anger flashed in his eyes. 'You haven't let yourself.'

She knew he believed that. She wasn't sure the words existed to convince him otherwise. She sighed and released his face. 'You think I'm going to have a revelation just because you stick your prick inside my cunt: "Oh, God. Tommy's the love of my life. I think I'll marry him and bear his children."'

She'd gone too far. A silence fell, shocked and leaden.

'Christ, Audrey,' Tommy said.

He was a hair's-breadth from tears. Seeing the emotion glittering in his eyes, the anger and the hurt, she wanted nothing more than to hold him and kiss him and never, ever harm him again. She also knew that, where she was concerned, never wouldn't last very long. 'I'm sorry, Tommy. As sorry as I can be. I wish I knew why you weren't enough for me, but I don't. God knows, you're better than I deserve.'

The set of his jaw was mutinous. 'That is not true.'

Then why did I leave you for a man like Sterling? she cried inside her head. Why do I still crave what he gave me? Why aren't I more ashamed? But Tommy, of all people, didn't have those answers.

'You're welcome to visit,' she said instead. Hands shaking, she reached for her fallen shirt. 'You can make sure Patrick and the she-male haven't locked me in a closet and made me their sex slave.'

'Fuck,' Tommy said, his face blotchy from the effort

90

of holding back tears. 'If all you meant to do was torture me, why did you bother coming back?'

Audrey closed her eyes. 'I thought you were the only one who could save me.'

'Then why won't you let me?'

The question rang with a decade of pain. Audrey balled a shirt in front of her chest. When she spoke, her throat felt like sandpaper. 'Maybe I don't want to be saved, after all.'

As soon as she said it, she knew it was true. She wanted to explore the mystery Sterling had begun to open inside her. She prayed she wouldn't turn to someone like him to do it, but she wasn't ready to abandon the adventure altogether. On many levels, sex with Sterling had been the most rewarding experience of her life. There had to be a way to touch that fire again without getting burnt. The realisation that she wanted to try was simultaneously frightening and liberating, as if she were perched on the edge of a cliff with a pair of untried wings. Cynthia had said she seemed as if she'd dare anything. If that were the case, how could she not dare this?

But none of this lessened Tommy's pain. 'If you walk out of here tonight,' he said, 'don't come back.'

Audrey gasped at the unexpected blow. 'Don't say that.' She curled her hand behind his neck and kissed his rigid cheek. 'Tommy, I need you.'

Her plea broke the last of his patience. He grasped her head, palms to ears, and pressed an angry kiss to her mouth. 'You need me, huh? For what?'

He kissed her again, forcing her lips apart with his jaw. His tongue jabbed inside to stroke her own. There was more anger than mastery in his actions, but they worked on her all the same, triggering reactions she could not control. Sterling had trained her too well. Heat flowed over her skin, weakening her knees, quickening her breath. She cupped his shoulder blades, pulling him to her until her breasts flattened against his chest. He jerked in reaction, then lifted her off her feet and shoved her against the wall. His body pushed hard, his pelvis grinding hers in urgent imitation of intercourse. His mouth slanted for a deeper kiss. Audrey moaned and hooked her foot behind his calf.

'I'll show you what you need me for,' he said, attacking his zip seconds before he tackled hers. He went to his knees just long enough to pull her jeans down her legs. The panties came with them. As he rose, he nipped the muscle of her thigh. Were it not for the hot after-throb of pain, she'd have thought she'd dreamt the bite. Evasion was impossible. Her ankles were trapped by the jeans. He shoved her thighs apart like a pinned frog, the position awkward, unbalanced. She couldn't pull away without falling over. As she teetered, he shoved his own jeans as far as his hips. His cock sprang out, red and thick. She was panting for it, not even thinking because she wanted him inside her so badly. He pushed his shaft against her mound and cursed to find her wet.

'Whore,' he said, meaning it as Sterling never had. His crown probed her folds, searching for entry. Finding it, he drove inside, one swift, hard stab of angry flesh, weakening her spine, melting her crotch, making her groan with a pleasure too extravagant to be contained. Her head fell back against the wall. Then he stopped. His cock remained inside, beating with hungry life. 'Audrey,' he said, beginning to tremble, preparing – she knew – to apologise for the dreadful sin of taking her without sweetness filling his heart.

'No.' She curled her nails through his T-shirt and into his sweating shoulders. 'Do it, damn you. Do it. I've kept you hanging for ten years. Surely you're angry enough by now to give it to me rough.'

'Audrey –'

'Do it!' she demanded, pounding his buttocks with both fists so that his cock jarred deeper inside her. He drew a sharp breath, staring at her in disbelief. 'Do it,' she said, lower this time, more dangerous. She twisted her hands into the tangle of his briefs and pinched the hard, small muscles of his cheeks. 'Do it, Tommy. Fuck me.'

His eyes slid shut. Temptation twisted across his face. He pushed deeper, struggling to reach her furthest limits. But he didn't thrust. That was what she needed: deep, punishing thrusts that would pound her sins to oblivion.

'Do it,' she said. 'Do it. Ten years, Tommy. Ten fucking years watching me sleep with more men than you could count. Men who didn't love me. Men I didn't love. Men whose names I can't remember today. Why shouldn't you take what they did? You know I want it. You can feel me dripping down you. You can feel my pussy twitch. This is your chance, Tommy-boy. You'll never have me this way again.'

'Damn you,' he gasped. His tremor sharpened but her need had aroused him. His cock stretched inside her, longer, thicker. He cursed and drew back. The ridge of the helmet hovered just inside her brink. Her muscle tightened. 'Jesus,' he said, and shoved into her hard. Sensation shimmied outward from the blow. Again he hammered, and again, his speed increasing with her moans. Still thrusting, he tore off her T-shirt, then his own. His mouth was greedy on her breast, her throat, her mouth. He nipped her lips, making them heat and swell. She dug her nails into the meat of his buttocks. His body quaked. 'Bitch,' he said. 'Christ, I love you.' Then, with a rough, tight cry, he came.

The spasms shook him to the bone. From his shoulders to his hips, his body buffeted hers. Then, just as quickly, he calmed. His head dropped forward, brow braced against the wall, cheek pressed to hers. Audrey was too shocked to move. Her sex pulsed with unsatisfied desire. 'Shit,' he said, then: 'No.' His jaw clenched beside her ear. He dragged her down the wall, still inside her, still hard enough to stay. 'No, that's not it. It's not over.' He manoeuvred her under him on the carpet, her ankles bound by her jeans, her legs wide, her body trembling. He began to thrust again, slower now, but with force. Almost at once, he returned to full tumescence. 'Come with me,' he said, his tone making it an order. 'This isn't over until you fucking come.'

She didn't have to struggle to obey. The rise came steadily, strongly, in thick, growing waves that spread outward from each plunging drive of his cock. Her pleasure was fluid, wetness calling to wetness, heat firing heat. He'd slipped one forearm up between her shoulder blades until his hand cradled her head. He muttered demands between his kisses: told her how hot she was, how tight, how he wanted to fuck her until she cried, how he'd never be done with her, never. His own urgency returned and soon they were striving together towards release.

He told her to lift her knees; to open all the way. He told her to suck him deeper with her cunt; begged her to touch him the way he'd always dreamt she would. She didn't know how that was, but she touched him as if she might never touch him again. She ran her fingers through his hair, down his spine; probed the crack of his arse, the swing of his scrotum, the sweaty tendon of his inner thigh. One of his knees swung sideways and upward, bracing against the floor as if he meant to climb inside her. He gripped her hip with his second hand. He was strong enough to control her, to tilt her up as he drove himself in and down. He went so deep her womb jolted with the blow. She tightened around his thrusts, straining, longing, her climax just out of reach. For a moment, his cock was her prisoner. Then he growled and pumped more determinedly through her hold.

The increase in force was all she needed. The ache of pre-orgasmic tension spiked. She gripped him, inside and out. Her neck arched. The small of her back left the floor. 'Now!' he said, slamming through the last resistance. Her tension broke in heavy, cream-drenched swells. Sweetness rolled through her, his climax a drizzle of chocolate atop a scoop of caramel swirl: the last necessary component for perfection. He pulsed and gasped and sank exhausted to her breast.

She combed her fingers through his hair. How good it had been surprised her as much as how little her feelings had changed, despite her claim that they wouldn't. He was still her friend, but he was neither more nor less her friend because they'd screwed each other limp.

He mumbled something against her neck, an endearment, she supposed. From the looseness in his limbs she knew he was drifting towards sleep.

'Tommy.' She kissed his ear, then pushed him off far enough to slip free. He rolled on to his back and stared up at her, his forearm shading his eyes, his expression guarded. 'I have to go,' she said.

He scrubbed his hands over his face and left them there. 'Then go.' His voice was dull but calm, as if he'd fucked out all the emotional energy he had.

She nodded and pulled on her clothes, so shaky she fumbled over every garment. By the time she finished packing her bag and snapped it shut, he was sitting up, propped against the side of the bed. He touched her calf to hold her a moment longer. 'I didn't mean what I said about not coming back. I'll always be here for you. Always.'

Her throat was too tight to speak so she nodded again. Maybe it would have been better if he'd meant the ultimatum. She wished she hadn't hurt him. She wished she didn't feel like the stupidest woman who'd ever lived. Most of all, she wished she wanted to stay more than she wanted to go.

Patrick usually looked forward to coming home. His penthouse overlooked a muddy curve of the Potomac River, scenic and restful. A trendy development had sprung up nearby, complete with restaurants, shops and a lively boardwalk. Patrick's residence was more low-key. He lived in a young building, nondescript modern on the outside, sleekly luxurious on the inside. Its discreetly helpful doorman wore a suit rather than a uniform. Despite the building's exclusivity, neither the famous, nor those who wished to be famous, lived there – an oddity in status-conscious Washington. Patrick knew his fellow residents well enough to exchange nods, but not well enough to call them by name. For the last five years, the tenth floor had been his retreat.

Sharing it did not come easily, regardless of the incentives to do so. His shoulders tightened instinctively when he heard Basil rattling around the spacious kitchen. Rather than greet his temporary roommate, he eased the front door shut, slipped off his shoes, and padded silently to the windows that formed one wall of the lofty living room. The night sky was overcast, grey rather than black. Lights from a building across the river served in place of stars. That very morning, his father's investigator had informed him that Audrey's watcher had taken a flat on its eleventh floor. Patrick was certain a high-powered telescope was trained on him now. From this moment on, his every move would be watched: his and Basil's.

Basil had not baulked at the news that he would have to stay in character. Patrick suspected his amusement was exceeded only by his evil glee.

Resisting an urge to grind his teeth, he turned to face the inevitable. Apparently, Basil had heard him come in. He was watching Patrick with one shoulder propped against the entry to the kitchen. His ridiculous grey fuzzball was cuddled against his neck. The kitten yawned, displaying needle-sharp teeth that would no doubt wreak havoc on Patrick's home. Not that Basil would care. With a smile that boded mischief, the singer pushed off the wall and began to walk towards his pretend lover. Barefoot, clad in worn jeans, Basil crossed the thick, fringed rugs with a deceptively lazy swing to his hips. Patrick had seen male flamenco dancers use that stalk. I can fuck you, it said. I can fuck you slow and long. The stroll was hard to look away from, no matter what one's gender. Reaching his goal, Basil laid a hand on Patrick's shoulder and kissed his cheek. 'I was just warming Newton's supper,' he said. 'Did you have a nice time walking your sweetie home?'

Oh, Patrick did not want to get into that. He grunted, shrugged out of his braces and dropped to the cushioned leather sofa. Unfortunately, Basil's interest in conversation was not so easily discouraged. He sat beside him, knees angled to brush his, like a woman who wants to flirt. His hand stroked the sleepy kitten's back, the movement sensual and slow. The creature's purr was startlingly loud. 'What you told Audrey was quite poetic,' he said. 'How you knew she was destined to be important to you. Nice delivery, too. I almost believed you meant it.'

Patrick had meant it, as much as a man who'd had more women than birthdays meant anything. But Basil wouldn't understand that feeling something interesting for a woman and making a big damn deal out of it were two very different things. Patrick was not in any danger of falling for the girl.

'Screw you,' he said, and reached for the *Washington Post*.

'Any time, anywhere,' Basil chirped. He pulled the edge of the paper down. 'I don't think you should be reading now. I think you should be learning how to feed this hungry kitty.'

Patrick wrestled the paper back. 'You feed it. It's your damn cat.'

'I'm doing you a favour, dearest. You have no idea what the sight of a big strong man with a helpless kitten can do to an impressionable young woman. You did say you wanted to sneak past her defences.'

'Fine.' Patrick dropped the newspaper and put out his hands. 'Give me the damn fuzzball.'

'His name is Newton. After Sir Isaac.'

'Yeah, yeah. Cats and gravity. It's a perfect match.' With a sigh, Patrick accepted Newton's negligible weight, along with the warm, doll-sized baby bottle Basil pulled from his shirt pocket. A more ridiculous feeding implement would be hard to imagine, but Patrick took it without comment. After a moment's fumbling, the kitten latched on to the rubber nipple. He immediately began to knead Patrick's hand with his paws. The gesture did something to him. Heat flashed behind his eyes. He thought of his mother, then just as quickly pushed the thought away. 'Christ,' he said. 'Where did you get this runt?'

'In the rubbish behind my building, but I told Audrey you found him, so don't contradict me.'

'In the rubbish? You mean someone threw him away?' Before he could stop himself, Patrick cradled the kitten closer.

Basil smiled and scratched Newton behind the ear. 'All's well that ends well. The vet says as long as we keep him warm and fed, he should be fine. Next week we can try solid food. Can't we, Newton?'

A knock sounded on the door, signalling Audrey's

arrival. Patrick's heart beat a fraction harder. Hands full of kitten, he met Basil's smiling coffee eyes. Now that Audrey was here and his plans were, so far as he could tell, proceeding on course, he felt inexplicably uncertain. He'd never mastered a woman who hadn't agreed to the process beforehand, nor had it ever seemed so important that he succeed. His pride would not allow him to let his father down.

'Do you need help answering the door?' Basil's query was an insinuating croon. His hand slid up Patrick's thigh until it cupped the slumbering weight of his balls. Patrick's mouth fell open. Not the least bit shy, Basil's thumb moved, polishing the flare of Patrick's glans through three soft layers of cloth: trousers, shirt-tails, underwear. He might as well have been naked. A muscle jumped at the side of his groin and then, helplessly, embarrassingly, his cock began to swell.

'I've got it,' he said, jumping up more abruptly than he'd intended. The kitten cheeped in complaint as the bottle joggled in its mouth. Patrick barely noticed. His erection would not subside. It was rising in surges, thickening in direct opposition to the strength with which he willed it down. 'I've got it,' he said again, and turned towards the door.

'You certainly do,' Basil agreed with a throaty alto chuckle.

By the time Patrick unbolted the locks, he was blushing worse than the time Sister Mary Catherine caught him spanking Claudia Simpson in the broom closet at school. He'd had an erection then, too, and it had lasted through the scolding and beyond. It seemed too much to hope that this one would prove less stubborn.

From the outside, Patrick's building hadn't impressed her. It was nothing but poured concrete and faceless security windows. The interior was a different story. There, marble floors, soft Indian rugs and beautifully restored turn-of-the-century lighting combined to make Audrey feel completely out-classed. The lift had a hammered brass door and an illuminated stained glass ceiling. Like the rest of the decor, it glowed in shades of gold and cream. A tasteful smattering of plants added the necessary money green.

What the hell am I doing here? she wondered. She knew, though. Staying with Patrick was the lesser of two evils, the greater being staying on with Tommy and ruining his love life. I can handle this, she told herself, and rapped on the only door the tenth floor held.

Patrick opened it with his orphaned kitty curled in his hand. Its fur still feathery, its eyes milky blue, the creature was so small the Irishman's palm was all the cradle it required. It was slurping at a doll-sized milk bottle. Audrey had sworn to keep her employer at a distance, but the sight tugged at her heartstrings. The message was elemental. The kitten trusted Patrick and Patrick, in turn, gave the kitten everything it needed.

'Let me take that,' he said, reaching for her satchel.

The gesture both flustered and pleased her. It marked the difference in their generations. Men her age rarely held doors or carried luggage. Their idea of being a gentleman was buying their own condoms. I'm too young for him to take seriously, she thought. No wonder he hadn't hesitated to ask her to stay.

He led her through a dim, round entryway with an inlaid marble floor. Slices of pale and dark stone formed the same sunburst pattern she'd seen on the lift door. She smelt fresh-cut flowers and floor polish and then they entered the brightly lit living room. Basil Arch was draped across its toast-brown sofa like an adult version of Patrick's pet. The laughter in his eyes, coupled with a lingering flush, told Audrey her entrance had interrupted more than the kitten's dinner. Her gaze darted to Patrick. His colour was high as well. Even more telling, he had a boner that misshaped his trousers like a policeman's baton.

'Here.' He handed the kitten to Basil. 'You finish feeding Newton while I show Audrey around.'

'My pleasure,' Basil purred, and stroked his lover's left hipbone.

From what Audrey could see, Patrick's erection didn't need the encouragement. She tried not to stare as he led her around the penthouse, but the occasional glimpse of its distension was enough to swell the tender folds of her sex. He hadn't flagged since she'd arrived. Her muscles quivered. Her moisture flowed. She didn't care that this penile prodigy wasn't for her. It was big. It was sturdy. It made her want to howl at the moon with her legs splayed wide.

Instead, she swallowed her lust and complimented him on his home. In other circumstances, her surroundings would have held all her attention. The living room was a marvel. It rose two stories and was circled on three sides by an iron-railed gallery, the scrollwork reminiscent of the French Quarter in New Orleans. Oriental rugs lay in a pleasant scatter across the polished, wheat-gold onyx floors. Most of the furniture was leather, dark and comfortable. He favoured Matisse, she saw, and Manet and one childishly amusing Paul Klee. All his reproductions were nicely framed. They were painted reproductions rather than posters. Audrey actually had to ask to make sure they weren't real. Out on the roof, he had a small swimming pool, a garden, and a view of the light-spangled Potomac that was tailor-made for lovers. Basil was more likely to benefit from the ambience than she was, but it was hard to suppress a shiver of anticipation.

Her room, the guest room, opened off the lower

level. Though large, it was furnished simply with a futon, a bedside table, a plain wooden bureau and one ladderback chair. Compared to the rest of the house, it was spartan. In lieu of a closet, a metal pole stretched across an alcove on one side of the room. Audrey found that odd, but she supposed the architect had his reasons. The window overlooked a car park full of Mercedes.

Beyond that, in the distance, the stately white dome of the Capitol Building glowed like a beacon in the night. The sight added an extra kick to her pulse, reminding her that Washington was a city of history, dead and living – the most important city in the world if you listened to the natives. Maybe that was claiming too much, but anyone who'd lived here, who'd seen life bustling past and through its monuments, knew DC was more than the sum of its parts. For a small town girl like Audrey, Washington was better than a trip to Disneyworld.

'There's a bathroom next door,' Patrick said, recalling her from her thoughts. He cleared his throat. 'Basil and I will share the one on the second floor.'

'That's very thoughtful,' she said. 'You've both been so kind to me. I don't know how to thank you.'

He stopped her with a click of his tongue. 'You've thanked us already. We're happy to have you.'

His voice was husky. Audrey looked up and met his gaze. She should have known better. A wave of lust poured through her at the contact. His eyes were hot blue beams of sexual energy. They shot hooks into her body and tugged at muscles nothing but his cock should have been able to reach. They were hard eyes, wilful eyes. They called to everything inside her that yearned to submit. As she trembled before their power, they began to twinkle. His hand rose; touched her face. His palm was lightly callused, as if he lifted weights. In her imagination she could feel it spanking, then caressing her, his fingers slipping down to paint themselves with her desire.

The corners of his mouth curled as he stroked a lock of hair behind her ear. His fingertips were smooth and warm. 'Why don't you get me and Basil a beer?' he said. 'Since you're feeling grateful.'

She didn't understand how he could make such a quiet request sound like an order, but he did. Responses Sterling Foster had honed to a fine edge kicked to life. She wanted to say she wasn't his servant. He could get his own damn beer, and she could find a hundred other places to live.

She uttered none of these protests. In her current state of arousal, fighting would feel too much like foreplay. She might do something inappropriate; might betray her weakness. Rather than risk that, she smiled as brightly as she could. 'I'd be happy to get you a beer. I assume it's in the refrigerator.'

He nodded and pointed imperiously towards the kitchen. She had to cross the living room to get there. Basil was sprawled on the couch with the kitten. He smiled knowingly when Audrey passed, then swung one leg aside to make room for his lover. The leather creaked as Patrick sat within the harbor of his lap. She heard them murmuring to each other in low, cosy tones. The back of her neck prickled with the first warning burn of anger. Was this their game? To make her their mutual slave? To taunt her with what she couldn't have?

She stopped with her arm braced against the refrigerator, breathing hard to push her emotions down. The appliances were black, the tiles blood red. The colours buzzed across her nerves like acid, beautiful but dangerous. She wiped her sweating upper lip on the shoulder of her white T-shirt. She had to stay calm. She had to control herself. She had no idea what was really going on here.

'Use glasses,' Patrick called, 'and don't pour too much head.'

'Don't pour too much head,' she mouthed, drawing two Pilsners from a lacquered black cabinet. The way Patrick was pushing her buttons, he'd be lucky if she didn't pour the beer *on* his head. She pulled two icy bottles from their carrier inside the door, then popped their tops with the corkscrew that hung from the scarlet-tiled wall. Her motions were sharp, but controlled. She could do this for tonight. She could. And if it got out of hand, she would leave. Patrick couldn't make her do anything she didn't want to do. No one could. She was the master of her fate, the captain of her frigging ship.

When she finished pouring, each tall, flaring glass contained an inch and a half of foam. She carried them into the living room. The kitten was gone, tucked away safely, she hoped. Patrick's upper body reclined against his lover's chest. One elbow supported his weight on the couch's arm. The other draped Basil's neck. Basil was playing with Patrick's close-cropped hair. They couldn't have looked more intimate if they'd been naked. Audrey did her best to remain blank-faced. She set the beers on a low satinwood table. 'There you are,' she said, her voice only a little tighter than she would have wished.

Neither man moved to take the drink. Patrick's brows arched towards the raven commas of his hair. 'Don't put it there,' he said, scorn dripping from every word. 'Hand the glasses to us.'

She looked at them, lounging like pashas on the expensive leather, their mouths curled in identical spoilt-bastard grins. She couldn't hold her temper, no matter what the cost. Screw this, she thought, and dashed the closest Pilsner in Patrick's face.

He blinked, but didn't gasp; didn't even lift his hand to wipe the streams of bubbly gold that poured down his face to his pristine pin-tucked shirt. His eyes narrowed, their gaze seeming to nail her to the floor. 'Clean it up,' he said.

It was a tone she knew well: not anger but sheer, unadulterated will. In that moment, she knew he wasn't some chauvinist male ordering a convenient female around. He didn't care about the beer or where she put it. He only cared that she obeyed him. The last of her doubt shredded like tissue in a storm. Patrick Dugan was a dom. Patrick Dugan wanted to master her.

Panic sent her heart careering against her ribs. Sterling's ice was nothing to this man's warmth, warmth like a trail of honey luring her to her doom. 'I'll get a towel,' she said, grasping one last straw as her teeth chattered in reaction.

Patrick grabbed her wrist. The unbreakable hold flushed her through and through with heat. Fluid flowed from her core, shameful and delicious. She could smell her own excitement, musky and rich. When Patrick's nostrils flared, she almost came. 'I want you to use your mouth,' he said. 'I want you to clean me with your tongue.' She glanced at Basil, but he didn't seem upset by his lover's behaviour. In fact, he wore a faint, ironic smile. 'Don't look at him,' Patrick ordered. 'He owes me for that stunt he pulled in the dressing room.'

Audrey yanked her hand away. 'You want me to believe this is about payback?'

Patrick spread his hands, as if to say 'what else could it be?' His eyes were not so innocent. Hot with lust, hard with determination, they told the truth about his intentions. 'Now,' he said, and put a spine-tingling growl into the sound.

Oh, God, she thought. How do I get out of this?

# Chapter Seven

*T*here was no getting out of it, of course.

Patrick ordered her to open his buttons with her teeth. She knelt between his thighs to do it, her body vibrating with the adrenaline rush that declared her nature more surely than words. Basil remained curled behind his lover. His dark eyes flashed at every fumble as if it were a sweet he was eager to consume. Consume he did, for she could not control her agitation. The task was harder than she'd expected. Each button required a war of teeth and tongue with her cheek pressed tight to the beer-soaked linen of Patrick's shirt. To her surprise, he did not scold or threaten; he simply held her wrists behind her back. He was strong enough to cuff her with one hand.

This close, he seemed huge, his size alone a menace. Beneath her cheek, his muscles felt like bricks, his masculine scent more pungent than the beer. She drew his essence into her lungs even as she swallowed back tears of frustration. She would not give him her tears. She was tolerating this act of mastery, not throwing herself into it headlong.

Her heart jumped. His third button had fallen open.

Coils of black hair lay matted against his chest, glinting with blue highlights. The sight struck her hard, resonating deep between her legs. This was a man's chest, adult and powerful. She wanted to rub her face in his curls, to run her tongue around the dark risen centres of his nipples. She knew that, without permission, either of these acts would be punishable. Naturally, the mere thought of risking it sent a sharp, forbidden thrill down her spine.

Behave, she told herself. You don't need to make this any worse ... or any better. With a grimace, she freed the button that lay above his waistband. She'd reached the bulky arch of his erection, trapped still by his trousers. Heat rose from the cloth to touch her neck, a strong, animal heat. Nerves failing, she sat back on her heels. She couldn't look away. The fabric clung so loyally to his shape it wasn't difficult to trace his lines. His penis was large and thick, the glans big enough to make her swallow at the thought of him forging up her cunt. His zip was soaked with beer. It needed cleaning, too. She licked her lips, swayed by temptation. Before she could lower her head, Patrick gathered her hair in his fist and pulled back. 'You haven't earnt that right,' he said, low and stern.

Oh, he was perfect: the force with which he held her, the threat in his words, the slight rough edge that betrayed his arousal. She could not resist such sinister charms. When he pressed her face into his chest, she whimpered with excitement. She wanted this, wanted him. She licked the smooth, hot skin beneath his hair, the rosy buds of his nipples, the stretch of his collar bones. The stubble on his neck rasped against her tongue. She licked his face from brow to chin, tasting the beer and him beneath it. As she progressed, a current of wanting seemed to flow through his body, making him restless. His grip shifted on her wrists. She licked his mouth, teasing the tip of her tongue over its plump lower curve. His lips were smooth and warm. They twitched beneath her exploration, but did not open for the entry she craved.

She could have sold her soul for that kiss. But, no, she was not so weak. She would not beg, not for him, not tonight. Tonight she would give him obedience, nothing more.

At his urging, she began her descent, trailing small wet kisses down his breastbone, over the rippling muscles of his belly. Here his skin was smooth and vulnerable. Goaded by an evil impulse, she took a tiny fold between her teeth. His hold tightened on her wrist, verging on discomfort. Was the grip a warning? A scold? Tingles of pleasure flowed outward from the point where his hand compressed her bones. Defiance and an urge to share this gift rose inside her. With her teeth, she caught the tab of his trousers and tugged. She wanted him in her mouth, wanted that fat, full crown quivering against her tongue. She tugged harder. The fastening pulled free. Behind him, Basil drew a soft, eager intake of breath.

Patrick pushed her firmly away. 'No,' he said. 'You haven't earnt the right to see me, yet.'

'But –'

He slapped her in reward for her protest, a light, warm sting of palm to cheek. 'Lick me through my trousers. That's all a greedy child like you deserves.'

She knew he wanted more. She knew he wanted the wet silk of her tongue on the hot bare satin of his cock. She could read the hunger in his eyes, as potent as her own. If they'd been alone, she thought, he might have let her do it. But perhaps the rules of his and Basil's relationship forbade too much intimacy with strangers.

'I'm waiting,' he said, gently cupping the cheek he'd just struck.

Her wrists were free. She placed her hands at the

midpoint of his thighs, squeezing once for the pleasure of feeling his heavy muscles shift. He was so strong. She lowered her head with the sense of sinking into a dream. Her body was simultaneously fluid and taut. She had to do this. This was what her master ordered. This was her destiny. She lapped the cloth over his crotch as forcefully as she could, raking his hard, straining outline with her tongue. He made a sound, a muffled but heartfelt groan. His hips cocked forward, pressing towards her mouth. She knew the stimulation wasn't enough, not for her and not for him, not when they could have been sharing so much more.

He pressed the back of her head. 'Teeth,' he said, just the one harsh word. She understood. She pushed the edge of her teeth into the material, using them to squeeze his balls, to drag up and down his shaft, to rake the sensitive swell of his crown.

'There,' he said. 'Faster.'

She did as he asked and soon he began to blow, an athlete's quest for a few more seconds on the razor's edge of bliss. A hand covered hers where it lay on his thigh. It was too small to be Patrick's, and too smooth. Basil was squeezing her fingers. Basil was plastered to Patrick's back as if he, too, were about to come. He was humping Patrick's ribs the way he'd humped her mons that day in his dressing room. His motions were urgent. His hands clamped Audrey's like iron.

Patrick slapped his palms over the singer's. 'Fuck,' he said, and jammed his cock into Audrey's teeth.

Basil cried out, an unmistakably orgasmic sound. His coming touched off Patrick's. Patrick growled as if in anger, but he was past the point of no return. His hips bucked against her mouth. Fluid pulsed through his zip, copious, musky, changing the taste, the temperature, the very meaning of what she did. This breaching of the barriers between them created an intimacy she had not foreseen. His seed touched her tongue. She knew his taste. In that moment, he was not her master, he was a man: one individual man with one individual taste. The substance of their intercourse, the tiny particles of thought and feeling, were forever rearranged.

She lay her cheek across his sodden crotch, affected so unexpectedly she could not define her emotions. She only knew that if he wanted her, she was his.

Then he pulled his hands from the sandwich the three of them had made.

'You may go now,' he said, his breathing ragged but steadying.

Shocked, she rocked back from his lap. 'I can go?'

Patrick had sagged into Basil's arms. His eyes were tightly closed, but he did not look satisfied. He looked impatient, angry even. Basil was stroking his chest with a faint, possessive smile, his fingers twirling among the curls. Audrey's throat tightened.

'I've had all I need from you,' Patrick said.

She shook her head, loath to believe him. But this was his game. What right had she to question it? Some might say she deserved her own orgasm, but she would not stoop to ask for one. She pushed to her feet; forced herself to walk stiff-legged to her room. With every step, her pussy throbbed with unrequited lust. Turn back, it said. Make him give you what you need. But she wasn't prepared to argue, not yet – not until she knew what tricks the canny Irishman had hidden up his sleeve.

As soon as she'd left, Patrick pushed his back off Basil's front. He slumped over his knees, his brain seeming to spin inside his skull. It had been a long time since he'd come that hard, or wanted to come again so soon. She shouldn't have had that effect on him. He hadn't done half of what he'd wanted: what he would have done if they'd been alone. He rubbed the heels of his palms over his forehead. This whole situation had thrown him off keel. He wished he didn't have to master her this way, without her full cooperation. He wished he didn't find her so appealing. Above all, he wished he could snap his fingers and make Basil disappear. The heat of the man's erection lingered in the small of his back, taunting him with the knowledge that a minute ago he hadn't been disgusted in the least. Patrick's usually stellar control had burst like a soap bubble when Basil came. He could only hope the man didn't guess how aroused he'd been.

'You're very cruel,' Basil said now. 'Telling that girl you had all you needed from her.' Patrick grunted. Undaunted, the other man pulled Patrick's collar from the back of his neck. Patrick thought he was straightening it until he felt a tongue drag up his vertebrae.

'Hey.' He hunched his shoulders. 'No need to get carried away.'

Basil nuzzled the wet line he'd just drawn, causing warmth to ooze down Patrick's spine. 'I have to do this,' he said. 'I saw something flash across the river. I think the man with the telescope is watching.'

'You saw no such thing.'

Basil massaged his shoulders. 'Sure you want to bet on that? Especially since he may have seen our guest playing oral laundress on your crotch.'

'Shit.'

'Forgot about that, did we? Tut tut. The heat of the moment must have carried you away.' Basil's thumbs did something bone-melting to the knots in his trapezius muscles. 'I wonder if our little guest suspects how much power she has.'

Patrick tried to pull free, but Basil's arms were caught inside his shirt. 'That's enough,' he said, more

111

concerned that Basil should not suspect how much power he had.

'It's not nearly enough,' Basil said. His hands worked lower, over Patrick's shoulder blades, down his ribs. 'You wouldn't want our watcher reporting your latent heterosexual tendencies.'

'There's nothing latent about my tendencies. I'm straight.'

Basil leered at his crotch. 'Straight as a bone.'

'Basil,' Patrick warned, despite the fact that it was true. He had risen again the moment Basil licked his neck.

The singer pouted, but did not seem rebuked. 'How can I resist you when you're such a bad, bad man?' He mimicked Patrick's stern expression. '"You must earn the right to see me. Greedy girls like you don't deserve to lick my cock."'

Patrick frowned. Laughing would only encourage the man. Instead, he wrenched free and stood. He stared down at the smaller man. 'Come with me,' he said in the low, firm tone he'd spent years perfecting.

Despite his irreverence, Basil shivered. 'Are you going to ravish me?'

'No,' he said. 'I'm going to show you the end to which my cruelty leads.'

The guest room, formerly Patrick's dungeon, had been stripped of intimidating paraphernalia in honour of Audrey's stay. Beside it was a storage closet. He led Basil here and gestured silently for him to wait. A practised flick of his fingers released the hidden locking mechanism. The door opened without a creak. When they entered, they triggered the electric eye. A red darkroom bulb blinked on automatically, its light dim and lurid. Inside, amid the shadows and the dust, the tools of Patrick's avocation were stored. Bondage frames, costumes, whips, paddles and

112

restraints of every description shared the long, narrow space. A tall mahogany cabinet, its drawers lined in velvet, held a collection of dildos, nipple clamps, and other exotic toys. A silk scarf trailed from a partially open drawer. Basil stroked it, though not in the manner of one who had seen the ingenious ways it could be used. 'Good Lord,' was his only comment.

Patrick steered him by the elbow to one of two stools that stood by the lefthand wall. Sitting on the other, he depressed a small button. With a faint, electric hum, the mirror atop Audrey's bureau became a one-way glass. It was wide enough for both of them to watch in comfort.

'Good Lord,' Basil said again. Audrey was muttering to herself as she dug through the contents of a leather satchel. A pair of khaki trousers hit the floor, followed by a rumpled yellow T-shirt. Patrick reminded himself to do something about her wardrobe. Less concerned with her fashion sense, Basil pressed his hands to his mouth. 'She looks angry.'

'She looks horny,' Patrick corrected. 'But she seems to have found what she was looking for.' To his amusement, she had pulled from her bag a glittering purple dildo. Leave it to a twenty-two year old to choose such a garish plaything. The flare at its base was as wide as her palm. He did not guess what it was for until she thwacked it against the wall beneath the empty clothes rail. When she let go, the suction cup held the dildo firmly in place. Now it looked as if a stiff purple cock were growing from the opposite wall.

Wide-eyed, Basil edged so close to the mirror his breath misted the glass. 'That dildo is too big for her.'

It was rather large, but Patrick wasn't concerned. In his opinion, large was good; large indicated a fondness for being well and truly filled. For all he cared, she might be a size queen. In fact, he hoped she was.

Patrick had reason to know that fear was best reserved for other causes than the size of a man's dick. He heated at the thought of unveiling his own overlarge organ, of working its girth inside her humid sheath. 'I'm sure she knows what she can take,' he said, and polished the glass with his sleeve.

She stripped off without ceremony, pushing the low-slung jeans down her hips, peeling the plain white T-shirt over her head. He'd known she was attractive, but the removal of her clothes was like blasting a layer of grime from the Venus de Milo. Rid of its camouflage, her young, nubile body glowed. She was a luscious, dewy rose, a gilded peach, a ripe, red strawberry begging to be caught between the teeth and licked to the point of tears. No strap marks marred her sun-browned curves, no misplaced weight, no blemish. Her hair fell to her waist in glossy waves. Impatient with the heavy mass, she twisted it on top of her head and secured it in a knot. Sprays poked out from the top, a fetchingly girlish mess. She seemed the personification of health and youth and innocent sensuality. Only the piercings in her nipples suggested more decadent tastes. The dichotomy made him grit his teeth at a painful surge of lust. He wanted both of her, the girl and the wanton. Most of all, he wanted them now.

Her arms lifted. She gripped the closet rail, never dreaming how many women had gripped it before her, with similarly carnal intent. Her shoulders wriggled as she tested its ability to hold her weight, like a gymnast preparing to launch a routine. Both he and Basil drew a breath and held it.

'Look at that back,' Basil murmured. 'I haven't seen curves like that since I saw that Ingres at the Louvre.'

She was indeed the proverbial violin, lush and smooth and toothsome. Patrick gnawed his lower lip as she lifted herself over the dildo. She tested it a moment, caressing her slit, perhaps bracing for its size. Then she relaxed her arms. With a mutual gasp, he and Basil watched the massive dildo slide inside her body; watched the muscles of her back writhe with pleasure as it stretched her. Slowly, she lifted back to the tip. The soles of her feet flashed white as she went on tiptoe. The head was still inside her. She hesitated, tensed, and then she took it hard, using her grip on the pole to sling her body up and down the glistening toy. Her pace was brutal. She fucked the dildo as if it were alive and could take pleasure in her abandon. They could actually hear the dull percussion of her body against the wall. Patrick's hands curled into fists in front of his hipbones. He wanted to be that dildo. He wanted to feel that wet, reckless plunge.

'She'll hurt herself,' Basil said, though he didn't shift from his riveted pose.

Patrick should have reassured him. Instead, he wished him to perdition. To have watched Audrey's wild ride with his hands on his cock and his palms squeezing tight would have been a sweet indulgence. 'What's the matter?' he said, frustration sharpening his voice. 'Never fucked a woman that hard?'

'Certainly not!' Basil's fingers pressed the glass. 'In light of this demonstration, however, I may rethink my position.'

'She won't hurt herself,' Patrick said, grudging the attention it took to do so. Audrey had shifted angles and closed her eyes. Her strokes were growing longer, faster. Her thighs left sweat streaks on the wall. She wanted this bad. He had teased her to desperation and now she was taking her relief as forcefully as she could. Waves of sympathetic steam enveloped Patrick's skin. If Basil hadn't been sitting beside him, he didn't think he could have stopped himself from rushing into the other room. But he had to get a grip on his reaction. The last thing he needed was for Basil to realise how turned on he was. He blew out a steadying breath and finished addressing his concern. 'She's not a masochist in the true sense of the word. She's got too much fire to want a pain that doesn't enhance her pleasure.' He shook his head. 'Honestly, she's the perfect submissive.'

'Well.' Basil rubbed his thighs as if he wished he were rubbing something else. 'Clearly, this S&M business is more complicated than I thought.'

'S&M isn't the only factor. Lots of women like a good hard fuck. It pushes different buttons: physically, emotionally . . .'

Basil wasn't listening. He had his nose pressed to the glass. 'Look, she's slowing down.'

It probably wasn't a good idea, but Patrick returned his attention to Audrey. She'd switched to a one-handed grip on the bar. Her back rolled in sweat-gleamed undulations. Her free hand cupped her vulva. The motion of her elbow suggested she was masturbating. Her head lolled on her neck and her ribs moved in deliberate, rhythmic swells. Patrick thought she must be holding herself on the edge of orgasm.

'She's teasing herself,' he said. 'She wants to make herself suffer before she comes.'

Audrey wasn't the only one suffering. Patrick's cock was so stingingly sensitive he could count each fold of cloth straining between his legs. His balls hurt as if he hadn't just emptied them ten minutes before. He would have sold his soul to be inside her now.

Then Basil sat straighter. He tapped the window. 'I think – yes. That dildo has a vibrator in it. I can see her arm shaking. She must have turned it on. God, what that must feel like!' He bit his knuckle. 'Oh! She's pushing her clit against the side. I think she's coming!'

She was indeed. Her head snapped back with the force of it, hair tumbling down her back, cries muffled by the thickness of the wall. Patrick's heart pounded in his throat, too fast, too hard, but there was nothing he could do to calm it. She came as if she meant to drain every drop of pleasure, with her whole heart and soul. When the orgasm ended, she lifted herself free and tugged the dildo from the wall. Its glitter was dulled by her juices. She pressed it to her breasts and swayed as if she were light-headed. Still holding the toy, she staggered to the bed and curled up beneath the sheets.

Patrick closed his eyes and listened to the blood rushing in his ears.

Basil found his voice first. He cleared his throat and gestured to the bulge inside his jeans. 'I don't suppose you'd care help me with this.'

'In your dreams.'

Basil tossed his head. 'Heterosexuals have been known to trade hand jobs. It wouldn't rob you of the right to call yourself a big hairy he-man.'

'Basil.'

'It's a waste not to. You know we'll be doing it by ourselves, the minute we leave. It's a friendly thing, Patrick, not an engraved invitation to the poofter parade.'

His scorn took Patrick by surprise. It seemed to have deeper roots than this particular rebuff. Just how long had Basil been angry at him? And why? Because his attraction wasn't returned? Patrick had a hard time believing that. He didn't know much about Basil's private life, but he knew he and his lover had been close. Basil had barely had time to mourn him; certainly not enough to develop a *tendre* for his boss. They'd never been friendly enough for that. It simply didn't make sense.

But maybe Patrick needed to make sense of it. 'I'm sorry,' he said. 'I'm just not made that way.'

'Fine. I'm an amoral bastard who'll screw anything that moves. But you're the one who spied on our guest without permission. Doesn't that break some sort of dominators' honour code?'

Patrick crossed his arms. 'Are you planning on reporting me?'

'She never said you could watch her. She never gave you permission to play these mind games. Don't you feel the least bit guilty?'

Patrick examined the bare red bulb that lit their spying post. Did he feel guilty? Or was he secretly, shamefully, titillated by the hair-thin line he was treading? If Audrey had known he was watching, he sensed the knowledge would have aroused her. Her explosive orgasm was proof she found his games exciting. She certainly hadn't asked him to stop. Was that enough to constitute consent? He thought it was but, truth be told, he wasn't certain. 'I regret the conflict she's experiencing,' he said, hoping the words didn't sound as stiff to Basil as they did to him. 'I wish I weren't obliged to keep her in the dark about my motives, but I am.'

'If you really wanted to, you could explain what's going on.'

'Not yet. Her attachment to me isn't strong enough to challenge her trust that way. She might not believe my explanation.'

'So you can't tell her the truth because you haven't rendered her spineless, yet? Forgive me, oh Great One,' Basil drawled, 'but that line of reasoning sucks.'

Patrick shrugged off an annoying prick of shame. Basil had watched as enthusiastically as he had. He had no right to point fingers. 'You know my situation,' he said. 'What would you have me do?'

This was not a good question to ask. Basil swung towards him on the stool, his face creased by a devilish grin. 'Turnabout,' he said.

Patrick blinked. 'You think I should let her watch me masturbate?'

'No. Watching you masturbate would even the scales for her, but I've decided I need a reward for my cooperation. I think you should let her watch while I get you off.'

Patrick could only shake his head. 'Why would you want to do that when you know I'd rather not?'

'Because I don't know you'd rather not. I only know you think you'd rather not.' Basil patted Patrick's shoulder and squeezed past the bondage rack to the door. His erection not so accidentally brushed Patrick's knee. 'Don't look so glum, dearest. You will enjoy it and, after all, it is the right thing to do.'

Patrick muttered a curse. Basil's departing chuckle was not the least bit reassuring.

Audrey woke to the sound of a door opening. For a moment, she couldn't remember where she was. Then the scent of Patrick's soap reminded her. His shadow moved into the room. With a blush, she patted her wall-mounting vibrator to make sure it was hidden by the covers. Metal clinked as Patrick hung something on the closet rail.

'Audrey,' he whispered, the sound brushing her nerves like smoke. She sat up with the covers clutched to her chest. 'I thought you might be lonely. I brought you a friend.'

To her delight, he brushed the purring kitten down her cheek. Newton stretched and mewed, but curled into a ball as soon as Patrick laid him on her pillow. His nose was hidden in his paws, his tail tucked around his body. Patrick stroked him in parting, his big hand momentarily swallowing the little cat.

Audrey's chest tightened at the sight. Then his hand rose to smooth her hair. With the same gentleness he'd shown his pet, his thumb swept the curve of her cheek, back and forth, as if he meant to polish it. She wished she could make out his expression. The gesture felt wistful somehow. She couldn't think why. It was hard to imagine him being sad; he seemed as if his world were entirely in his control. But maybe his relationship with Basil didn't give him everything he needed. Maybe he was lonely. The possibility made her want to reach out to him, to connect with him the way she did with Tommy.

'Keep Newton warm,' he said, and began to pull away.

'Wait.' She caught his forearm. His skin was bare and warm, his hair silky smooth. He stopped moving forward, but he didn't turn back. To her dismay, she found she didn't have the nerve to ask him to stay. 'What, um, what did you hang up over there?'

'Clothes for you to wear tomorrow,' he said. 'My women don't run around in jeans.'

The words were spoken so lightly they didn't register until the door clicked shut behind him. When they did, she trembled. It's starting, she thought. He's going to tell me what to wear, how to speak, what to think. He's going to master me. She couldn't be mistaken. But maybe she wished she were. Did she really want to submit to a man who inspired such lust she nearly humped herself raw? Fuck yes, said the woman who'd hung from Sterling's chains. Fuck no, said the woman who'd run from them.

As she lay back, lost in thought, the kitten squirmed up her hair to nuzzle her cheek. She stroked his fat, milk-fed belly, loving the pat-pat-pat of his heart, the warmth of his sighing breaths, the sweet animal sanity of his sleep. He was just what she needed to calm her jangled nerves. Apparently, Patrick was good at being kind. If it was all an act, it was a far better act than Sterling's.

Across the river, in a one-bedroom flat with carpet the colour of decomposing mice, the watcher slouched in a dusty armchair, thumbing through his collection of Polaroids. At intervals he turned his head to the eyepiece of a high-powered telescope. When the window on which it was trained remained dark, he returned to his monotonous shuffling. His appearance was no more prepossessing than his actions. He wore the same ripped jeans he'd worn all week. Since he had no partner to complain, he didn't particularly care. Tomorrow would be soon enough to wash them. His boss didn't pay him to loiter at the laundrette.

He also didn't pay him to loiter at the peep shows on Fourteenth Street, but after a long, dull day of surveillance a man was entitled to his diversions. It wasn't as if he'd missed tonight's big revelation. Their client might not like hearing his bird was living with the bartender, but he'd be fascinated to hear he was gay. The watcher had crystal clear shots of the man receiving a touchy-feely back rub from his lover. He also had shots, taken earlier, of the lover wearing a girly get-up. The watcher would send scans of both to his boss before morning.

He fingered a loose shirt button, his grin stretching the skin of his face. He knew how these things worked. No matter how people blabbered about tolerance and equal rights, DC was an old-fashioned town. A senator with a gay son might not raise eyebrows, but a senator with a gay son whose lover dressed in women's clothes was news. The kinkiness alone would warrant extensive media coverage. The watcher was sure their client would appreciate the leverage this information could afford.

His smirk faded as he rubbed a questing finger

down his zip. There was one downside to tonight's discovery. Due to the bartender's leftward swing, the entertainment value of this assignment was dropping like a stone. Their bird was a sweet little piece of Generation X pussy: tits, arse, a belly a man could cover with one hand. He wouldn't have minded watching her get horizontal with her protector.

One couldn't have everything, though. He glanced at the tracker, beeping quietly in its gunmetal case. Such nice toys he had. If their bird walked down the street to buy a paper, he'd know about it, and she would never know he knew. Even if she discovered she were being tracked, she'd never guess how. The awareness of his power sent a tingle up his thighs. No doubt about it, the watcher loved his work.

## Chapter Eight

$S$he dreamt she was smothering and woke to find Newton draped across her mouth.

'Newton!' She lifted the little grey cat until he dangled from the end of her arms. His eyes were wide, his pointy tail curled between his legs. He looked so surprised she laughed and rubbed their noses together. 'You're a bad kitty, sleeping on my face that way.'

Unimpressed by the scold, Newton yawned and dug his claws into her T-shirt to stretch. Apparently, his talents did not yet include retracting his claws. He proved so difficult to disengage, she took off the shirt with him still attached to it. 'You're a pest,' she said, setting him on the bed. With great fascination, he eyed her dangly nipple ornaments.'Oh, no you don't. Those aren't toys, Newton.'

Before he could get any brilliant ideas, she grabbed a bra from the tangle on the floor. She'd forgotten to put her clothes away. And speaking of clothes . . . Her heart gave a thump as she turned towards the alcove closet. Patrick's black suit bag hung from the rail. 'My women don't run around in jeans,' he'd said.

I'll just open it, she thought. Then I'll decide what to wear.

As soon as she saw the bag's contents, she knew she was in trouble. From behind the long zip, a tunic and trousers emerged. Sewn in heavy Chinese silk, the tunic was sky blue, exquisitely embroidered with yellow and scarlet butterflies. Braided frogs fastened the front, the sort one rarely saw on modern clothes. A stiff mandarin collar, black and gold, matched short cap sleeves. The trousers were yellow with blue satin-stitched flowers. Fitted at the waist and ankles, the cloth flowed loose through the legs. Exotic though it was, for a slave's outfit, it had dignity. Audrey had never owned or thought to own anything like it. She stroked the cool, slippery silk. I'll just try it on, she mused. See if it fits.

It fit as closely as if she'd stood on a stool and let the seamstress stitch it on to her body. Amazed yet again by Patrick's eye, she backed to the opposite wall to catch the full effect in the bureau's mirror.

She noticed at once that her underwear ruined the line. She undid the frogs again. What the hell. In for a penny, in for a pound. Her daring proved beneficial. Without the bra and panties, the outfit was perfect. She looked mysterious. She felt pampered. She swept her hands down the tunic. The bodice was tailored to cup the weight of her breasts. They swayed when she walked, but the motion was subtle. The shape of her nipples and the jewels that pierced them were lost among the embroidery; enough, at any rate, to wear these clothes in public.

The removal of her panties revealed another surprise. The trousers' seam was open between the legs. When she moved her feet apart, a breeze flirted with her curls. Then her stomach rumbled. The same air current had carried the scent of frying sausage to her nose. Someone else must be awake, someone who might want to see her in these clothes. Her pussy brimmed at the thought of Patrick's reaction. She closed her eyes. Yes. She was ready to obey. She was ready for whatever lay in store.

The plan was simple: throw breakfast on the stove, wait until they heard Audrey moving around, then pose Basil making a meal of his host. Patrick could not claim disinterest. If nothing else, the thought of being watched added weight to the swing of his cock. All he needed now was a serving of nerve.

'I don't see why my clothes can't stay as they are,' he said.

Basil frowned at him. 'No one gets a blow job wearing a tie.'

'I have. It adds an air of authority.'

'As if I cared about your authority.' With a snort of impatience, Basil loosened the knot and spread the halves of his starched white shirt. 'We're following my aesthetic today, and my aesthetic calls for you to look as if you couldn't wait to get mussed.' He dealt efficiently with Patrick's belt and zip, each rattle and rustle increasing his alarm. For some reason, the more nervous Patrick got, the more blood rushed to his groin. Basil's hand slid inside his black silk boxers. A grin creased his face, and it wasn't due to Patrick's choice of undergarment. 'My, my, what have we here?'

Patrick cast his gaze towards the ceiling as Basil drew out his erection, nearly full from the feel of it. The singer's hands were smooth and warm. Only the size of his knuckles marked them as male. Basil wrapped his fingers around the base of Patrick's cock, then pulled them gently to the crown. The ensuing flare of pleasure made him stumble back into the kitchen table.

'Lubricant,' Basil said, with a decisiveness Patrick

125

could not like. Basil grabbed the bottle of toasted sesame oil that was sitting on the counter. Jesus, he was going to smell like a Chinese restaurant. He tried to retreat as Basil approached, but the table blocked his way. He clutched the backs of the chairs on either side.

'Don't be such a baby,' Basil said. 'You can't expect me to shove that whole monster down my throat. I'm not complaining, mind you. A hard-on that size is an inspiring sight, but I'll have to do some handwork and handwork means oil. Unless you prefer being rubbed raw?'

Patrick clenched his jaw. 'Just do it.'

Damn Basil for enjoying this. Eyes glinting with mischief, the singer pushed his boxers out of the way, then filled the cup of his palm with the fragrant oil. He pressed his hands together to warm it, then grinned when his victim's erection surged. 'Very nice, dearest. Very nice indeed.'

Patrick tensed at the approach of his hand. 'Shouldn't we wait until we're certain Audrey is awake?'

Apparently, Basil didn't care about that. He clapped his hand around Patrick's balls. This time the slow, wanking stroke started under his scrotum. The pull was slippery, of course, with a knee-weakening corkscrew added to its upward rise. Patrick's teeth were grinding by the time Basil pushed his fist back down, not stopping until he cupped Patrick's balls. Gently, he kneaded the heavy sac, rippling his fingers as if he were practising scales. Already Patrick's scrotum was pulling up, and the massage didn't relax it at all. 'I hope this isn't too much for you,' Basil said, as arch as his name. 'You wouldn't want to lose your grip before Audrey gets her eyeful.'

'Not a problem.' Patrick ignored the sweat that trickled down his back. 'I'll be fine.'

His bravado was wasted. Basil's attention was fixed on his cock. He widened the gap in Patrick's trousers, then shook his head to himself. 'I think we'll have to drop these to your ankles. I need more access to do this properly.'

Great, Patrick thought. Now the man wants access. He dug his nails into his palms as Basil dragged his trousers down his legs. The black silk boxers followed. Goose bumps broke out along his thighs. Basil rubbed them briskly. 'Cold?' he said, on his knees now. They both knew cold had nothing to do with it. Patrick could feel his cock bobbing with the force of his lust. Basil pursed his lips and blew a stream of air across the tip. 'Not to worry,' he cooed. 'I know just what will warm you up.'

Warming up was not the problem. Restraining his impulses was. Basil handled Patrick's cock as if it were his own, without shyness, without fear of going wrong. He widened Patrick's knees with his shoulders and rested his forehead against his belly. Just make yourself at home, Patrick thought, but didn't trust his voice to say it aloud.

He'd discovered what Basil meant by access.

The singer's clever, oily fingers were working him over from perineum to anus, finding every crease, every gathering of nerves. The pleasure was soft and thick, almost soporific, but Basil did not intend for him to drowse. First, he gripped the shaft. Then, ringing the base of his scrotum between finger and thumb, he shocked Patrick awake by pulling his cock and balls in opposite directions. Two snug circles of fingers dragged smoothly over the oil, the skin going taut as he pulled, then loose when he released. The effect was astonishing. No one had done this to him before, nor had he thought to do it for himself. The top of his skull seemed to float up and down with each stroke, as if something more profound than flesh were being stretched. Heat suffused his groin. His head sagged on his shoulders. Ooh, this was good. His toes were curling on the floor. He almost forgot to tense when Basil brought his mouth into play – though it was extremely difficult to ignore.

'Jesus,' he said, as Basil's tongue added a sweet wet friction to the double pull. Tempted to grab Basil's head, he took a death grip on the upper rungs of the kitchen chairs. He had to control himself. He couldn't touch him, couldn't guide him, couldn't push deeper into the strong-soft heat of his mouth. If he did, Basil would know just how devastating his talent was.

Assuming he didn't already.

Now he was doing something with his thumb, pushing it up into his mouth so that it rubbed the nerve centre under Patrick's glans. Patrick's vision began to blur. His balls were buzzing. His blood was singing. His climax approached like a thundering train. 'Slow down,' he said, his eyes screwing shut at the intensity of the messages pounding through his cock. 'Damn it, Basil. Slower.'

Basil lifted his mouth and grinned. 'Not so bad, is it?' His thumb was still drawing circles on the neck of Patrick's shaft, light enough to send a horde of shivers down his spine.

'No,' Patrick admitted, the word fighting past his gasp for air. 'It's pretty good.' He clenched his thighs. He couldn't deny he wanted more, much as he would have liked to. 'Put your mouth on me again. Slowly this time.'

Basil obliged. Patrick tried to delay his orgasm but, slow or fast, Basil was a fellatory genius. His hands twisted and rubbed; his tongue licked and warmed; his exhalations washed like steam across his skin. His panting breaths betrayed just how thrilled he was to have his mouth on Patrick's cock. God help him, even that was exciting. Patrick couldn't wait for Audrey.

He could barely remember why he'd wanted to. The orgasm started rising from the heels of his feet, tingling up the back of his legs, tensing his buttocks. He used every trick he knew to stop it: relaxing his sphincter, counting heartbeats, controlling his breath. It was like trying to stop a tidal wave. Basil knew the end was near. His mouth descended, swallowing, sucking, until the need for release made Patrick's eyes tear. A second more was too much, a millisecond. With a low moan, he let the pressure burst. Basil groaned in answer, drawing hard, teasing each wine-sweet flutter into an ache. He sucked everything from him, every bloody drop, until Patrick felt as if his heart were draining through his cock.

Breathing hard, he touched Basil for the first time, just his fingertips on his hair. It was half thanks, half warning that he couldn't bear more stimulation. With a grin Patrick could feel, the singer let him slip free. Patrick opened his eyes.

His heart jumped like a landed trout.

Audrey was standing in the doorway, eyes round, mouth agape. She wore the Chinese tunic he'd left her the night before. Newton was cradled to her breast. He had no idea how long she'd been there, but she couldn't have looked more stunned if she'd walked in on a murder. Heat flooded his face. He couldn't control the flush any better than he'd controlled his climax. If he'd ever been more embarrassed, he couldn't recall it now.

Sensing a change in the air, Basil turned on his knees. 'Well, well, our guest has awakened. Enjoy the show?'

Audrey's lips moved as if she meant to say something. Then she turned on her heel and left. Patrick pressed his hand to his solar plexus. This was not the reaction he'd hoped for. It was, however, the reaction he should have expected. Audrey had no idea she

129

was supposed to walk in on them. No doubt she was as mortified as he was.

Idiot, he thought. How could he expect her to play his game when he hadn't told her the rules? Obviously she was too inexperienced to guess. 'I've got to go after her,' he said.

Basil waved him off with the tips of his fingers. 'By all means, dearest, go.'

He found her perched on the end of the guest room bed. She looked like a teenager who'd just been told her parents were splitting up. Her head was bowed and she'd twisted her hands between her silk-clad knees. In the corner, Newton pounced on a sunbeam as if his little legs were made of springs. So much for animal sympathy. Audrey's eyes rose. The confusion in her gaze made his vocal chords close in on themselves.

'I heard you talking,' she said. 'Why would you pretend to be gay if you're not? Why go to such lengths to make a fool of me?'

Poor Audrey. He should have known she'd think they were mocking her. In her place, he would have. Shaking his head over this unaccountable failure of judgment, he sat beside her and pulled her hand on to his thigh. 'I'm sorry, Audrey. It was a stupid idea. I thought you'd lower your guard if you thought I was interested in men. I knew you were nervous about me dominating you.'

'You could have asked.'

The words were plaintive. He chafed her cold hand. The moment had come to tell her the truth, whether he wanted to or not. Only confession had a chance of winning her over now. 'There's something else,' he said. 'The man you ran away from knows you're here. He asked me to look after you.'

'Sterling?' Her expression was so dumbfounded it

130

was blank. 'I don't believe it. He wouldn't send me to you. He wouldn't want another man to master me.'

'He doesn't know what I am,' he said. 'Mastering you was my father's idea.'

'Your father's?'

He didn't have a choice. He told her everything: about the threat Sterling had hung over the senator's head, about the watcher across the river. Face hot, he even explained the *quid pro quo* Basil had shamed him into accepting because he'd spied on her without permission.

Her lips twitched over that, but she soon grew solemn. She gazed at her lap. 'Sterling never used to ask, either,' she said.

The melancholy in her voice shamed him worse than Basil's taunts. She sounded so resigned, as if – because of her nature – being manipulated against her will was now her lot in life. It wasn't true. No submissive should ever believe it was. He curled his hand around the back of her neck, her hair smooth and cool beneath his palm. 'I'm sorry,' he said. 'I shouldn't have treated you that way, no matter what. If you want to leave, I'll understand. I'll hire a real guard for you, for as long as it takes to get Sterling off your back.'

His offer seemed to increase her tension. She rose and paced to the window. She pressed one knuckle to her lips. 'I know I shouldn't trust you,' she said. 'I know I should leave.'

He heard forgiveness in her voice. It rang as sweetly as a bell to a punch-drunk boxer. Reprieved! His shame fell from him as his smile grew. She knew she shouldn't trust him, but she did. Even better, she wanted him to convince her to stay. He moved behind her. He put his hands on her shoulders and rubbed their taut curves. Her weight shifted. The back of her head brushed his chest. Bit by bit, muscle by muscle, she was melting in his hold. He kissed the soft hollow at her temple.

'Let me prove myself,' he said. 'Let me show you how good the right master can be.'

'The right master?' She turned in his arms, her chin tilting up for a kiss.

He didn't think. He didn't worry that he might want this too much. He stared at her fresh young mouth. He took what she offered and sighed.

It was a kiss to swoon over. Patrick explored her mouth with the most delectable patience. Pull by tender pull, he increased the pressure only to let it fall away. Still connected, she could feel his pulse beating in his mouth, a subtle tremor transmitted by liquid warmth. His fingers burrowed in her hair, drawing circles on the back of her head. She inhaled deeply and held her breath.

'Audrey,' he whispered. His lips began to move again, slowly, as in a dream. His tongue reached; stroked her own. She stumbled at a sudden failure of her knees. He smiled and wrapped one arm around her back, pulling her against his larger, harder body. The embrace was so welcome she thought she might dissolve. He was aroused, extremely so. The ridge of his erection pressed her belly. Rather than grind her into it, he shifted slowly, rubbing it over her clothes like a cat marking his possession.

She could not fear him when he kissed her this way. Pleasure drowned her fears, pleasure and gentleness. He wasn't like Sterling. Sterling wouldn't have apologised. Sterling wouldn't have wasted so much time on a kiss.

His mouth was delicious. If she'd had the will, she would have clasped his face and dragged it closer. Instead, she clung to his shoulders and let him kiss her as he wished, a drugging play of lips and teeth and tongue. She could barely open her eyes when he set her from him.

'You are not to do anything,' he said. 'I'll see to it all.' He took her hand and led her to the rumpled bed. She climbed on, scooting backwards until she reached the stack of pillows. She waited with bated breath for him to follow, but he remained where he was, watching her with heavy-lidded eyes. Stars of blue shone through his lashes, his irises the centre of a flame.

'I have to leave for a short while,' he said, his voice deep and whiskey-rich. 'I want you to think of me while you wait. I want you to remember what you saw this morning in the kitchen. I want you to remember how I looked, how I sounded when I came.'

She stared at the slabs of muscle that showed through his open shirt. He'd been big, she remembered, impressively so. The hair at his groin had been as black as a fine mink stole. Basil's hair had seemed pale beside it. She recalled their mingled groans and fever swept her skin.

Patrick noted her flush. 'Very good,' he murmured. He turned to go.

Her throat tightened to call him back, but she managed to stop herself. She would be good. She would be what he wished. For today, for now, she would give herself as his toy. The walls of her pussy thickened at the prospect. She imagined their soft, juicy swell and a trickle of cream slid from her lips. Never had surrender seemed so desirable.

He returned with a long black jeweller's case, a small brown bottle, and an assortment of scarves, all in hues to complement the tunic and trousers he'd ordered her to wear. Without warning, her consciousness shifted. She felt neither American nor modern, not with that heavy Chinese silk encasing her skin, not with her master looming over her smaller, more

133

vulnerable form. No. She was a creature from a pillow book, a moonflower, a servant of whom anything might be asked. She trembled as Patrick sat on the edge of the bed. His lips curled upward at the corners, but somehow his face was stern. He set his playthings on the mattress beside her hip. With gentle, steady fingers, he released the frogs that fastened the front of her shirt.

'I'm very pleased with how you look in this,' he said. 'I think we'll leave it mostly on.' He spread the tunic's halves to bare her breasts. Her nipples ached for his touch, but he reached for the jeweller's case instead. The velvet box contained a long gold chain with a key at the end. When he fastened the chain around her waist, the length that held the key was just long enough to touch her clit.

He gave the chain a tug. 'This symbolises your desire to please me. We won't say you'll always obey, because we know what a rebel you are, and we know you need discipline. Of course –' he bent until his lips brushed her ear '– we know I like to administer discipline, so if you must be naughty, that will please me, too.'

His voice alone, with its tender, smoky threat, called a rush of moisture from her sex. 'What shall I call you?' she whispered.

'Call me Patrick,' he said. 'To you, "Patrick" will be the same as "sir." '

Her body quivered. 'Yes, Patrick,' she said, and the name did indeed seem to hold a spell.

He reached for one of the scarves, sheer silk splashed with yellow and scarlet. 'Put your arms above your head, Audrey.'

When he said her name, it was charged as well: by his tone, by the dark intent in his eyes. She lifted her arms. He tied her wrists, one to the other, then arranged her hands behind her head as if she were lounging in the sun. 'Be careful not to move,' he said. 'Struggling will tighten the knots.'

Her legs were next. He pushed them up and back until her knees pressed the side of her breasts. With two sapphire scarves, he bound them to her shoulders, then passed the last scarf behind her back to secure all the ties together. The arrangement didn't allow much movement but held her in surprising comfort. It also bared the slit in her trousers. Behind it, her sex gaped, the lips stretched, the mouth wide and wet. For reasons she didn't understand, she felt more exposed than if she'd been naked.

With lazy, laughing eyes, Patrick reached inside to pet her sticky curls. One long finger slid into her, eliciting a moan of longing. He drew the finger out and sucked it. Her blush deepened. 'This is very good, Audrey. I'm pleased you enjoy being bound. I think, however, that your body needs more provocation before it's ready to take me. I am, after all, somewhat larger than the average male.'

He must have known she'd be compelled to look for confirmation. Fingers spread like a peacock's tail, he rubbed the front of his trousers, gluing her gaze to the rigid bulge. A wave of summery heat rolled through her chest. She knew it was childish, but she loved well-hung men; loved how desired they made her feel; loved the challenge of squeezing them inside. 'Do you want to see it?' he purred, as if he guessed precisely what was going through her mind.

She bit her lip and nodded. His grin was a flash of boyish charm, surprising, endearing. He opened his trousers and pushed them down his legs, boxers and all. He stepped free of the tangle. A small, helpless sound uncoiled in her throat. She had not seen him clearly from the kitchen door. His cock was big and solid, with a thick, meaty strut arching up from swollen balls. She supposed it should have been ugly:

all those veins, all that dark curling hair. To her, it was a sight to sigh over. His colour was deep, almost rusty. A runnel of fluid was seeping from his slit, evidence of an excitement even he could not contain. The head was a substantial mouthful on its own, and never mind the shaft. An instinctive female panic knotted in her chest. I can't take all that, she thought. But she knew she could. The desire to try made her sex spasm with greed.

Eyelids shuttering a smile, Patrick reached for the small brown bottle that lay by her hip. It bore a white label, hand-lettered in emerald ink. THREE SPICE, it said. BATCH 17. When he unscrewed the top, the scent of cinnamon filled the room. He held the bottle up to the light with his thumb on the bottom and his middle finger stoppering the top.

'This,' he said, 'is a mild irritant in a base of soothing oil. It produces a slight burning sensation, an itch which stimulates a woman's natural lubrication. It wears off within a quarter hour but, until it does, the user experiences an uncontrollable urge to be rubbed with great vigour wherever the oil is placed. Shall we try it, you and I?'

The strangled sound Audrey emitted was more moan than acquiescence, but Patrick's eyes twinkled the same as if she'd jumped for joy, which – in a way – she had.

'Excellent. I'll start first, shall I?' His grin hooked the end of his Roman nose. 'I love coming to these encounters eager.'

The bottle had a narrow opening. He shook six drops down the length of his staff, then used both hands to rub the mysterious substance in. Audrey didn't know if the oil or the massage were to blame but, within seconds, his skin had flushed a deeper, hotter red. 'One more for good luck,' he said. With his tongue pressed between his lips, he shook a seventh drop on to his glans. He blended it swiftly with the moisture already there.

Overcome with excitement, Audrey closed her eyes.

'No.' Patrick gripped her jaw, forcing her to look at him. 'I want your eyes, Audrey. Your eyes belong to me.' So she watched as he rubbed the oil around the piercings in her nipples, down her belly, and around the swollen folds of her sex. The last drop he massaged into the hood of her clit, easing the itch even as he raised it.

As soon as he stopped, it became impossible not to squirm.

'Careful,' he said. 'You'll tighten the knots.'

She groaned at the reminder, gnashing her teeth at the wild, flicking burn that was teasing the sensitive tissues of her body. If he hadn't issued his warning, if she hadn't been tied, she'd have thrashed in desperation. She'd have squeezed her thighs together with her fingers driving hard inside her cunt. As it was, however, her knees were bound to her shoulders and her hands behind her neck. She could not touch herself. She dared not move. Patrick was her only hope for relief. Looking like the cat that ate the cream, he closed the little brown bottle and set it on the bedside table.

'I need you,' she growled, past worrying over master–slave etiquette. 'I need you inside me.'

The bastard had the nerve to laugh. 'As it happens,' he said, with a nod towards his flaming cock. 'I need you, too.'

Still chuckling, he stood and tore off his open shirt. She should have been pleased, but his nudity offered its own torment. He was seriously built. Leanly muscled, lushly haired, his legs made her mouth water all by themselves. They were runner's legs, with deeply incised muscles and beautifully rounded buttocks.

She wished she were naked, too, naked and free to touch every inch of his gorgeous form.

'Not this time,' he said, reading her mind. 'Next time, you can touch everything I own. This time, you belong to me.'

He swung on to the bed, his hands by her shoulders, his knees below her bent and open legs. He kissed her deeply, breathing hard against her cheek, strafing her tongue with his teeth. She groaned into his mouth because the heat he stirred increased the prickling irritation of her sex. 'It only gets worse,' he said. 'When I fuck you, I'll drive the burning deep inside. It's all over my cock, Audrey, and soon it'll be all over you.'

'Now,' she demanded, craning far enough to bite his shoulder. 'Do it now.'

His pupils swelled. His knees shifted. She felt the head of him, wide and wet, against the opening of her sex. It pressed but did not enter. 'Now?' he said. One dark brow slanted up his forehead. His hips swivelled, pushing the firm corona over her clit. Sweat beaded his darkened cheeks, but he did not drop his taunting pose. 'I don't hear you begging, Audrey.'

She groaned. 'Please, Patrick. Please fuck me. Please.'

He smiled and pushed and then he was groaning, too. The width of him stretched her, burnt her. At once, the oil began to work, a million pinpricks, a million tiny fires. Her body gushed to put them out but all they did was spread. He reached the halfway mark and cursed, his limbs trembling almost as violently as hers. 'Am I hurting you?' he said. 'You're so tight.'

She shook her head. 'It's good. Push harder. Give me all of it.'

He worked his arms beneath her body to brace her

shoulders. Sweat rolled down his chest and tiny noises issued from his throat. With a grunt of effort, he pushed. 'Just a little more,' he gasped and then he was there, thick, hot, throbbing like a second heart. She wanted to savour the feel of him joined to her, his bulk, his vibrance, but even as he hilted, the itching prickle seemed to explode inside her body. She wriggled beneath him, whimpering with a need too huge for words.

He kissed her, an unmitigated taking of her mouth. Even if she'd wanted, she couldn't have fought that marauding tongue. She gasped for air when he set her free. 'Count to thirty,' he ordered. 'Then we'll move.'

He counted with her, slowing her, pinching her sharply when she rushed ahead. Twice he made her start over, though he was trembling himself, muscles twitching like a restive racehorse. He was huge inside her; so hard the clenching of her muscles only made him swell the more. But he would not move. He would not thrust until she finished counting. She thought if she could not rub that burning itch, she'd die.

'Thirty,' she said, her voice as rough as if she'd screamed herself hoarse. 'Thirty, damn it.'

His grip tightened on her shoulders. He arched his back to reach her mouth. He caught her lower lip between his teeth. 'Thirty,' he said, and slammed into motion.

She came within seconds, wailing at the deep, hard stab of pleasure. He must have felt her spasms. A growl rumbled in his chest. He pumped faster. Like an animal, his lips drew back from his teeth. He wrenched one hand from beneath her back and rolled her oil-singed nipple. His fingers pressed the bar inside, sending an ache straight to her clit. She came again with a startled gasp. He tried to reach her breast with his mouth, but the position hampered the action of his hips. That neither of them could tolerate. She tried to help him, tried to roll her pelvis against the net of scarves. His entry deepened.

'Careful,' he warned, though his face contorted with what looked to be excruciating need. He released her breast and gripped her bottom, tilting it for his thrusts. 'Later. I'll get your nipples –' His voice broke. His hips jarred forward. Warmth flooded her sex. He'd come. She knew from the vibration of his sigh. But he was still hard, still moving, just very slowly.

'It's all right,' he said, as heavy as a sleepwalker. 'We're not done here, yet.'

To her relief, he continued to stroke. His face was beautiful as he moved above her, his mouth relaxed, his skin flushed, his short hair clinging in sweaty arcs. His cock grew firmer, fatter. She could feel each thrust; appreciate each incremental easing of her distress. The prickle began to fade, frustration turning pure, going gold. Her squirms slowed, lascivious now, like a snake stretching its back. He smiled and moved both hands over her breasts. 'Together,' he said, kneading the last of the itch away. 'We come this time together.'

Even this was his to order. Her arousal rose at his command, reaching, yearning. The synchrony was effortless. When he groaned with hunger, hunger throbbed through her. When he swelled, she tightened. He read the signals of her body as if it were his own. She hovered closer, closer. The hand that held her bottom moved, one finger tickling her anal bud. She gasped as it slid inside. The tip was oiled. A new heat sprang to life inside her. He rubbed her, drawing his finger from the first knuckle to the last, a quick, smooth motion that changed the itch to a buzz and the buzz to a burn. Her pussy caught fire again,

140

touched off by the unfamiliar spark. She moaned and it sounded barely human.

'Now,' he said, through the roaring of her blood. 'With me.'

He pumped her back and front. Sensation crashed. Up, up. She was dizzy, helpless, squeezed by the first sweet pulses of an orgasm harder than any she'd ever known. She felt him stiffen and shoot and then her climax flared too high to sense any pleasure but her own. She soared, blinded, almost frightened by the strength of what she felt. At last, when it had shaken the teeth in her skull, the orgasm eased.

She opened bleary eyes to find Patrick cutting the scarves. His hands shook but they did not fumble. When she was free, he chafed her tingling wrists until warmth returned to her hands. Then he pulled the sheets up from the foot of the bed and curled his long, hard body around her back. Her eyes widened in surprise. Hadn't he been on his way to work? She could understand him delaying his departure for sex, but for a snuggle? With her?

'Something wrong?' he asked, running his hand down her arm.

She let the stiffness drain from her body. 'No. Everything's wonderful.'

'Good,' he said, his voice already sleepy. 'You did very well.'

She stroked the arm that cradled her neck. His fingers were lax, as trusting as a child's. She could hardly believe they were his. She touched the calluses at the top of his palm. There was his hardness, there. She closed her eyes. Deep inside her, in the recesses of her soul, something sparked and began to burn like a tiny candle. The something had never been there before: not for her father, who cared more about hockey than he did for her; not for her mother, who was dear and sweet but as alien from her daughter as she could be. It hadn't been there for any of her ex-boyfriends, or for Sterling, who – truth be told – was barely a person to Audrey. Nor had it been there for Tommy, her best friend, though of all the people she'd known, he'd come the closest to lighting it.

If she'd suspected how small and fragile the something was, she might have blown it out. As it happened, however, she barely registered its presence. She certainly didn't know what it was. Consequently, as Audrey slept in Patrick's arms, the little flame burnt merrily, a sneak thief, a harbinger of things to come.

When Audrey rolled out of bed for the second time that day, Patrick was gone. Sadly, her tunic and trousers were crumpled beyond wearing. She folded them and added the dry cleaners to her list of errands. She didn't regret the absence of Sterling's servants to whisk the clothes away. Pleasures like this morning's were worth some inconvenience.

She showered quickly, donned the nicest of her sundresses and headed to the kitchen to scare up a meal. To her surprise, Basil sat in the living room, sipping coffee from a delicate porcelain cup. He wore a suit, a man's suit. Its muted green set off a pale gold shirt. A matching handkerchief peeped from the breast pocket. Newton snoozed on his knee. Minus the cat and plus a few inches, he could have stepped off the cover of *Gentleman's Quarterly*.

He lifted his cup in greeting. 'Yes, I'm still here. The gig may be up as far as you're concerned, but wool remains to pull over our spying friend across the river. I'm here for the duration, whatever that might be.'

With neither food nor coffee in her veins, Audrey couldn't make sense of his tone. She managed a nod and continued to the kitchen. There she filled a mug with hot Sumatran, ate the cold sausages that remained in the pan and grabbed a navel orange from a dwindling bowl of fruit. Food shopping jumped to the top of her mental list. She was a guest here, not a sponger.

The orange and the coffee accompanied her return to the living room. She took the corner of the couch next to Basil's chair. Ignoring her, he pinched his lip and stared out at the rooftop garden. Newton yawned and nudged his hand. When Basil began to pet him, he purred.

'Are you angry with me?' she said.

He blinked, but didn't turn. 'No.'

She spread a napkin across her lap and dug her thumbnail into the orange. 'Are you angry with Patrick?'

Basil sighed and smoothed the crease of his trousers. He'd crossed his legs the way a woman would, calf to calf. In spite of this, he looked more elegant than effeminate. 'Do you know what my dear departed boyfriend used to call Patrick? The Dominator. He used to tease me for having such a lech for him. Said if I wanted to be spanked, I ought to call my mum.'

'Where is he now?'

'Patrick?'

'Your dear departed boyfriend.'

Basil's laugh was harsh and startled. 'I'm afraid that wasn't a joke. That big train derailment last spring: he was killed in it.' He shielded his eyes with the side of his hand. 'When they found him ... in the wreckage ... they saw he'd thrown his body over a little girl. Five years old.' This time his laugh had a break in it. 'She survived. A concussion and a fractured leg. She sent me a card on her birthday. Crayon and glitter and every second word misspelt. She wanted me to know what a hero my friend had been.'

Audrey squeezed his arm. 'I'm sorry. You must miss him a lot.'

Basil pressed his lips together. When he lifted his head, his jaw was hard. 'I must have been insane to think Patrick could help me forget. All he'll give me is more grief.'

'Oh, Basil.'

'No, no.' He patted her hand. 'I'm not in love with him if that's what you're worried about. I've merely got a private bone to pick, and I will, when the time is right.'

'If you want to talk about it . . .'

He smiled. She saw he was calm again. His habitual, ironic wit shone from his coffee-coloured eyes. 'You're a nice girl, Audrey Popkin. You be careful with Patrick. He's got charm to burn, but he only lets people so close. That's the way he's comfortable. That's the way he runs his life.'

Audrey thought of Tommy, of the way she could never quite love him enough. She thought of her conservative Midwestern mother, whose love inspired more guilt than appreciation. She thought of all the ex-boyfriends who'd fallen by the wayside, unmourned and unremembered. Had she ever loved anyone the way Basil loved his friend?

'Patrick and I might have that in common,' she said.

Basil pinched her cheek. 'You can wish, dearest, but wishing doesn't make it true.'

# Chapter Nine

*T*he next few weeks were as close to idyllic as Audrey could conceive. Her job was still new, still challenging and – as Cynthia had predicted – more interesting than she'd imagined. She met many of the city's bigwigs, some associates of Patrick's father, some Patrick's own acquaintances. She amused herself by trying to guess which were part of his spanking crowd. Patrick would not tell her, nor did he involve anyone but himself in her training.

'You're mine,' he explained. 'Unless you express a burning desire for a crowd scene, I intend to keep you to myself.'

The possibility that she might influence the course of their relationship by expressing a preference had not occurred to her. A mixture of fear and excitement coursed through her veins. She assured Patrick she was happy to be kept as private stock.

He kept her well, he and Basil both. Neither allowed her to cook or clean, her incompetence at the tasks earning identical expressions of disgust from the men. They relegated her to shopping. Since she enjoyed shopping, she made no complaints. She and

Basil had a running bet that she could buy any ingredient he could cook. Thus far she'd only missed one and it was just as well, because he'd requested a part of a pig she knew was better left uneaten. As punishment, Basil made her pay for pizza. In thanks, Patrick installed an Arabian Night-ish canopy over her bed. From then on, embroidered silk curtained her sleep in midnight blue and gold.

This was not the last of his redecorating. Bit by bit, the guest room lost its spartan air. Patrick covered the floor with small Persian carpets, at least a dozen, all soft as velvet underfoot. A comfy armchair took up residence beside the window, a bookcase for her mysteries, a Chinese screen to hide the infamous closet rail. Pictures adorned the walls, one of them a real Degas. The quick charcoal sketch displayed a dancer tying her shoe. Audrey's heart beat faster every time she saw it. That Patrick trusted her with it amazed her. He said he'd hung it to remind her what true discipline was, but his eyes had been twinkling, and she'd thought ... she'd suspected he'd done it merely to please her.

He was full of surprises. Every morning the black suit bag contained a different outfit. He hadn't repeated one yet. Sometimes the clothes were exotic, sometimes elegant, sometimes whimsical. All were feminine and all made her feel cosseted, like the favourite in a harem.

Of course, concubines didn't wait tables five nights a week.

He never tried to top her at work, not since those first few days when he'd teased her that he might. If she made a mistake, he treated her the same as his other employees: with patience and humour. One night, he called in one of the part-timers so she could enjoy Basil's performance without distraction. That was a treat. Basil was so good, so fun to watch. He

146

became Basha when he sang, a sultry chanteuse with a gleam in her eye. Come and get me, the gleam said, if you're man enough. A large portion of the audience seemed to wish they were.

'You were man enough,' Patrick teased when she shared her impressions.

'So were you,' she countered. He grimaced but did not scold. He reserved his master persona for home and, even there, he often let it slide. For long stretches of time, they played no roles at all. At first, the lack of scripting threw her off balance. She didn't know what to say, how to act. He knew so much. He'd done so much. Compared to him, she was a silly, green girl. When shyness overcame her, Basil's presence helped immeasurably. He could talk to anyone about anything. Gradually, watching him, and Patrick's response to him, she realised he didn't expect her to be anyone but herself.

She began to know her master as a person. He was charming but moody, and in a mood he wanted no one near him but the cat. He had a keen grasp of politics, but did not care about it as she or Basil did. He worked hard, but he came from money. Like Cynthia, he had the unconscious arrogance that could bring. He didn't understand her pleasure over finding asparagus on sale. He admired her concern for her future but did not see it as urgent. He saw no reason to apologise for any of his opinions. His likes and dislikes were strong. He hated all TV except the news. If she and Basil wanted to watch, he'd leave the room. He loved music, any kind of music but most especially jazz. He and Basil spent long hours conversing about musicians she'd never heard of. Audrey would tuck herself under his arm and read mysteries while their voices flowed over her head, one low and rich, one mild and smooth.

'We're boring her,' Basil would warn.

Audrey always shook her head and smiled. There was something so comforting about curling into the solidity of his body. She loved to run her hands over him when he'd let her, usually after they'd played whatever game he'd chosen for the night. She'd smooth her palms down his arms, over his legs, admiring each muscle and curve. She'd comb her fingers through the hair that trailed from his chest to his groin. She loved to pet his flaccid sex, the skin silken under her hand, the muscle lax. The big head would loll between his thighs, still wet sometimes with seed and cream. She could wipe him clean with the tips of her fingers, the curve of her thumb. Or she could bend to drag their tastes across her tongue, counting his pulse with the tip pressed into his slit, seeing if she could rouse him one more time.

He'd lie quietly while she stroked him, eyes closed, mouth curling faintly at the corners. Sometimes his body would arch and stretch like the cat's and she'd sense he was purring inside. She liked that as much as the times he'd swell beneath her touch and take her again, lazily, like a heavy-laden ship easing into port. Like waves he'd lap in and out, thumb circling her pleasure point to compensate for the indolent pace.

'You're a greedy little thing,' he'd say, sounding pleased. He'd thicken inside her, more and more, until the stretch of her walls made her moan with need. 'Say please,' he'd tease and, when she said it, he'd fill his lungs and pound in hard and deep. His strength amazed her: the control he had over his own body.

But some responses even he could not fight. On the nights she coaxed him to this extra lovemaking, he would sleep almost as soon as he came, his final sigh of pleasure drawn out like a yawn. She couldn't say why she revelled in this, but she did; maybe because his surrender to sleep seemed so trusting. She could not truly hurt him, of course, so his trust was an illusion. Regardless, holding him as he slept gave her great satisfaction. No other man had calmed her like this. In its way, the peace he inspired was as addictive as the excitement. Together, they filled her life. She couldn't remember having been so content. She could almost forget Sterling Foster's existence.

The watcher, however, remained.

Patrick and Basil developed a ritual to keep him lulled. At some point every evening they would stroll through the garden on the roof, pause beneath the trellis, and kiss for the benefit of the telescope. Some nights, Basil managed to keep Patrick out a long time. 'He's all yours,' he'd say when they returned, and Patrick's flushed face would flush darker with annoyance.

Basil relished his power to arouse him. Sometimes Patrick would be hard to satisfy after these necking sessions. One night he took her three times, one after the other, no frills, just straight, hard-driving sex. Audrey didn't mind. Any sort of sex with Patrick was exciting. He never lost his aura of danger held in check.

And the snuggling afterward; she would never tire of that. Even if he didn't spend the night in her bed, he'd hold her until she fell asleep. If she woke and he'd remained, she'd get the oddest feeling, as if she'd just been born and didn't know her name. The blue and gold canopy would twinkle in the dark like a sky full of stars, a universe of unknown magic beating against her skin. With a sense of wonder, she'd lie on her back and listen to him breathe. I could be anyone, she'd think, anyone at all, and so could he. The mystery of what had drawn them together, what drew anyone together, filled her with a pleasurable, trembling awe.

Other nights, when she remembered Basil's warning, she'd wonder if he held all his submissives this way.

One day, on the off-chance Basil might shed light on the topic, she climbed the stairs to ask him. He had his own room off the balcony, where he'd installed a digital piano. Audrey had come to loathe his practice scales as much as she loved his singing. Not sorry to forestall the torture, she propped one shoulder against the wall and shoved her hands into the pockets of the tight moleskin jeans Patrick had left for her that morning. The matching black silk blouse slid smoothly over her skin, cool as a mountain stream. 'Tell me about his girlfriends,' she said. 'The ones before me.'

Basil dragged his thumb down an octave of keys. 'Never met them.'

'Never met them! Why not?'

'Patrick and I aren't bosom buddies. Before I moved in, we barely knew each other.'

Audrey rolled this over in her mind. It was true she'd never heard them discussing personal matters: their childhoods, their dreams. But why would Patrick enter this charade with a man he barely knew? Was it easier for him to play boyfriend with someone to whom he didn't have ties? Or was the truth as Basil claimed: Patrick simply wasn't close to anyone? Since coming to work for him, she'd met many people who knew Patrick and were fond of him. None seemed as intimate with him as Basil. Perhaps what Basil said was true. Perhaps Patrick, charming and personable though he was, didn't have friends.

The thought made her eyes prick. Could that truly be the way he wanted to live? She clenched her hands in her pockets. If it was what he wanted, she didn't have the power to change him. She'd be a fool to forget it.

150

Basil was watching her with calm, curious eyes. She said the first thing that came to her mind. 'Why did you agree to help him? Since you say you weren't close.'

He shrugged. 'He's my boss. I didn't want to lose my job.'

'That's not an answer. He wouldn't have fired you. Anyway, you're good enough to perform anywhere. Maybe even to record.'

Basil played a teasing riff, his expression wry. 'I'm a singer, not a freak. If people found out Basha was Basil, that's all they'd see. Patrick's good at keeping secrets. He respects my privacy.'

*Unlike you*, was the unspoken implication. But if Basil could push where he wasn't wanted, so could Audrey. 'Would coming out be so horrible? Maybe you'd seem like a freak at first, but eventually people would get used to the idea and just hear your voice. It could even be a marketing point.'

'No,' Basil said. His fingers settled on an emphatic chord.

He's afraid, she thought. Afraid he'll try to succeed and fail. Or maybe the illusion of being Basha was so precious to him he couldn't bear for anything to break it. Either possibility saddened her. But who was she to call him to task for a lack of ambition? Where was her brilliant career? Giving up, she turned to leave.

Basil caught her attention with a ripple of notes. 'You wanted to know about Patrick's girlfriends.'

'Yes,' she said, though suddenly she wasn't sure.

'I don't know much,' he warned. 'In fact, I don't know anything. I'm not certain Patrick has had actual girlfriends since I've known him. None of his playmates ever came into the bar.'

Playmates. Was that what Audrey was? She shook

off the thought. Nonsense. She wasn't a playmate. She was a project.

The distinction was not particularly heartening.

'I want to swim on the roof,' she said.

Patrick looked up from the *Washington Post*. It was Monday. The bar was closed, the day was bright, and Audrey's pout added a biteable fullness to her mouth. His penis stirred beneath his black silk robe. He forced his expression to remain stern. 'I don't want you out there where the watcher can see you.'

'But I'm tired of jogging.'

For the past week, Patrick had coaxed her into running along the towpath to the C&O Canal. He'd known she wasn't fit enough to enjoy it, but this was the first time she'd complained. He folded the paper and set it on the kitchen table. 'I never ordered you to exercise.'

'I'm not saying I want to quit. I just need a break.' The pout had left her voice. He stroked her cheek, amused by the way she tried so hard to be a grown up, harder than some grown ups tried, truth be told.

'I don't think he can see the pool,' she said. 'Not with the wall in the way.' She pursed her lips and vamped one shoulder. 'I do have a nice collection of swimwear. You could join me.'

He considered the invitation. He doubted the swim would remain platonic, knowing Audrey, and knowing himself around Audrey. To betray the chemistry between them might be foolhardy. He wasn't ready for a showdown with Audrey's old master. She was far from completely his – not that he expected her to be. Patrick's methods were slow and graduated. If forced to choose, he wasn't sure she'd cleave to him with the totality his father hoped would humiliate the blackmailing banker. On the other hand, the arrogant SOB might benefit from a test to his nerves.

'Very well,' he said. 'I'll change and meet you there.'

The pool was a small, round jewel of aqua ripples. Half a lap in diameter, it glowed within a circle of sun warmed brick. Flowers spilt from the surrounding beds: azaleas, hot pink and heavy with blooms; orange trees growing gamely in wooden pots; roses so sweet their scent seemed as warm and soft as the water that lapped her skin.

With one hand grasping the rim, Audrey relaxed until her feet floated up and her toes broke the surface of the pool. She wore her favourite bikini, purple pansies on a yellow ground. It went well with Patrick's chain and key. The tiny top tied behind her neck, making her aware of the weight of her breasts. The bottom was a triangle of cloth leading to a thong. Wearing it demanded a close and thorough shave. She ran one finger down the smooth channel beside her hipbone and shivered with sensual enjoyment. This was the way to spend August in DC, not huffing down some stinky canal, so sweaty she could send the humidity up a point by herself. She closed her eyes and let the late summer sun bake their lids. A jet broke the silence of the sky and traffic rumbled in the street below. Here in her head, though, Audrey was in heaven.

The glass door slid open. She slitted her eyes to see if it was Patrick, then jerked to her feet with a splash. He was naked, head to toe. He strolled across the patterned red brick as if Basil weren't a room away practising his scales, as if the world had never held a pair of uninvited eyes.

He stopped before her, godlike, then lowered himself to the side of the pool. He did not dabble his feet but sat sideways, stretching his muscular legs along the rim. His cock curled large and slack across his hairy thigh. Its eye seemed to stare at her, though with considerably less astonishment than she was experiencing. Without a word, he commandeered her suntan lotion and proceeded to oil the white marks at his groin.

'Stay where you are,' he said when she lifted her arm to help. He used his master's voice, firm and low. She could only swallow as he oiled his pale, sleeping cock. Its softness taunted her. She was pulsing with readiness. She wanted him to be, too. Most especially, she wanted to caress that slippery serpent and make it stiff. She waited, hoping for instructions, but he did not give them. When he'd oiled his legs and chest, he lay back and closed his eyes.

'Grab that pool chair,' he said, gesturing blindly to a styrofoam lounger that floated near the steps. Striped navy and white canvas stretched across the buoyant frame. 'I want you to lie on it with your feet facing my head.'

She did as he asked. After a few more instructions, she was positioned to his satisfaction. He'd barely looked at her. His arm moved with the lassitude of a bored sultan. His hand slid up her legs, found its way under the gusset of her suit, and entered her waiting sex. Gentle as the insertion was, it called a longing whimper from her throat.

'Quiet,' he ordered. 'I'm going to tell you a story. You must be silent as you listen, silent and still. Your body will tell me which parts you like best. You need not utter a word.'

He worked two fingers deeper inside, curling them to follow her curves. His thumb he perched on the swell of her clit. He did not rub the little bead, merely pressed it, as if preparing to count her most intimate pulse. Audrey bit her lip and fought a compulsion to work herself against him. She hoped the story wouldn't torment her too badly but feared very much it would. Patrick was Irish, after all. He'd know how to spin a tale.

'Once upon a time,' he began, 'by a great oasis in the desert, there lived a stern and righteous king. Rich, he was, in water and in gold. The minarets of his palace shone with that sunny metal, and its windows were rimmed with jewels. In every courtyard a fountain played. In every tree a bird sang out with joy. So mighty and so blessed was this king that he had forty wives, each lovelier than the last. These forty wives bore forty strapping sons, all of whom were officers in his army. Together, they formed a formidable force. As a result, the king but rarely went to war. Strangers sent him tribute before a drop of blood was spilt. Most often, he used his troops to keep his neighbours from squabbling amongst themselves.

'On the king's fortieth birthday, in gratitude for settling a dispute, one of his vassals sent him a gift.

'"My youngest daughter, Zaphie," wrote the lord on the scroll that accompanied her. "The apple of my eye, a creature so beautiful, grown men tremble to look upon her. Only you, our mighty king, are strong enough to tame her. Only you can face her beauty without fear."

'The daughter, the gift, stood before the king's throne swathed in cloth of gold. Her head was veiled and bowed, but she did not kneel as was the custom, nor did her stance convey aught of humility.

'"Well, well," said the king, amused by her pride. "Let us see if this paragon lives up to her reputation."

'The courtiers held their breath as he approached the girl and drew his sword. Even then she did not fall to her knees. With three long slashes, the king disrobed her. The crowd let out a sigh. The lord's daughter possessed an enchanting form, more enchanting perhaps than any of the wives. Flush and

155

firm with youth, ripe with sensual promise, her beauty caused many a hand to slip beneath a robe to soothe a twitching sex.

'The king was not so easily impressed. "Very nice," he said. "Let us see if the face matches the body." So saying, he flung off Zaphie's veil.

'At this, the king was speechless. He had expected the cool proud polish of a mountain snow. What he found was a rising sun. The girl laughed at him without saying a word; laughed at him, her sovereign lord. Her eyes sparkled. Her soft mouth curled. Her cheeks were as rosy as a peach. A bolt of lust struck the worldly king. Beneath his royal robes, his cock grew painfully hard, stiffening as it had not done since his youth.

' "Come with me," he said gruffly. Grabbing her wrist, he pulled the naked girl behind him, striding so swiftly from the hall she stumbled in his wake. So hard did his desire for her ride him, he could not wait to reach his private rooms. A hundred steps from the audience chamber, in a shadowed prayer chapel, he pushed Zaphie behind the statue of a god, hauled out his mighty cock, and took her without delay.

'When her maidenhead broke across his fleshy sword, something snapped in his mind. Her cries inflamed him. He was hurting her, she said. He was breaking her in two. His climax ripped from him with the force of a sandstorm. He could not hold his groans inside. Fearing the courtiers would hear him, he muffled them against her breast. He came and he came, until his seed was drained. Even then he could not bear to leave her body's soft embrace. His sword remained unvanquished. His motions slowed only; grew coaxing and sly. He slipped his hand between their bodies and tickled her tender pearl. Zaphie gasped and wound her arms behind his neck. The king kissed her pomegranate mouth. "Oh, my," she murmured. "What is this magic you do to me?"

'The god whose shelter they had sought smiled kindly on the flowering of Zaphie's joy. He sent its ripples deep into her loins, so deep and sweet she clutched the royal shaft as if she'd never let it go. "Again," she cried, all gasps and sighs. "Again, your Majesty. Please."

'For forty nights, they gave themselves to madness. The king sought no other but her; wanted no other but her. He took her with the ferocity of a camel bull in heat: on her back, on her belly, in his bed, on the floor. They mated in his bath. He mounted her across his throne. He fucked her in every position the gods proclaimed as wise, and a number they had forbidden. He spilt in her an ocean of royal seed. In short, he took her like a man who had lost his reason. No bed was softer than her breast, no food sweeter than the honey of her desire.

'Finally, his advisers called him aside. "Honorable Majesty," began the eldest, "we are delighted to see your vitality undiminished by your years. Your neglect of your forty wives, however, concerns us. Naturally, when you are happy, they rejoice, but is this the respect they are due for bearing loyal sons? Moreover, shall those sons, loving their mothers, understand you mean no disrespect by your behaviour?"

'Once he had swallowed his ire, the king saw that they were right. He spent the next forty nights with each of his wives in turn. He showered them with gifts and kindness, making love in his old gentle way, listening to their stories and their plaints. Then, satisfied that peace reigned again within the palace, he returned to Zaphie's chamber. The spring in his step was that of a much younger man.

'She greeted him with tears of rage. "I gave you my

innocence," she wailed. "You made me believe you loved me."

'"Hush," said the king, his hands spread in conciliation.

'Zaphie broke a priceless vase across his brow. The king touched the wound. He stared at the blood, then at Zaphie. Zaphie trembled with fear but her eyes flashed fire. "I don't care," she said. "I will hate you forever for breaking my heart!"

'Two things happened to the king upon hearing her reckless declaration. First, his soul exulted to discover this exquisite creature loved him. Second, his determination to master her grew implacably firm. If Zaphie could not learn her place, the welfare of his household would oblige him to set her aside. That he did not wish to do.

'In a motion too quick to evade, he bound her delicate hands behind her back, ripped her gown from her body, and turned her over his knee. "Your heart is mine," he said in his most indomitable tone. "Mine to cherish or break as I please. You will cease, at once, to protest anything I do."

'"I won't," she cried, wriggling like a frantic eel. "I won't, I won't, I won't!"

'He answered with the flat of his hand. He, who had never spanked a living soul, beat Zaphie's round white bottom until the sun rising over the dunes did not flush a deeper pink. Her tears soaked her face. Her cries singed his ears. Her heart pounded wildly where the softness of her breast pressed his leg. The king's arousal had not flagged since he'd turned his steps towards her rooms, but now he felt something which squeezed the blood so fiercely through his cock, he feared his pleasure would burst.

'Zaphie's juices were running down her thighs. Despite her tears, despite her cries of outrage,

Zaphie's desire for him flared as hot as he had ever seen it.

'At once, he threw her face down on the carpet. There she writhed, hands bound behind her, cheek pressed to the floor, hips lifting in a silent plea. He needed no more invitation. He covered her, lunging into her from behind, filling her velvet channel with his iron shaft. He seemed to have known no pleasure since they'd coupled last. No: he seemed to have known no pleasure in his life. The king was larger than other men and now his organ was so swollen with lust, she could barely contain his width. He wrenched her leg higher, opening her body for his thrusts. Her hands curled into fists beneath his belly. She whimpered. She squirmed. He curled his longest finger across her slippery bud.

'"Now," he shouted, feeling the end rushing nearer. "Come with me now!"

'Her body convulsed at his command, dragging pleasure down his cock in a seething river of fire. On and on it went, blinding streaks of bliss. The force of it astonished him. He lay above her, panting, feeling as if she'd pulled his soul out through his loins. "You see," he said, when he was able. "I love you still. Now be a good girl and do not raise a tempest when I visit my other wives. They have stood by me these many years. They have given me sons and succoured me when times were hard. They deserve a night in my arms."

'Zaphie's body stiffened beneath him. "I hate you," she said in a muffled, teary voice. "You are a cruel and heartless man."

'The king was stunned. Never had anyone said such a thing. Never had anyone dared. He rose and pulled his rebellious young lover to her feet. "You have not learnt your lesson," he said. "But I will teach you my will is law."

'A golden leash lay on a table beside her bed, such as ladies of the court used to lead the temple cats about the grounds. The collar was just large enough for Zaphie's slender neck. The king fastened it and pulled her naked from the room. "Say another word," he warned, "and I will gag you with my belt."

'He led her to the weapons room, where his guards were suiting up for their daily exercise at arms. They fell to their knees as soon as they saw him, but even their respect was not great enough to keep their gaze from straying to his beautiful captive. "Rise," he said, their lust as pleasing as their homage. "One stands here with greater cause to kneel than you."

'They rose, their eyes hungry and wary, their eager young cocks beginning to lift beneath their braies. Few wore more than this snug article of clothing and Zaphie's own gaze slid from one powerful torso to another. The king forced her to her knees.

'"How may we serve your majesty?" asked the captain of the guard, one of the king's eldest sons. Colour had risen to his cheeks with his arousal. Nervously, he licked his lips.

'"Untie your braies," ordered the king, "and take them down. This girl is here to serve you, one after the other, until she learns the meaning of obedience."

'"No!" Zaphie cried, begging him with her eyes.

'The king beat her lightly with the leash that chained her neck. He pointed to another guard. "You. Take that leather scabbard and lash her about the bottom while she pleasures my son with her mouth."

'After a brief, staring silence, the guards sprang into action. Zaphie trembled at the first stinging smack of the scabbard, then moaned at the brush of the prince's rampant cock across her lips. Its helmet glistened with the juice of his excitement, making it slide as if in oil. Ever since Zaphie arrived at the palace, the memory of her naked beauty had fuelled fantasies among the guards. Never, however, had they dreamt they'd be permitted to sample her treasures themselves. All watched as the prince's huge, blood-flushed organ slid between her lips. All imagined the moment they would be allowed to follow.

'"This is the fruit of my loins," said the king. "You must show him the same care you would offer me, the same respect you owe the woman who bore him."

'For once the king's admonition was not needed. Zaphie's pomegranate mouth cosseted the young man's shaft as if his pleasure were her dearest desire. Since her hands were bound, she could not stroke him, but from no other kindness did she shrink. Up and down her head bobbed. In and out her tongue flicked. She seemed famished for the taste of him, nor did the steady spanking of her bottom dull her enthusiasm. To the contrary, it heightened it, until the desperate prince twisted and groaned like a man being stretched on the rack. All around the stony room, sweat rolled down sympathetic faces and hands adjusted swollen shafts. They wanted her, all of them, but they also wanted to watch. Driven to his limit, the prince gripped the base of his shaft and began to thrust into Zaphie's mouth. So forceful was his need, her lips grew bruised, despite his care. He drew a long, moaning breath. He gripped his balls and squeezed. Then he came, shuddering from head to toe with unprecedented bliss.

'He was but the first. One after the other, Zaphie pleasured all the guard, each taking her as he most desired: in her mouth or sex, between her breasts or against the simmering mounds of her bottom. They were animals in their lust, inflamed by each other's exploits, each man egging his fellows on. The king lost count of how many peaks Zaphie ascended. Her voice was hoarse from crying out. Their seed shone on her naked skin, on her hair and on her mouth. The scent of the guards' emissions rose from her body like rain steaming off a sun-baked stone. The king had never wanted her more. His knuckles whitened where they clenched the end of her golden leash. In some mysterious fashion, every man's pleasure had become his own.

'Finally, the last guard's will was done. Zaphie prostrated herself before the king and kissed his feet. The soldier who beat her had taken care not to break her skin, but her back and buttocks glowed from the blows of the scabbard. The sight pleased the king immensely.

'Now she is humbled, he thought. Now she is a mistress I can keep.

'She stroked the top of the royal sandal. "You should not have done it," she murmured, weary and strangely calm. "You should not have left me so long without a word. Forty nights, my lord. Would not your heart have broken, too?"

'Her quiet speech shook his certainty. Was she correct? Had he been cruel? She was young. No doubt she had been sheltered and spoilt. Perhaps he should have shown her more care.

'But, no, he could not afford this weakness, not in front of his guard, not when her future depended on his mastering her. "Take her to the dungeon," he said. "Chain her with her face to the wall."'

'No,' Audrey whispered, unable to stop herself. All through Patrick's story, her sex had twitched and wept. This, however, was more than she could bear. Anything but chains. A dark, heavy ache tightened her sex on Patrick's fingers. They stiffened inside her, but did not move. 'No,' she said again, and shook her head from side to side.

'Yes,' Patrick insisted, the word hissing with determination. He slid into the water in a single fluid move. Pulling Audrey from the raft, he turned her to

162

face the wall, just as the king had chained his slave. His chest pressed the back of her shoulders. His cock strafed the small of her back. With unforgiving hands, he manacled her wrists to the edge of the pool. 'Yes, Audrey, the king chained her in the fearsome oubliette. His heart was heavy, but he had no choice. She had to be broken or all was lost.

'He sent a trusted maid to feed and bathe her, to salve her injured skin. For three nights, Zaphie wept for his cruelty. For three days, she turned her face from him when he came to see her in her prison. Then, on the fourth night, the storm inside her ceased. Empty of tears, she found herself as pure and clean as the desert sky. Her soul was light, her body calm. She saw the midnight star that burnt in the centre of her being. Nothing could extinguish that flame: not rage, not sorrow, not fear. Unbeknown to himself, the king had shown Zaphie her power.

'When he arrived for his visit, she spoke to him in tender tones. She thanked him for his care. She said all he loved were loved by her. If a chain around her neck could bring him joy, she welcomed its embrace.

'The king was moved beyond speech. He clasped his beloved, still in her chains. He kissed the humbled curve of her neck. His manhood wept at the brush of her silken bottom, begging more, begging all. He could not wait to unchain her. Flinging off his kingly robe, he bent his knees and slid his aching phallus into her sex. The sheer relief of entry shocked him. Their four nights apart might have been a year. His cock was stone. Her sex was velvet fire. Together, they pulsed and throbbed with hunger for release, not solitary release but one that was shared. Fluid poured from her walls, from the flickering tip of his crest. The conflict they'd passed through had increased their yearning as the sun increases the crops. The king knew they would walk this road again. They would

163

clash and kiss and the fire that linked them loin to loin and heart to heart would never dim. Moaning her name, he pulled back and thrust slowly, strongly forward. Tears of joy wet Zaphie's cheeks. Their hands tangled together among her chains. Again he thrust, and again, and then the sublime crescendo locked them in its grip. This was their secret home. This was the slavery to which they had sold their souls.'

Audrey trembled at the final words. Patrick pressed his lips to the back of her neck and licked the shivery, heated skin. It was not enough. It was not half of what she wanted.

'Love me,' she said, her voice husky and hushed. 'Put your cock inside me now. Be my king.'

A shudder ran through him. With deliberate force, he tore her thong at its weakest point and laid it on the side of the pool. She felt his knees bend; heard the focused intake of his breath. He pushed inside her, immense and smooth and hot. Her flesh gave, stretched. Her sigh of relief came from the heart.

'Thank you,' he said as he thrust in steady waves. 'You've told me all I need to know.'

She tried to regret the discoveries he'd made, but she couldn't. Nor could she stop her body from betraying her again. She climaxed before he'd thrust a dozen times, not once but a chain of spasms, each burst a brilliant silver link. Her only consolation was that he could not hold back his own release. He swelled inside her and stiffened and clamped his hands like steel around her wrists. With a groan of luxuriant regret, he gave up the ghost and came.

Sterling Foster sat at his computer, downloading the latest batch of scans from Washington. He was fully prepared to yawn his way through them just as he had the last. Sterling had nothing against homosexu-

164

als. Men were as enjoyable to play with as women, sometimes more, because their egos were bigger. This lovey-dovey crap, however, made him want to gag.

The third picture in the queue brought his spine erect. It showed Audrey and Patrick in a rooftop pool. Only their heads were visible, but their rapturous expressions left no doubt as to what was happening beneath the water. Sterling drew a quick, tight circle with his mouse. He hadn't intended Patrick Dugan to become Audrey's lover. His instructions had stipulated that the senator's son was to provide an extra barrier of protection. That was all. Until Audrey returned, she was to be kept safe. Naturally, her return was inevitable. Audrey's appetite for punishment was extraordinary. A girl like her wouldn't last long without her erotic drug of choice. She might, however, be distracted by a buff young Irishman with a pike that swung both ways.

The compound's cooling system hummed, keeping the Florida night at bay. Sterling looked at the picture again and sneered. Rear entry. How very imaginative. No doubt the bisexual angle sparked her interest, but this saccharine saphead would soon bore a woman of Audrey's ilk. Her long-term satisfaction demanded a relentless iron hand.

He snapped his fingers for one of the maids to pour a drink. While she jumped to obey, he traced the image of Audrey's face with his nail. He told himself he'd inspired that expression many times, that expression and others more intense. To worry was an insult to his skill. To interfere would have been ludicrous. No cause existed for intervention yet. The more he thought about it, the surer he was. Audrey needed a lover with whom to compare him. When he offered to take her back, her gratitude would run all the deeper.

The maid set his Singapore Sling on a cut glass

coaster. A fresh hibiscus shivered on the rim. 'Will there be anything else, sir?'

Her voice trembled. He looked at her. She was a young Mexican with eyes like a doe and skin the colour of buttered toast. He'd played with her before. She was too biddable to provide much entertainment, but she was delightfully sensitive to humiliation. 'You can lick my feet,' he said. 'And if you're very, very good, I'll let you lick my cock.'

# Chapter Ten

'Meg is off, tonight,' Patrick said. 'You'll have to handle the upstairs party yourself.'

He'd walked into the employee lounge just as Audrey was clipping down her braces. Her piercings had healed, but the moment she first fastened the straps was always sensitive. She looked up at Patrick, knowing her cheeks were pinker than they should have been. 'Is it a big group?'

'A dozen. They'll be in the gold room. We're bringing in buffet-style dishes from Filomena Ristorante.' Though his expression gave nothing away, his gaze followed her hands as she smoothed the braces. In his own hand, he held a sack which he was swinging back and forth like a metronome. The cloth was crushed velvet, royal blue.

She resisted a prick of curiosity. 'I'm sure I can manage a dozen,' she said. 'Especially if the food is settled. Who'll cover the downstairs?'

'I've called in one of the part-timers.' Back and forth the sack swung, dangling from the tip of his finger. He drew her attention to his face by clearing his throat. 'You may as well take off those braces. In fact, you'd better return to the bathroom. I have a present for you and I need to see if it fits.'

He had a present for her? In that crushed velvet sack? Audrey backed distractedly towards the bathroom. She'd grown used to work being off limits for their games. The change rattled her too much to do anything but obey.

Patrick followed her into the small tiled room. With a mock flourish, he emptied the sack. Two balls of pale green jade rolled into his palm. Their surface was carved with Chinese dragons, the reliefs intricate but shallow, the quality that of fine art. A smooth satin cord linked the spheres together.

'Let's wash these,' he said, and soaped them under the hot water. Audrey watched his beautiful hands move through the foam, her sex gone supple and thick. She didn't need to be told those balls shared the same diameter as his erect penis, or that he intended to push them up the same passage. He shook the last of the water from the jade, his smile deceptively pleasant. 'Do I need to oil them?'

A surge of blood warmed Audrey's cheeks. 'Um, I don't think so.'

If anything, her wetness exceeded her expectations. Moisture squelched as he pressed the first globe gently up her sheath. His actions jarred the tiny key that hung from her waist. She hadn't removed it since he'd put it on. She liked the chain's delicate golden weight, its symbolism, and the fact that she wore it voluntarily. He'd never asked her to. Its presence was a gift, a silent, subtle promise. She was his by choice, regardless of how ephemeral his commitment to her might be. She pressed her lips together as the second ball slid inside. Her sense of internal pressure increased by sumptuous degrees.

'Not too large?' he asked. He smiled when she shook her head. 'Mind, they're a bit heavy. You might have to squeeze them up now and then.' Experimenting, Audrey tightened her vaginal walls. The jade felt wonderfully substantial inside her, harder than a cock and growing warmer by the second. The weight, coupled with its threat of possible loss, made the intrusion all the more appealing. As for the texture, the smooth, slightly raised curves of the carving entranced her hidden nerves.

Patrick tugged the knotted end of the cord. 'That feels secure to me. How about you?'

'Yes,' she said, and he kissed her open-mouthed and sweet, perhaps in appreciation for the rough-edged longing in her voice.

He drew away slowly. His starry blue eyes held mysteries she could not read. She knew, though, despite his controlled demeanor, that he was as aroused as she. 'Tonight's guests are special,' he said. 'They're a bachelor party and they've hired a very expensive stripper to perform for them.'

'Here?'

'Yes, here.' He stroked the curve of her cheek. 'Remember I told you how important privacy is to Dugan's patrons? Tonight you'll see it in action.'

She was certainly going to see something in action. A stripper. And a roomful of randy, drunken men. The back of her neck prickled. She remembered the story he'd told her about Zaphie and the palace guards: the golden leash, the soldiers she'd pleasured at the behest of the king. Surely Patrick didn't expect her to play that role for his customers!

Whether he did or not, he didn't hurry to explain. With a fey smile, he retucked her shirt and zipped her trousers. 'I want you to remain with the guests. You may leave to fill their drink orders, but that's all.'

'Patrick –'

'Hush.' He pressed the pads of two fingers to her worried lips. 'You're only to watch, lass. I want you

169

to study their arousal. I want you to know to the millimetre how long each man's erection grows. If you find it pleasant, I want you to watch the stripper. Most of all, I want you to do this without betraying your own excitement. The men will be drunk, you see, and won't have their normal inhibitions. I don't want anything to happen that might embarrass you or them later on. These are good customers, Audrey. Valued customers.'

Audrey nodded her understanding, but her nails dug into her palms and her palms themselves were hot. The pulse between her legs, magnified by the two jade spheres, felt strong enough to shake the world. She was not entirely confident she could do as Patrick asked.

The party took over the gold room at the top of the stairs. Two round tables filled most of the space, plus a platform for the dancer, who had yet to arrive. Audrey brought a round of drinks for the men, clearly not the first of their evening. Then she returned downstairs to bring up the platters from Filomena's. Eric the busboy was kind enough to help her, or perhaps the smells drew him. The lobster linguini made her mouth water. The mushrooms with crab-meat stuffing brought tears to her eyes. Behind her, Eric sighed over the *insalata di salmone*. She knew the seafood couldn't have been fresher if it had crawled on the plate a minute before.

'I didn't know you could get takeaway from Filo-mena's,' Eric said as they set the platters on the cloth-covered sidetable.

'Trust me,' Audrey assured him. 'If you've got enough money, you can get takeaway from the White House.'

They both spoke too quietly to be overheard. With their crisp navy blazers and their drunken air of

170

entitlement, their guests didn't invite hobnobbing from the hired help. To make matters worse, their manners were atrocious. They ate the beautifully prepared Italian food as if it were burgers from McDonald's. They snapped their fingers for service. They joked about the size of the bride-to-be's breasts as if Audrey weren't there, as if the groom could not conceivably take offence. In this they were correct. That chivalrous fellow merely laughed.

Compared to them, Patrick didn't seem spoilt at all. Son of privilege he might be; son of idiots he was not.

The stripper was too good for them. Audrey knew this, the moment she saw her. Like a businessman's wet dream of a secretary, the woman sashayed into the room. Conversation stopped. She had wavy blonde hair and the soft, wide cheekbones of an old-fashioned film goddess. Her sedate navy suit clung to curves as generous as her scarlet mouth. For the first time since she'd started serving, Audrey felt a flutter of interest between her legs. This was not the blowsy tassel twirler she'd expected.

'Well, hello,' said the stripper in a breathless, Marilyn Monroe-ish voice. 'Who's ready for some entertainment?'

Hoots and grunts were all the answer she got. Pigs, Audrey thought, but the stripper beamed like a proud mama. Was she for real? Or was she one of Patrick's whips-and-chains friends acting out a fantasy? Whatever her origin, she didn't waste time.

'Loosen your ties,' she crooned. 'You're going to need all the air you can get.'

She turned on her music, oddly enough something loud and raucous by Chinese Burn. To this head-banging, hard-driving noise, she pranced to the small platform at the front of the room. The music pushed her in jerks and curves. Off came her lustful-secretary jacket, then the straight, narrow skirt of her suit. Her

171

dance was standard bump and grind, but well done, and no one could fault her enthusiasm. Beneath her sheer white blouse, beneath her lacy white bra, her nipples stood out like raisins.

Thankfully, no one paid Audrey any notice, because her own breasts tightened in sympathy. The pressure between her legs, kept alive by the pale jade balls, began to beat a more demanding refrain. She backed towards the wainscotting, distancing herself even further from the slavering men. She didn't want them to know what was happening to her; didn't want their leers and obnoxious comments.

Meanwhile, the stripper peeled off her sheer white blouse and tossed it over the groom's head. 'Look at me, love,' she said. 'I'm a bride.'

She was all in white: bra, panties, silk stockings and heels. Pink satin roses dotted her lingerie, very much what an innocent bride might choose. But the stripper made a burlesque of innocence. Back and forth she strutted, batting her lashes, jiggling the goods, taunting the men, only to skip out of reach. With difficulty, Audrey remembered Patrick's instructions. She was to watch. She was to measure. Her gaze slid over the men's crotches. All but one were hard, and he was so glassy-eyed she doubted he'd keep his feet for long. By far the largest erection belonged to a brutish fellow with mile-wide shoulders and a dark beard shadow. His jaw was heavy, his hands huge. When the stripper teased one bra strap off her shoulder, he put two fingers in his mouth and whistled.

'Take it off,' he said. 'Take it all off.'

The stripper pressed one finger to the dimple in her cheek. 'What,' she asked, 'will you give me for it?'

'Anything you want,' promised the brute. Two of his companions went for their wallets.

'No, no, no.' The stripper shook her silver-clawed

index finger. 'I don't want money, I want meat. You show me yours and I'll show you mine.'

Some of the bachelors gaped, some guffawed, and some exchanged nervous glances. The stripper wasn't interested in their misgivings. She planted her hands on her nipped-in waist. 'Come on, boys. Whip 'em out. I want to see how good a job I've been doing.'

Audrey was willing to bet they wouldn't agree, but the stripper coaxed them, shamed them, and finally laughed them into baring all. Soon the dozen men surrounded her, their pricks poking through their open zips. Each looked as hard as he could get. Even the bleary-eyed drunkard had risen to the occasion. The stripper strolled down the queue, twanging each erection with her nail. The men jumped but did not soften. Two of them giggled.

'Very good,' she said when she'd flicked the final cock. 'This calls for a reward.'

With yet more twists and bumps, she teased off her bra. She swivelled to face the men, palms covering her nipples, lips pouting. Then she revealed her glory. Her breasts spilt free of her hold and joggled in the air. She'd painted them with silver glitter, but they needed no gilding. They were beautiful as only natural breasts can be, round and weighty and topped with puckered rose-pink nipples.

'Come to Papa,' moaned the biggest brute, his cock an astonishing brick-red pole.

'You want a taste?' said the stripper, feigning shock. 'Do you all want a taste?'

'Yeah!' rumbled the besotted crowd.

She let them touch her, let them gobble at her swaying breasts. When the biggest fellow took his turn, she gazed at Audrey over his head and winked. The unexpected communication sent a zing through her veins. She'd been watching, passive, but with that wink the woman claimed her as a sister. She was inviting Audrey to share the enjoyment of her power.

'Enough,' the stripper said, shoving the black-haired brute away. 'Or don't you want to see the rest?'

They did, of course. Like a pack of obedient schoolboys they watched, jaws slack, eyes bulging, while she squirmed out of her tiny white panties. Her mound was covered in fluffy blonde curls; dyed, Audrey suspected, but they made a pretty picture in the frame of her white suspenders. Turning once more, she bent over with her bottom facing the crowd and spread her spectacular high-heeled legs. Her calves were muscled, her thighs firm. The folds of her pussy were clearly visible. She was a centrefold come to life. 'Who wants a taste of this?' she cooed.

The men roared. Before they could mob her, she spun around and shook her teasing finger. That slender digit seemed to wield more power than an AK-47. The men stopped in their tracks. 'What,' she said, her voice dripping a very sly brand of sex, 'will you give me for it?'

Audrey's pussy throbbed with a spike of excitement. She squeezed the jade balls, wishing more than anything for release. Whatever the stripper had in mind, she knew it would be good. Up on the little platform, she crossed her arms and planted her bridal heels as if they were a general's boots.

'Hands on your pricks!' she exhorted. 'I want you to beat that meat, gentlemen. I want you to flog that five-fingered flute. And when you reach that magic moment –' her hands slithered over her breasts towards her thatch '– the one who shoots the furthest gets to kiss my pretty clit.'

Silver nails agleam, she pulled her labia back to display the shining pearl. This must have been the last straw for the men, because twelve sweaty hands

174

began wanking twelve rigid cocks as if their lives depended on obeying. Audrey couldn't believe it. They'd all lost their minds. Not one of them seemed embarrassed. In fact, they were sneaking looks at each other, probably measuring how they stacked up against the competition. Most weren't anything to write home about but, still, they were so excited – by each other, by the stripper, by the steady squeeze and pull of their hands – that it was impossible not to catch a bit of their fever.

More than a bit, actually. Audrey's pussy felt steamed. She clenched in rhythm on the jade balls, grinding her buttocks as hard as she dared without being obvious. The first man shot his wad and two more lost it seconds later. The stripper licked her lips and ran one finger along her slit. Another man groaned and sprayed the edge of the stage. 'Three feet!' chortled the stripper. 'Who'll give me four?'

Audrey pressed her thighs together as three men moved to stand hip to hip. They were pulling hard, dragging that stiff red flesh out from their groins. 'Now!' said one of the men and they shot in unison, long strands of white like wedding confetti. Audrey's arousal was excruciating, but she couldn't make herself come without shoving her hands between her legs. Unwilling to betray herself, she watched the remaining men: the looks of concentration on their faces, the individual motions of their arms, the colour and thickness of their jerking cocks.

'Oh, God,' said the groom. 'Oh, God –' and splattered semen across the satin toe of the stripper's shoes.

Four men remained. Audrey's money was on the black-haired brute. Lord, he was big. Bigger than Patrick. He was working himself slowly, more pressure than speed, storing up his explosion. Shrouded in thick black fuzz, his balls were hanging low. His glans was wide, saucer-like, as if the crown would blast off when he shot his load. No man needed to be that big. No woman in her right mind would want a man that big. But to look at, oh, his body was the most primal of male threats. That threat spoke to Audrey as if he were whispering up her cunt. His slit began to drip and she couldn't look away. The other men might as well have disappeared. His pre-ejaculate was as generous as the rest of him. It hung from the tip in a glistening stream and Audrey couldn't decide if she were repelled or just enthralled.

What if all that juice were for me? she thought, and the muscles of her pussy leapt in consternation.

She must have made some sound, some motion, because the black-haired man chose that moment to turn his head and look at her. Her heart jolted with shock. His eyes were squinty and dark, bright as jet. His lips moved on a word. She thought . . . it couldn't be . . . but she thought it was her name. He left the circle and came towards her. Her limbs began to quake. One of his companions called after him, but they were too drunk and too engrossed in the stripper's game to care what he did. He shoved his giant cock back in his trousers and carefully pulled up the zip.

His walk was bow-legged, distorted by the discomfort of his arousal. Her gaze slid to the bulge, then to his brutish face. He kept coming until he was close enough to touch her. Part of her wanted him to touch her, but he didn't. His big, hairy hands remained by his sides, both curled into fists. He stood and he stared, his gaze boring through her, heating her face, heating her pussy. She couldn't guess what the look was meant to convey. He lifted his clenched left hand. Slowly, one by one, he opened the fingers. In the centre of his palm lay a tiny gold key, a twin to the one that dangled from Audrey's waist.

Her breath whooshed out of her. 'You're part of the spanking crowd.'

He chuckled, a surprisingly pleasant sound. 'Yes, but I'm not one of the spankers.'

My God, you should be, she thought, but it seemed rude to say so. He shifted on his feet and suddenly she deciphered his expression. She'd seen it on her own face in the mirror: it was the hope of being found worthy to obey.

'If it would please you,' he said in a beautifully humble tone, 'I'd like to perform a service for you. Patrick said you might need relief and I would be honoured to provide it.'

'Patrick said.'

'Yes.' He lowered his eyes and crossed his hands over the mountain at his groin. 'He said my talents might amuse you.'

Talents! More likely his gargantuan phallus. Audrey tried not to laugh at her own susceptibility, or Patrick's skill at reading it. She couldn't regret his insight, not with that insistent desire pounding between her legs. This man offered relief and she was more than ready for it. 'Not here,' she said. 'Follow me to the end of the hall.'

The crowd broke into applause as someone won the stripper's challenge. Neither she nor the brute turned to see who'd collected the reward. They moved in synchrony, quick, focused strides that took them to the lounge almost as quickly as if they'd run.

'Does it lock?' the brute asked, nodding at the door. When Audrey shook her head, he wedged an armchair under the knob. He moved the heavy seat as if it were a piece of kindling. Then he resumed his servile pose. My God, Audrey thought, he could crush me in two.

'What are your talents?' she asked as steadily as she could.

He smiled. His teeth were sharp and white. The front two overlapped, but the effect wasn't boyish. This was not a polished specimen, his teeth seemed to say; this was an animal. He gestured towards her clothes. 'It would be better if I demonstrated. May I take down your trousers?'

She told him he could. He was so tall that when he dropped to his knees, his head was level with her shoulders. His movements were respectful, almost laughably so. She couldn't help picturing his big, rough hands at more aggressive tasks. But he did seem to relish what he was doing. His chest, huger than any she'd seen up close, rose and fell with excitement. A growing dark spot marked the front of his straining zip. The sight acted as a whip to her arousal. Her pussy was so wet, the jade balls slid up and down with each contraction of her muscles. Gently he pulled her trousers and panties down.

'You should sit,' he said, tugging lightly at her hands. 'I want you to enjoy this.'

She tried not to collapse on the couch, but her descent was not graceful. Not that it mattered. The brute sighed with pleasure as he spread her knees. The couch was deep blue velveteen with a curved Deco back. He pulled her forward until her elbows and tailbone were all that supported her torso. Her buttocks hung over the edge of the seat. The brute inhaled, scenting her arousal. Goose bumps swept her flesh. He was like a stallion sniffing after a mare. With reverent fingers, their ends spatulate but smooth, he stroked her gleaming, sticky folds. Within them, he found the satin cord that secured Patrick's playthings. His gaze rose to hers. 'What does this lead to?'

She could barely answer. 'Two jade balls.'

His skin darkened beneath the shadow of his beard. 'Do they feel good?'

'Very.'

'Then we should leave them where they are while I pleasure you.'

She nodded, shakily, and with that permission, he lowered his head and began to exercise his talent. It was indeed impressive. He seemed to read what she needed through the surface of his tongue and lips. Focusing on her clitoris, he brought her to one quick orgasm, then another, and then – her immediate needs satisfied – he began to play. His hands roved her body, spreading the sensations his mouth was wringing from her sex. He smoothed her breasts through her shirt; squeezed her calves; trailed his fingers down the bend of her inner arms. With his mouth, he twisted her tight, then let her float on the edge. He teased her slowly, endlessly, then toppled her with a single, feather-light stroke of his tongue. He played a symphony on her nerves, complete with crashing chords and haunting sweeps of melody.

'Enough,' she said in a pleasure-thickened voice.

He withdrew and clasped his hands behind his back. His eyes were downcast, his head bowed. With a tiny thrill, she realised he was awaiting further orders. It wasn't over yet. He was still her obedient servant. 'There is one more thing I'd like,' she said. He looked up, face shining with hope. 'I want your cock inside me.'

His hands flew to his groin as if she'd threatened to cut it off. 'No. You're just a little thing. I'd hurt you.'

Audrey could not accept his demur. She'd been dreaming of cocks like his since she'd known what a cock was. She would not lose this opportunity. 'I'm ordering you to do it,' she said. 'A big brute like you must have practice being careful.' She softened her voice the way Patrick would, the honeyed iron hand. 'I'm sure you know how displeased I'd be if you hurt me. Or if you disobeyed.'

179

He shivered and his breath came faster. She knew this was his fantasy, then: to take a fragile flower of a woman, to be forced to be gentle, no matter how hard his cock wanted to plunge. With shaking hands, he opened his trousers and pushed them to his hips. His erection sprang free, a marvel of divine engineering. His veins were ropes, his colour astonishingly dark. The massive head cast a shadow across his navel. The eye was a slowly dripping slash. Unable to resist, she pressed the tip of her little finger into the sticky pool. He made a sound, a raw tenor vibration. The delicate skin of his hole seemed to grip her finger as if he wanted her to fuck him.

'Like that?' she whispered, turning her pinkie from side to side.

'Please,' he said, then panted. 'Please don't excite me any more. It's too much. I need to – I need to put on the condom.'

Reluctantly, she withdrew her hand. He was so hard he had to pull the shaft away from his belly to roll the prophylactic on. He carried his own supply. She supposed he had to, big as he was. The sheer white latex fitted snugly. It was lubricated. My, yes, he was prepared.

'You could stay right there,' he said, his eyes zeroed in on her sex, his voice dreamy. 'You could drape your knees over my arms.'

'I could. And I will. But first you'll have to remove my toy.'

He wound the satin cord around his finger and sank his crooked white teeth into his lower lip. 'I don't want to hurt you,' he said. 'You're such a little thing.'

He tugged so gently, she thought the balls would never pull free. Chinese water torture was not more agonising, nor more delicious. When the jade slipped out at last, her pussy tingled in reaction. She was

180

aware of every inch of her sex, from the outer reaches to the hidden depths. She was swollen but empty, and she longed to be filled with warm, throbbing flesh. She reached for the brute's big arms, coaxing him closer. He hulked over her on the couch, radiating heat and smells and an incredible vibration of life. His was an animal charm, leashed by a man's imaginative psyche.

'Tell me if I hurt you,' he said, and pressed the fat, hot crown to her gate.

She could not pretend it wasn't heaven. Sighing happily, she wrapped her arms around his shoulders. With a concerted, careful push, he wedged the flare in, first one side, then the other. Even that small penetration must have felt good to him. His breath rushed out. He pushed again and took another inch. He stopped. Apparently, her angle wasn't right. Murmuring apologies, he shifted her position as if she were a porcelain doll, splaying her legs, tilting her hips just so. When he was satisfied, he settled his elbows at her sides and pushed, gently, feeling his way. Inch by inch, he worked his mammoth organ into her sheath. Audrey could not take it all, but she could take more than he thought. When they'd reached another impasse, she crooked her legs over his arms. He slid in another fraction. Ah, she was stuffed, deliciously stuffed and bathed in luscious sexual heat. The head of his cock felt as if it stroked her spine. She stretched her back, revelling in the pleasure of it. The brute groaned.

'I don't dare move,' he said, his voice trembling as violently as his arms. 'I want to so, so badly, but I don't dare.'

His confession had the tone of a ritual, words his fantasy compelled him to say. She wondered if she should order him to move. It didn't seem wise. He really was very large, not to mention aroused. She didn't want to risk breaking the hold he had on his impulses. Instead, she dragged her nails down the warm, damp back of his shirt. The phrase 'broad as a barn' took on a new, more carnal meaning. 'I'll move,' she said. 'You stay as you are.'

This was the right thing to say. He gulped and set his jaw. His cock, already huge, jumped inside her as if it had been shocked. She gripped his shoulders to pull herself up. Despite his tremor, he was as sturdy as a boulder. Gradually, thrust by thrust, she built a rhythm that slid him from crown to midpoint inside her. Freeing one arm, she reached between them and massaged the part of his shaft her body could not encompass. He shuddered and closed his eyes. 'Good?' she said, pleased with herself. He nodded and released a moaning sigh. She was glad. Her own interest was rising and this thick warm flesh stimulated every pressure point she had. What they were doing was almost, but not quite, enough to send her over. On the next upward stroke, she ground her clit against her thumb knuckle.

'I can do that,' he gasped.

'No.' Her voice was sterner than it had been before. 'This is my show. You're here to enjoy.'

He quivered at the verbal lash. 'Yes, ma'am,' he said. 'Whatever you say.'

She laughed. She'd never expected to hear that worshipful tone directed towards herself. Because she liked it very much, with this man, on this day, it sent a frisson of pleasure to her core. She thrust faster, hips swivelling smoothly. Sounds rose from the jointure of their bodies, wet and slick. The brute began to huff. Her pace was pushing his limits. She, on the other hand, was not yet where she needed to be. 'You must hold on,' she ordered. 'You must not come before I do.'

'Yes, ma'am,' he said through gritted teeth. One of

his hands caught her hip, gripping it hard, but not changing its movements. He seemed desperate for some way to express the need boiling up inside him. Despite that need, he obeyed; he didn't come and he didn't thrust. The next time she withdrew to his crown, she tightened and gave it a tug. 'Oh, yes,' he breathed. 'That's sweet.'

But sweet was as sweet did. She slid her left hand down his back, under the waist of his open trousers and over his stone-tight buttocks. He cried out when her fingers dug in, not pain but panic. 'Soon,' she said, working him harder, working him deeper. 'Not much longer –'

She came in a long, fluttering trill of feeling, a purely physical pleasure unmuddled by emotion. She thought he would join her at once, but the brute had his own ambitions. The veins on his neck stood out like a weight lifter's. 'A little more,' he pleaded. 'Can't you take just a little more?'

She blew the air from her climax-tightened lungs. She was warm, she was wet, and he had been very good. He was entitled to her best effort. Relax, she told herself. Relax. She changed her grip on his root to two fingers and a thumb. His raphe felt like steel, barely giving under the pressure. She wanted this. She could do it. Relax, she thought, and pushed. He slid deeper, almost another inch. He shuddered like a tree beneath a logger's axe.

'Ah,' he said. 'Don't move.'

She remained as she was while he throbbed inside her, clasped as deeply as her body would allow. His buttocks tensed and relaxed, tensed and relaxed. Then he began to move, not forward, but in circles, his motions growing faster and faster until he was breathing so hard she feared he'd pass out. His glans especially he rubbed against her walls, altering his angle so that the crown gathered the lion's share of

183

the friction. The effect was dramatic. His pulse pounded like a wild thing. His breath rasped in his lungs. Knowing how badly he wanted release made her come again. Then he let loose. With a strangled squeal, he spasmed, his eyes rolling back in the ultimate delight. Even then, he didn't thrust, but shook and twisted and finally, with reluctant groan, rolled to the side to spare her his weight.

A moment later, before she even had a chance to feel embarrassed for what she'd done with a perfect stranger, he sat up and straightened his clothes. He wrapped the condom in tissues and tossed it in the trash. Apart from a sweaty spot on the couch, no one would know what had happened.

Someone had trained this brute very well. He rose and bowed.

'Thank you,' she said, taking his hand before he could slip away.

'Thank *you*,' he returned, kissing her fingers with European style. 'That was pretty damn good for a fellow sub.'

She laughed because he'd recognised what she was, because her body still hummed with satisfaction and, most of all, because Patrick had given her such a thoughtful gift.


She found her benefactor in the private dining room, clearing the remains of the bachelors' debauch. 'Sit,' he said when she moved to help. It was not a request. She swallowed her apology.

'Who's watching the bar?' she asked, lowering herself carefully to the chair.

'Eric. And he thanked me nicely for the privilege, so you can wipe that guilt off your face.' He finished loading glasses on a tray, then took the seat beside her. Audrey had clasped her hands together in her lap. He squeezed them with a reassuring smile. 'Did you enjoy your little escapade?'

'Yes,' she said, and blushed.

'You were meant to enjoy it.'

'I realise that, but it's sort of embarrassing to have you know me so well.'

He chuckled. One finger drew a circle over her knee. 'I suppose this means his talents were as impressive as reported.'

She remembered the brute's clever tongue and felt again the astonishing stretch of his cock. Her cheeks stung anew. Was it wicked to have enjoyed him so much? And, if so, why was this guilt so beguiling? Generally speaking, she was not a fan of the emotion, but if she and Patrick had been home, alone, she would have thrown him to the floor. Tender though her pussy was, she was more than ready for another roll. 'I didn't even get his name,' she confessed.

'What a depraved creature.' He kissed the peak of her hairline. 'We'll have to see what else we can do to bring out that side of your nature.'

Audrey contemplated this pleasant threat, then turned her gaze to his. His eyes were patient, amused, molten. 'He knew that stripper, didn't he?'

Patrick smiled. 'What an observant question. Yes, he did know her. He's sworn himself to her. She's his mistress. As the groom's best man, he set up the party and arranged for her to perform. And she gave me permission to ask a favour of her pet.'

'So she's not a real stripper.'

'In real life she's a motivational speaker, but she is very good at whipping a room into shape.' He studied her expression. 'Would you like to do what she did?'

'I don't think I could.'

'Perhaps not today, but someday.'

Someday. Audrey tightened her clasped hands. Someday was the future. Did Patrick mean to imply they had one? And why did her heart jump so fiercely at the thought?

He caressed her jaw with his thumb. 'You're troubled.'

'No. I just –' She searched for any explanation but the truth: that she wanted a future with him, that she feared she was falling in love. 'You wouldn't loan me to another master, would you?'

'No.' His thumb travelled to her ear and slipped around it. 'I chose this young man precisely because he's well and truly whipped.'

'Thank you,' Audrey said, and wondered what he'd do if he knew how relieved she was.

# Chapter Eleven

$A$t the time, Audrey considered Patrick's generosity a good thing. Looking back, she wasn't sure. What did it mean that he was willing to share her?

She brooded over this question as she lay sunning on his roof. Newton was her only distraction. He catnapped at the foot of her lounger, trying to beat the heat by stretching his little grey body as long as it would go. She couldn't believe how fast he was growing. He didn't fall over when he licked his back paws anymore. He could jump on to chairs by himself, though he hadn't yet mastered the kitchen counters. Newton was living proof that time was passing, day by day, week by week, and she still hadn't sorted out her life.

What did it mean that Patrick was willing to share her?

She frowned at Newton's gently twitching tail. Was Patrick tiring of her? No doubt she seemed tame, compared to his usual playmates. Was protecting his father's reputation the only reason he'd stuck with her? But maybe he wanted her to feel insecure. Maybe he thought it would make her easier to control.

And maybe he had shared her with the brute for no other reason than to please her. With a grimace of disgust, she twisted her hair off her sweaty neck and draped it over the top of the chair. She shouldn't torture herself this way. Patrick was fond of her, at least as fond of her as he was of Newton.

Audrey's snort woke the cat. He blinked as if to say, what did you do that for? 'For spite,' she cooed, gathering him up. 'For spite, you hairy beast.'

Settling him on her lap, she scratched him under his chin. His purr rumbled through her fingers. Life was easy for Newton. He didn't question why people were nice to him; he simply was glad they were. She knew she could learn something from that, but she didn't think she would.

From the shadows of the living room, Patrick watched her making faces at the cat and peeking under her bikini to sigh at her tan lines. He'd ordered her not to sunbathe nude. He hated the idea of the watcher seeing her, even if this did brand him an old stick-in-the-mud. Her brooding, however, worried him. Was she chafing under his rule? He couldn't tell. He'd never lived with anyone he'd topped before. Her mood might have been perfectly normal and he wouldn't have known it.

He hoped she wasn't bored.

He smoothed the lie of his tie, knowing he needed to leave for work. He wanted to speak to the distributor when he came, to make some changes in the wine order. The last case of merlot hadn't been up to snuff. If Patrick didn't catch him in time, he'd be stuck with the stuff for another week.

I'll leave in a minute, he thought, watching Audrey rub noses with Newton. He pressed his fist to a curious warm spot beneath his breast. She really was an unexpected pleasure to have around: a welcoming body, a pretty face, a quick mind when she chose to use it. She engaged him. He loved watching her charm the customers at Dugan's. He loved hearing her rattling off drinks: 'Gin and bitters and a pitcher, Patrick.' Each time she said his name, no matter how public the situation, he'd hear her remembering his claim that, for her, 'Patrick' was the same as 'master'.

But who wouldn't have delighted in her suggestibility? Or her inexperience. She'd been thoroughly adorable after her encounter with Marilyn's colossus, blushing like a twelve-year-old over Patrick's discovery of her secret kink. He chuckled at the memory. He'd known the little size queen wouldn't be able to resist. He rubbed the groove beneath his lower lip. It had pleased him to please her. He'd felt like a good person for offering that treat.

But maybe it was time to plan the next one. If Audrey had time to brood, she was ready for a challenge.

The day started well for Audrey. Dressed in nothing but a lavender bra and panty set, she bounced on her rumpled bed. Patrick, who sat beside her, had just handed her a neatly wrapped jeweller's box. 'Another present!' she exclaimed.

Not about to complain, she ripped the silver paper and gasped when she lifted the lid. Gold met her eye, gold so soft and yellow she couldn't help licking her lips. He'd bought her new nipple rings. Dozens of tiny leaves dangled from two gold loops. A third loop, this one sized to hug the underside of her nipple, flashed with emerald beads. It was the cleverest piece of jewellery she'd ever seen.

'They're from India,' he said. 'I sent the goldsmith your precise measurements. You should find that gauge quite comfortable.'

Knowing Patrick, she had no doubt she would. 'I

love them,' she said, stroking the shiny leaves. 'I just love them.'

She wanted to wear them that instant. Without thinking, she turned her back to take down her bra. Patrick put on a laughing brogue. 'Such modesty, lass!'

She blushed and offered him the rings instead. He changed them with care, bathing both her and the jewellery in antiseptic wash. She trembled at his gentle touch, her nipples beading up so strongly they hurt. He stroked the smallest loop. The half ring of emeralds clasped her to perfection, a pressure but not a pinch. The gold leaves shivered with her breaths. They'd lay flat under clothes, she thought, but she'd always know they were there. Now they tickled the lower swell of her areola.

When he'd finished inserting the second ring, Patrick dropped Sterling's trinkets into the empty box. 'There.' He snapped the lid and slipped the box into his pocket. 'Now I've dressed every bit of you.'

His tone was endearingly possessive. She lowered her head to hide her pleasure. He probably saw it anyway, because he pressed a kiss to her cheek. Then he stood. 'I'm giving you the night off. Don't wear the clothes I've left you until this evening. Spend the day relaxing. The rest of your instructions are on the kitchen table.'

Instructions for what? Had he planned another adventure? Confused, but excited, she asked him where he'd be.

He ran a finger down the length of her nose. 'Very close, sweetheart. Very close.'

The dress he'd chosen was velvet devoré, pewter, with a floral pattern burnt out from a background of silk. It clung to her curves, scooping over her collar bones, flirting with her calves, hinting at the next to nothing she wore beneath: two nipple ornaments, one belly chain, a minuscule charcoal thong, and a pair of real silk stockings. Two-inch heels in kid-glove leather cradled her feet. The shoes were Italian, a brand they'd never carried at Regina's. Regina had claimed their clientele couldn't afford it.

If I ever own a shop, Audrey decided, I'll court a few clients who can. Quality like this was meant to be shared.

She turned sideways before the mirror, sucked in her stomach and pushed out her chest. A surge of narcissistic pleasure rolled through her sex like heated oil. She'd never looked so seductive, or so grown up. Patrick would bust his zip when he saw her.

Of course, she wasn't entirely sure when that would be.

As if on cue, the cell phone he'd left her rang. She flipped it open.

'Your cab is waiting downstairs,' he said in a soft, smoky voice. 'Are you ready?'

'Yes.' The answer quivered from her throat.

'Good,' he said, and broke the connection.

The taxi took her to a tiny restaurant on Embassy Row, one she hadn't known existed. It occupied a corner of one of the turn-of-the-century mansions, a heavy arc of marble and pedimented windows, solidly rooted in the national earth. The entrance was hidden in the back beneath a pair of glossy green magnolias. The waiters were expecting her. Without requiring an introduction, they led her to a dappled courtyard, beautifully fenced in curled black iron. Audrey did not need to order. Course by course, they delivered her meal: asparagus frittata, a salad of baby greens and vinaigrette, lobster linguini and a chocolate tiramisu that made her sigh to let the last sweet bite melt across her tongue. The meal salved every smidgen of envy she'd felt for the piggish bachelors.

As she ate, alone at her tiny table, the other diners glanced at her. Audrey didn't mind. She looked like a million dollars, she felt like a queen, and she wasn't alone, not really. She stroked the sleek black cell phone where it sat beside her wineglass. Patrick might ring at any time.

As if he knew when the silky wine finished its euphoric journey to her veins, he waited until the sun sank towards the horizon to call. She answered in a voice thickened by sensual pleasure.

'I hope you enjoyed your meal,' he said, sounding as lazy as she did. 'I want you to freshen up, then head out for a stroll on Dupont Circle. Don't worry that any harm will come to you. I'll be close. But you mustn't try to find me. Think of yourself as Lot's wife. If you look back, you'll miss your chance at your reward.'

'I understand,' she said. He rang off with a quiet click. His abruptness didn't matter. The sound of his voice had left her tingling. He was thinking of her. Soon he would be close. After a quick stop at the ladies, she began her mandated walk.

Dupont Circle was DC's answer to Greenwich Village, a stylish, bohemian part of town. Since it wasn't far, she ambled east on Massachusetts, enjoying the warmth of the night and the perfect, decadent fullness that followed her meal. The food had not dulled her senses, merely lent the world a golden glow. The glow consoled her as the streetlights flicked on. Normally, she would have been anxious walking after dusk, alone, dressed to thrill. Tonight, the knowledge of Patrick's unseen presence kept her fears at bay. She reached her objective without incident.

Knots of teenagers, not much younger than herself, gathered near the plashing, goblet-shaped fountain at the centre of the circle. Dreadlocks seemed tonight's fashion choice, their snaky lengths woven with steel beads. One boy wore a knife lashed with leather to his ripped and sagging jeans. He could have been a criminal, or the wastrel son of a diplomat. Either way, he might have been dangerous. Audrey smiled with her eyes as she passed him, looking not at him but into the distance. He watched her, losing his place in the conversation, muttering something covetous under his breath.

She was very aware of the bareness of her breasts, of the new gold bangles circling their turgid points. The sensitive tips brushed the silk backing of her dress, teasing her and everyone who saw her. Her buttocks jiggled as well, reminding her that they, too, were nearly naked. She imagined how brazen she must look and her heart swelled to the limits of her ribcage. She had no desire to force Patrick to her rescue, but knowing he would defend her sent the most incredible charge through her veins.

Tonight her femininity was power rather than endangerment. She could draw eyes, young and old. She could make them want what they could not have. She winked at a man in a suit and he dropped his briefcase. A woman in a gauzy brown outfit, obviously waiting for a date, eyed her up and down. Why aren't you nervous, the woman's look seemed to say, and where the hell did you get that dress? Audrey lengthened and slowed her stride. Wouldn't you . . . like to know?' said the swing of her hips. Wouldn't you . . . like to know? Turning up Connecticut, she sauntered past the busy window at Kramerbooks, its orange neon sign flickering across her bosom. Browsers looked up from the shelves, curious, admiring. Audrey laughed and spun in a circle. The night was hers. Patrick had given her the night.

The phone she'd stuffed into her little handbag rang.

'Yes,' she said, breathless, half laughing.

He quoted an address on Q street. 'When you get to the door, kneel down and wait for me.'

He used his steeliest tone. Her laughter stilled, replaced by a thick, serpentine pulse. She felt it in her temples, in her throat, in the soft, crushable flesh between her legs. She'd eaten the sweet and now he was serving up the bitter. Luckily, the bitter was bitter chocolate to her, dark but savoury. Desire was all the sweetener it required and Audrey had plenty to spare.

She turned off the bright, four-lane bustle of Connecticut Avenue and headed west on Q, past the Metro stop and down the quieter, darker street.

The small plaque at her destination's door proclaimed it the Willson Collection Gallery. She could see this museum had once been a private home. Its three narrow stories bore a soft limestone facing, greening now with age. The windows were arched and oddly Gothic, out of character with their stolid red brick neighbours. No lights shone from inside. Viewing hours were over. Shrugging to herself, and hoping she couldn't be seen by passers-by, Audrey dropped to her knees beneath the steepled stone awning.

When the cellphone rang, her pulse leapt in her throat.

'Close your eyes,' he said, 'and don't turn around.'

She closed her eyes and waited. People drifted by, two by two, three by three, chatting about shows and dinner and who remembered where they'd left the car. Traffic hummed back on Connecticut. Leaves rustled in a breeze. A twig snapped, but it was only a squirrel leaping from a bush. No one's looking, she told herself. No one can see me kneeling like a freak before a closed museum. She screwed her eyes more tightly shut. It didn't matter who saw her. Patrick was near. Patrick would protect her.

But she didn't feel as safe as she had before. He'd

done it deliberately, she thought. He'd lent her his power and now he was taking it back. Her nerves began to stretch. When a step crunched on the walk behind her she almost turned around. No, she thought. It's Patrick. Don't ruin it. Don't open your eyes.

Hands touched her hair, stroked down her arms and lifted her to her feet. A velvet cloth teased each of her wrists, then lifted away. Did he intend to tie her? Would the world see her bound? The cloth covered her forehead, then her eyes. She felt the ends knot at the back of her head. The blindfold was thick and wide. She could see nothing around the edges, not even light. No one had blindfolded her before. The sudden descent of vulnerability stunned her. It was immense, an arctic night without a star. She could not walk without his help, nor would she know if anyone watched.

'You're mine,' he said and fitted a key into the museum's heavy lock.

The door swung open with a quiet hiss. When they stepped inside, their footsteps reverberated against the ceiling. The sound brought to mind an empty church. Audrey's shoulder brushed what she guessed was a glass-topped donation box. Where was the guard? Could Patrick have paid for his absence, or just his silence? What sort of power did he wield that he could arrange this after-hours tour? Would anyone come if she cried out? And if they would, did she want them to?

'This way,' he said, guiding her by the elbow. The surface beneath her feet changed from wood to marble. The air grew cooler, mustier. She smelled old things: metal, cloth, and a faint, animal scent. Humans, she thought, the humans who had passed between these walls.

They stopped beneath a doorway; she could tell

from the change in the sound. Patrick pulled something over her hands, a pair of cotton gloves. The
action mystified her until he tugged her to the right
and guided her touch to the top of a heavy pedestal.
He held each of her hands beneath his own, forcing
them over winged marble feet, up smooth marble legs
and finally on to a small marble penis. Audrey could
not resist its lure. This was something she'd wanted
to do since she'd seen her first nude statue as a girl.
With a shiver of purely juvenile pleasure, she ran her
fingers down the drooping marble foreskin, then
cupped the marble balls. The curls of the marble
thatch were frozen flames beneath her touch: forever
lovely, forever perfect.

'You see,' Patrick whispered. 'Small is beautiful,
too.'

She laughed and he pulled her through the archway
into a room paved with stone. Here, the smell of
metal was very strong. She stumbled over an irregu-
larity in the floor. Patrick caught her before she fell.

He peeled off the cotton gloves. One after the other,
they dropped like roses to the floor. Then she heard
the rattle of chains.

'No,' she said, her lips moving without sound. Heat
crashed over her skin. Perspiration broke out between
her thighs. Chains. For a moment she saw palm trees
swaying in the moonlight. Sterling's lawn. Sterling's
pool. Patrick lifted her hair and nuzzled the back of
her neck. She bowed her head, despair and wanting
tangled in her breast. Standing like a shadow behind
her, he drew his hand down the sensitive interior of
her arm. He lifted her wrist on two long fingers. She
knew he must feel her racing pulse.

'Do you want this?' he asked. 'I need your permission to continue.'

Did she want it? Her body said one thing, her mind
another. Her heart wavered in the balance.

He knew not to press her. His lips whispered up and down her nape, soft and persuasive, the front of his body brushing her back. His shirt was silk, his trousers linen, their placket stretched by his burgeoning erection. Could she face her fear that Patrick was at heart no different than Sterling? Could she let him chain her; let him see this brutal bondage demolish her control? Could she trust he wouldn't abuse his power? She wanted to trust him. She wanted to put her fate in his hands, and not just for tonight. The urge to submit frightened her. It seemed contrary to everything a modern female should desire.

'Do *you* want this?' she said, surprising herself.

He smoothed her hair over the front of her shoulder. 'Very much.'

She wanted to ask him why, but her lips wouldn't form the word. If he wanted her, she had power, too. That was enough for now. 'I'm ready,' she said. 'You may continue.'

He removed the patterned velvet dress, lowering the zip so slowly its descent was soundless. He knelt to slip the garment from her, then eased off her shoes. Cinderella had never felt like this. 'Turn around,' he said, low and serious.

Blindly she turned, the stone cool beneath her feet. The coverings that remained to her pressed more strongly against her awareness: the stockings, the thong and suspender, the tiny key and chain, the trembling, twenty-four carat leaves that dangled from her nipples. Her sense of these barriers intensified as Patrick pressed a set of shackles around her wrists. They were heavier than any she'd used before. Lined with padded velvet, their bolts shot firmly home.

Patrick's footsteps moved away. Gears turned. They sounded huge, clanking as the chains rolled up around their wooden teeth. Her hands were pulled upward, to her shoulders, above her head. She cried out, but not in pain. As her arms were drawn taut, sensations overwhelmed her, emotions she could not name. Heat flared between her legs, spreading outward in soft, breath-stealing waves. She wanted so badly to be filled, to disappear in a welter of hungry kisses. Her skin was nearly crawling with desire.

Patrick returned. He stood behind her to remove the blindfold. When he pulled it away, dozens of wavering golden lights caused her to blink. After a moment, her sight cleared and she saw the lights were candles. Great iron trees of them battled the shadows of a stony castle room. Suits of armour glinted in the flickering light. They stood, an army of silent watchers, beneath the low, rounded arches of a gallery. Faded tapestries stirred against the walls behind them. Picked out in tiny stitches, lords and ladies hunted deer while angels plied the clouds; full-grown angels, haloes aglow, gowns flowing over heavy, rounded limbs.

Audrey hung amid this antiquated glory, worse than naked, chained by the wrist with her arms stretched high above her head. Each iron link was bigger than her hand. She knew the chains had been used before, centuries before. The anguish of the captives they had held seemed to linger in the musty air. Spellbound, time slipped sideways in her mind.

She could not speak when Patrick stepped before her. A poet's shirt, white and ruffled, hung open to his waist. Between the fluttering halves, whorls of hair swept slabs of muscle. By the light of the candles, his face seemed a mix of troubadour and knight and devil. His brows were sable wings. His eyes glowed like stars. When he spoke, she could barely recognise his voice; desire had so tightened his throat.

'You're mine,' he said in that decimating rasp. He lifted his palms towards her breasts but did not touch them. 'Feel my heat, Audrey. Feel it roll over you.'

His words worked magic. A melting candle pressed to her skin could not have warmed her as deeply.

'Feel it,' he repeated, taking one step back, then another, his arms extended before him. The sensation of heat stretched but did not weaken. Audrey trembled. He backed to the wall, three, four body lengths away. Still the phantom warmth caressed her breasts. 'I am always with you. No matter what parts us, you are mine.'

She moaned in reaction. Long ago, a nightmare's age ago, another man had made that claim. Then it hadn't been true. Now – she shuddered – now she thought it might be.

He stroked her with the riffling heat, up to her shoulders, down to her knees, his arms rising and falling in graceful arcs. 'Close your eyes,' he said. 'Close your eyes.'

Lead weighted her lids. A pulse beat against the surface of her mons, like her own, but not her own. Her body went liquid. If the chains hadn't held her, she would have fallen. 'I want you,' she said, swaying like a drunkard.

'I'm with you.' The pulse moved to her thigh, slipped down the inner curve of her calf. 'Tell me where I'm touching you.'

'My left leg. My calf.'

'Good,' he purred. 'Now feel me touch the right.'

She felt him. She felt him as clearly as she felt the air current that stirred the ends of her hair. She knew when he began to circle her. She knew when his eyes brushed the curve of her bottom. Her pussy ached as if it had been bruised. 'I've never – I don't –'

'Hush,' he said. He'd slipped off his shoes. His feet patted bare across the stone. She wanted them to come closer. She wanted his skin, his living, physical touch. Instead, he stood behind her, unmoving.

'I want – I need –' She shook her head from side to side, reaching out with all her will. The effort must have accomplished something, because he gasped. Her eyes flew open. Her heart jumped with shock. Colour danced over her skin, gossamer flickers as faint as distant candlelight. In a more sensible frame of mind, she would have called it a trick of the eye. Tonight she could not. The colour tingled like liquid electricity, as if her limbs had fallen asleep. She wished she could believe they had. She feared the sensation was his magic dancing over her, his terrifying, unsuspected power.

How could she stand against a man who'd achieved a feat like this?

'Audrey.' He touched her with his hands, burnishing her skin with roving, greedy sweeps. 'Audrey.' He cupped the weight of her breasts; smoothed the quivering curve of her belly. He ripped the side of her thong and let it fall. His shirt followed, then his trousers, and then his naked front pressed her back. Oh, he was warm, like copper set next to a fire. His arms circled her belly. His cheek rubbed her hair. His cock pressed hot and damp along her spine, pulsing in quick, frantic rhythm. Fluid slid down the silky head, its abundance weakening her knees. His cock was crying for entry. Her head fell back on his shoulder. 'Audrey,' he whispered, making it a spell.

She heard the want in his voice, the overpowering, caution-robbing desire. Her own need was just as brutal. Rising on tiptoe, she rubbed her buttocks over his swollen, dripping prick. The head slipped over her crack, painting it with juice. 'Take me,' she said. 'Take me now.'

Groaning, he wrapped his right hand around her wrist. His left combed through her curls to find the ripened bud of her clitoris. He pinched it, pulled it out with finger and thumb, and rubbed it in between. A lightning bolt of pleasure streaked through her sex. She cried out.

The sound pushed him over some edge. He kneed her legs apart, rough and urgent. 'I meant to spank you first,' he said. 'I meant to – ah –' His crown brushed her point of entry, broad, hot, velvet-wrapped steel. He worked it between her folds, massaging the slippery furrow until she thought she'd die if he didn't push inside. 'I meant to beat you,' he gasped, and then he did push, in, in, in, losing his words, filling her with smooth, pulsating heat. He sighed and set his teeth to the side of her neck. 'Audrey. Tilt back.'

It was not request but command, dark and irresistible. She tilted back and he slid to his root. The rightness of the union brought tears to her eyes: his shape, his scent, his breath soughing in her ear. He was the man who fit her. He was her beloved king. He thrust, slow and forceful, and she gave in without reservation. She did not think of tomorrow, or yesterday, or all the words they had not said. Her soul had surrendered. Its tyranny she could not fight.

They climbed in step, each one's pleasure dragging the other along. His legs were strong, his hands clever. They angled their heads together to kiss, backs arching, hips beating out and in, out and in. The pace quickened, then slowed, then quickened again. Breath took on sound and urgency. Audrey licked the sharp peaks of his upper lip. His lashes rose. 'I'm yours,' she said. His eyes went black. His hand tightened on the skin beneath her shackle. He kissed her so deeply she lost her breath.

'Hold on,' he said. 'Hold on tight.'

All was fury then. His thrusts jarred her body to its toes. Deep. Achingly hard. He banded her belly with his arm. He groaned in her ear. He told her to take it, to take him. He'd fuck her womb. He'd fuck her till she cried. With punishing force, his fingers pinched her lips and clit. Spears of pleasure jumped upward through her sex, insanely sharp, insanely good. They leapt. They gathered. She bit her lip and screamed.

'Yes,' he said as she clamped in orgasm. 'Oh, God, I need to see you. I need to feel your heart.'

He lifted her off him so quickly she gasped. He spun her in his arms. The chains crossed, forcing her wrists together. With a grunt of impatience, he hiked her into position. 'Legs around my waist,' he ordered and took her almost before she could obey. He was thicker now, harder. The reach of him made her weak, the set of his jaw, the sweat trickling down his face. He had her buttocks in a death grip, working her up and down his cock as if he did not trust her to thrust as strongly as he.

'Let me help,' she said. Their eyes met for one breathless instant, his pupils black and huge. Her thighs tightened on his waist and then he kissed her. He kissed her with mewls and gasps. He kissed her with his tongue, with his teeth: gluttonous, desperate, aroused to the point of madness. He pulled her upper body tight to his. Their hearts thundered together even as their hips pumped in and out. The sound of each wet percussion, so quick, so crazed, drove her higher. Fire swept her skin. He was going to push her over again. Her sheath began to flutter in preparation.

'Not yet,' he growled. 'Wait for me.'

She tried to hold on, but it was killingly hard. She was making noises, like an animal, like a torture victim. Fluid gushed from her sex. When it hit his skin, he cried out as if someone were chasing him. His hips worked deeper, harder. The crown of his cock was a pummelling satin coal. His mouth closed on the side of her neck and sucked her skin against his teeth. She could not withstand the soft burst of pain. Her sheath convulsed, pulling him up and in.

'God,' he cried, 'God,' and then the madness burst for him as well. He held her so tightly she thought her ribs might crack. His hips ground against her, shuddering, slinging his ejaculation inward, and then, with a heavy expulsion of air, he relaxed.

'Audrey,' he murmured, kissing her shoulder, stroking her back. 'My God, you're a caution.'

She slumped against his chest, letting him hold her weight. If she was a caution, he was a mortal danger. Even now, her soul did not seem her own.

The tumbler of whiskey froze an inch from Patrick's lips, the fumes rising to sting his eyes. Audrey had emerged from her room. A tan leather satchel was slung over her shoulder. She wore her own clothes, disreputable jeans and a loose khaki T-shirt. Obviously, she was going somewhere.

'I need to get out of here,' she said, not quite meeting his eye. 'I need to think.'

'And where –' he set the whiskey on the black marble curve of the living room's bar '– were you planning to *think* at two in the morning?'

He knew he must sound like her father. She certainly faced him in the manner of an exasperated teen. The satchel dropped down her arm to drag from her hand. 'Tommy will be up. He always works late.'

A darkness he knew he ought to fight expanded in his head. 'Tommy. The boy you were living with before you came to me.'

'Yes,' she said, surly and stiff. Then, without warning, she relented. She crossed to him in half a dozen strides and clasped the knotted tendons of his forearms. 'It's not a bad thing. I just need to talk this out. Tommy's my best friend and tonight was kind of overwhelming for me: good, but – I don't know – I feel as if I'm losing myself, getting in over my head. I need to breathe. I need to think. Maybe I'm taking what's happening between us more seriously than I should, but I can't – I just need to talk it out with someone.'

Her words were a babble of noise. All he could think was: he's her best friend. *He's* her best friend. A dull ache speared his heart. Tommy was her best friend. Patrick was not. Rationally, he knew he had no reason to believe he might be. He had not worked for her friendship. Winning it had not been his ambition. Nonetheless, it hurt to hear her imply he did not have it.

He sat on the nearest barstool and massaged his breastbone with the heel of his palm. What did this hurt mean, this jealousy of her friend?

Tonight had been a singular experience. He'd tried touching energy once before with a woman he'd known during the seventies. She'd been a student of Tibetan Buddhism, a dedicated flower child. That attempt hadn't worked half as well as his with Audrey. Of course, the flower child hadn't been a suggestible young submissive. Audrey had responded beyond his wildest dreams. Didn't she know how rare the connection between them was? Didn't it mean anything to her? Why was she seized by this urge to go talk it out with Tommy? Surely she knew Patrick's ears worked just as well. He was a bartender, for God's sake. People were supposed to bring their troubles to him.

'Do you understand?' she said, her expression young and serious.

He hadn't heard a thing she'd said for minutes. He rubbed his palms down his thighs and nodded. 'You need to make sense of what's happened to you. You need to talk it out.'

She released a heartfelt sigh. 'Thank you.' She leant

forward to kiss his cheek. Her hands settled for a moment on top of his. Her palms were warm and damp. 'I won't be long. Not more than a couple of days.'

A couple of days! His throat resisted his attempt to swallow. Against his will, he recalled his mother's asinine quest to find herself, which worked so well she never bothered to return. Abruptly, he stood. 'Sure,' he said. 'You need some time away.'

He'd tamped his panic down, but denying it took all his strength. His face felt cold and hard.

Audrey smiled and squeezed his arm. 'I love you,' she said, softly, shyly.

What was he supposed to say to that? How could he take such a declaration seriously? He tried to remember if his mother had told him she loved him before she left. He had a vague memory of the hall to their old house. Fifteen. Too old to really need a mother, but young enough to miss one. She'd held both his hands with the suitcases stacked behind her. 'You understand,' she'd said. 'Mummy knows you understand.'

He shuddered. Words had nothing to do with love.

'Well, take care,' he said, and forced back the burning behind his eyes.

*Take care!* She'd said she loved him and all he could manage was take bloody care! Audrey controlled her tears until the door to the lift hissed shut behind her. The hammered brass blurred as salty drops spilt down her cheeks. She was an idiot. She never should have said she loved him. She wasn't even certain she did. She sniffed hard and tried to stem the flow by pinching her temples and holding her breath.

All she got for her pains was a case of the hiccups.

He didn't love her. She couldn't believe how badly that hurt.

# Chapter Twelve

*T*he hour was almost two by the time the cab reached Tommy's house. As she'd expected, lights burnt in the half-buried windows of the basement. Tommy was both night owl and workaholic. Knowing he'd never hear the bell, she let herself in with her copy of his key.

The muffled roar of a vacuum cleaner struck her ears. She gazed up the stairs towards the sound. That couldn't be Tommy vacuuming. Cynthia must be staying over. Audrey wanted to kick herself for not considering the possibility. How self-centred could she get: assuming Tommy would always be at her disposal, and alone to boot!

Frowning, she bumped her satchel against the front of her legs. She'd be damned if she'd scurry back to Mr Take Bloody Care. No. She'd call another taxi and stay at the Latham until she got her head on straight. Of course, if Cynthia walked in on her using the phone, she'd have some explaining to do. Better go upstairs, she thought, and announce myself straight off.

Wishing she hadn't been so thoughtless, she

climbed to the second floor. The noise of vacuuming grew louder. Now she could hear wheels rolling vigorously over the carpet. Cynthia was cleaning her little heart out. Come to think of it, why was she tidying up at two in the morning? If the neighbours weren't heavy sleepers, they'd be throwing shoes at the wall.

'Knock knock,' she called, halting at the door to Tommy's bedroom.

Cynthia looked up and gasped. Her face was streaked with tears. 'Oh,' she said, one hand covering her cheek while the other switched off the machine. She wore an oversized T-shirt, but it wasn't Tommy's; his wouldn't have been big enough to hang on her. Her straight, softly highlighted hair was smoothed beneath a periwinkle band. The colour brought out the blue in her hazel eyes. Despite her red nose and blotchy cheeks, she looked as pretty as a perfume ad. The legs her T-shirt bared were smooth and shapely. Her toenails had been painted a soft, tasteful pink.

'Did Tom call you?' she said, swiping at her nose and blushing.

'No-o.' Audrey eased into the room as if landmines might be hiding beneath the spotless navy carpet. She pulled a Kleenex from the flowered box on the bureau and handed it to Cynthia. 'Is there a reason Tommy would be calling me?'

Cynthia sat on the bed and blew her nose with amazingly little noise. 'I thought he might be upset.'

'You thought *he* might be upset.' Audrey sat beside her and looked around the room. Without Tommy's clutter she barely recognised it. Even the shades had been dusted.

'I know,' Cynthia said with a shaky half-laugh. 'I'm the one who's cleaning like a maniac. It's just –' Her delicate shoulders slumped beneath the oversized shirt. 'Everything's fine. I love Tom and we get along

207

great. But we, um, we've been having some trouble in bed.'

'Uh,' said Audrey, not sure she should be hearing this.

'It's not his fault,' Cynthia hastened to assure her, her hand clutching Audrey's thigh. 'He's a wonderful lover. Very considerate. It's just I've never been very good at relaxing. In bed, you know. Especially with Tom. I always want everything to be perfect. I guess it makes me uptight because I can't seem to . . .' Her voice trailed away and she wrinkled her flawless nose.

'You haven't had an orgasm with him.'

She hung her head. 'No. Not that it matters. I mean, the closeness is what counts to me, but Tom worries when I don't . . . Well, I think it bothers him.'

'I should think it would bother you, too,' Audrey said, a bit more sharply than she'd intended.

Cynthia shook her head. 'Oh, no. I mean, I read that lots of women don't, you know, during vaginal sex – which is not to say that's all he's willing to do.'

Cynthia's cheeks were as pink as if she'd described in detail what Tommy was willing to do. Audrey patted the hand she'd left on her thigh. 'Maybe you need to think less about Tommy's feelings and more about yours. If you just laid back and enjoyed when Tommy did those, uh, other things . . .'

Cynthia's lips thinned primly. 'That would be selfish.'

'Selfish isn't always bad. Selfish gives the other person a chance to be generous.' Audrey could tell from Cynthia's expression that she wasn't convinced. 'Cyn. You know what happens when you get two caretakers in a relationship? One of them is left without enough to do. That might not cause trouble when it comes to picking up his socks, but in bed, with a man like Tommy, you need to add some take to your give.'

Cynthia retrieved her hand and twisted it around the other in her lap. 'I just can't.' Her lower lip trembled. 'He didn't even want to sleep with me at first, not like I wanted to sleep with him. I can't ask him to go to all that trouble for me.'

'Of course you can.' Audrey hugged her. 'You said it bothered him that you didn't have an orgasm. Surely you can see he'd enjoy giving you pleasure.'

Cynthia sniffed and pressed the crumpled tissue to her nose. 'I'm not actually sure I can. I've come by myself, of course, but never with a man.'

'Oh, Cyn.' Audrey let her sympathy out on a sigh. Cynthia sighed back and snuggled closer. She wound her arms around Audrey's waist, her breasts pressed soft and small to her side. She smelled of sweet spring flowers and sudsing cleanser. They hadn't hugged each other this way since college. Audrey kissed the silky crown of her hair. 'I'm sure you and Tommy can work this out. It's just a matter of getting used to someone else's touch, and relaxing, and being patient.'

'Could you do it?' Cynthia asked, thready and girlish against her neck.

At first Audrey thought Cynthia wanted to know if *she'd* had an orgasm with Tommy. When she realised that couldn't be what she meant, her mouth fell open. 'You want me to give you an orgasm?'

'Oh, yes.' Cynthia sat up straighter. 'I think it would be easier to get used to another woman first.'

Audrey's head spun for a moment before she could respond. 'Look, I know you think I've had a wild past, but I've never been with another woman.'

'You've done it for yourself, though. It can't be that hard.'

Audrey stood and shoved her hair back from her

face. 'Women aren't carbon copies of each other. They don't all enjoy the same stimulation.'

'See. Already you've told me something I didn't know. Oh, please, Audrey, couldn't you try? I'd feel so much more comfortable with you.'

A laugh bubbled up from Audrey's chest. 'And you say I'm adventurous!'

Cynthia bounced like a puppy. 'You'll do it then. I knew you would.' She scrambled back on the bed and pulled down the neatly tucked navy coverlet.

'What? You want to do it now?'

Cynthia glanced over her shoulder, rump in the air. 'Why not? Tom will be glued to that computer all night.'

'Don't you think you should discuss this with him first?'

Her face fell. 'I'm not sure he cares who I sleep with.'

Despite her success with men, Audrey's pride had been trampled often enough to understand how badly the other woman needed reassurance. She climbed on to the bed and held her, petting her hair, letting her sniffle against her neck. 'I'm sure he cares, Cyn. I'm sure he does.'

Cynthia turned her head, nuzzling for her mouth. Audrey didn't resist. The kiss was soft at first, almost pleading, but when Audrey began to answer it, it turned hungry. Cynthia's hands slipped under her shirt, searching out her breasts. Audrey remembered what she'd said about having a crush on her at school. Did Cynthia know that Audrey and Tommy had made love? Was that part of her motivation: getting her own back, proving that Tommy wasn't the only one who could have Audrey? If that were the case, she doubted Cynthia would admit it, even to herself. Oddly enough, the possibility that Little Miss Perfect had a flaw opened a blossom of heat in Audrey's groin.

She told herself she was a small, petty person, but the scold didn't curb her upwelling of lust. She kissed Cynthia harder, then pushed her free. 'You aren't supposed to be touching me,' she said sternly. 'This is about your pleasure.'

Cynthia bit her lip. Her cheeks were flushed, her mouth swollen. Her nipples stood out beneath her thin T-shirt, trembling with the pounding of her heart. Audrey had done that to her, no one else. Power pumped through her veins. Was this what Patrick felt? Was this a master's joy? 'Pull that shirt off,' she ordered, 'and lie back across the bed.'

Cynthia did as she asked. Audrey positioned her limbs in a gentle splay, drawing her fingers down Cynthia's arms and across her palms until she quivered at the teasing of her nerves. Then Audrey pulled her flowered white panties down her legs. The gusset was wet and a new scent joined Cynthia's perfume. She was lovely naked: slim and smooth and pale. No clothes, however expensive, could do her body justice. Without a scrap of cloth, her demureness showed through: in the shy swell of her breasts, in the modest curve of her hip. Looking down at her, knowing this graceful girl was longing for her touch, Audrey felt a pleasure akin to pride of ownership. She dragged her hand up Cynthia's leg, then circled it over her hipbone. Cynthia's mound of Venus rose seekingly off the bed, as if she were incapable of being still. The light brown curls that covered her lips were spiked with dew. 'I'd like to hear you beg,' Audrey said, soft as thistledown.

Cynthia gasped and turned even pinker. 'I don't – I'm not sure I can.'

Audrey smiled and kissed her, deep and wet, driving her tongue so deeply Cynthia could not answer its thrust. 'That's all right, Cyn. You think about begging. That will be good enough.'

'Oh!' Cynthia jerked as Audrey's fingers found her labia. She stroked lightly up and down the plumping folds until the tip of Cynthia's clit peeped from its hood. Audrey flicked her nail across the tiny rod, a quick back-and-forth motion. Cynthia moaned.

'Does that tickle?' Audrey teased, licking a path around the shell of her ear.

Cynthia shivered and moaned again. Audrey loved that she was too befuddled to answer, absolutely loved it. She pushed two fingers between her slippery folds, rubbing the channel to either side of Cynthia's clit. Her motions were slow and firm. Cynthia's sex grew wetter, more fragrant. She began to squirm. Audrey knew she wanted to be touched more directly, but was too shy to ask. She laughed and slithered halfway down the bed. She kneed Cynthia's thighs apart and knelt between them. Cynthia closed her eyes.

'Embarrassed?' Audrey whispered. She opened Cynthia's labia with her thumbs, continuing her deep, slow massage. 'You're very pretty down here. You're rosy and flushed and your skin has little frills where it circles the mouth of your pussy.'

Cynthia's body arched with pleasure but, 'Don't look,' she begged, her eyes screwed shut with shame.

'Don't look, eh? Guess I'll have to find my way by touch.' Audrey slid her middle finger up Cynthia's glistening passage. Her sheath was soft and warm and mobile, closing eagerly around the penetration. One more finger, she thought, and added a second. 'Is that good? Do you like the sensation of being filled?'

'Yes,' Cynthia gasped, and Audrey could tell it was hard for her to admit even that much.

She pressed her mouth to the plump, silken flesh of

Cynthia's breast. 'If you were in my place,' she said, 'wouldn't you want me to tell you what I liked?'

Cynthia's head lashed back and forth. 'Touch my – touch my clitoris,' she stammered.

Audrey moved her thumb to the hood and worked it over the hardness inside. Cynthia groaned with relief. She was delicate here, but the small protrusion was cranberry red with engorging blood. Audrey experimented with different motions. 'Do you like it better when I rub you up and down? Or in a circle?'

Cynthia wriggled under her hand. She was biting her lip so hard, it whitened. 'Up and down.'

'Do you like it better when I rub this side or that?' Cynthia cried out sharply when Audrey moved to 'that'. Audrey chuckled. 'Ladies and gentlemen, we have a winner.'

Cynthia laughed with her, relaxing enough to open her eyes. 'Come closer,' she said, shy and soft. 'I want you to lie on top of me.'

Audrey left her hand where it was and moved over her friend. She still wore all her clothes. With someone else she might have stripped off but, crush or no crush, she imagined she'd challenged Cynthia's inhibitions as far as they would go. Instead, she clasped Cynthia's thigh between her own. She doubted the muffled friction would get her off, but it was enough to keep her from climbing the walls.

'How's the pressure?' she said, her lips against Cynthia's ear.

'Maybe a little harder. Oh! Yes, like that, like that.' Her hips began to rise and fall, intensifying what Audrey was doing. Her hand fluttered over Audrey's, then jerked away.

'Faster?' Audrey suggested, and heightened the pace. Cynthia groaned. The sound was not ladylike; it was rough and greedy and pained. It made Audrey's pussy clench and she could feel Cynthia's doing the same. Moisture slicked her working fingers. 'Ooh,' she said, grinding on Cynthia's thigh. 'You feel good. You feel tender inside and plump. You're clutching my fingers as if they were a cock. I love that you want this. I love how hot you are.'

Cynthia might not have been a talker, but she certainly liked being talked to. Her neck arched off the bed. Her hand clamped Audrey's wrist, jamming her deeper, closer. Audrey increased the pressure on the sweet spot beside her clit and pressed up on her pubis from inside. Cynthia came with a strangled wail. The first inch of her sheath fluttered with contractions. A gush of moisture drenched Audrey's palm. Amazing, she thought, even as she nursed the spasms with her thumb. Her own need was forgotten in enchantment at this discovery. She'd never thought a pussy could be so fascinating.

At last, Cynthia collapsed back on the pillows. Gently, Audrey withdrew her hand and squirmed off her thigh. They grinned at each other. If Cynthia's grin was a little sheepish, that was to be expected.

'Thank you,' she said. 'I really wasn't sure I could do that.'

'Neither was I,' said a voice from the open door.

Cynthia bolted up in horror, her palm pressed to her heart. 'Tommy!' Despite her claim that Tommy wouldn't care who she slept with, she looked as if she'd broken a sacred trust. From Tommy's wry expression, Audrey suspected Cynthia's first guess was closer to the mark.

'It isn't what you think,' Cynthia babbled. 'I mean, it is what you think, but she was just helping me. I was just –'

'Practising?' Tommy suggested, his amusement barely hidden.

Audrey knew if she met his eye, they'd both explode with laughter, not cruel laughter, but isn't-

214

life-ridiculous laughter. She'd been wrong to think Tommy would fall in love with Cynthia, just as Tommy had been wrong to think Audrey would fall in love with him. Now they both knew it. Only Cynthia remained in the dark. Poor Cynthia. But perhaps not so poor. Considering how successful tonight's experiment had been, their friend might have more adventures in store for her. Perhaps Cynthia had been wrong to dismiss her attraction to Audrey as a schoolgirl crush. Perhaps she'd turn out to be as omnisexual as Basil.

Audrey regarded her friends in turn. 'You know, I'm not entirely sure the lesson has taken. Cynthia here might need more practice.'

Her pupil stiffened with shock, but Tommy rubbed his chin and nodded. His trousers sported a noticeable bulge. 'You could be right,' he said. 'This may require a team effort.'

'Oh, no.' Cynthia squirmed back towards the headboard, her breasts bobbling, her cheeks bright pink. 'You don't have to –'

'Of course we do,' Audrey demurred. 'Lessons like these demand repetition.'

Patrick leant on the roof's ledge and watched the Potomac glimmer beneath a crescent moon. A snifter of brandy sat by his elbow. The cat draped his shoulder like a sack of beans, his ribs expanding in an occasional feline sigh. Newton was happy. His belly was full, his dreams sweet, and one of his favourite people was stroking his back. Patrick smiled – wistfully, he knew – and rubbed his jaw over the kitten's head.

People were right about cats. He'd grown up with dogs. Dogs won votes. But cats were calming creatures, easy to care for, easy to please in Newton's case. Newton loved any kind hand that touched him, no matter the flaws that lay behind it. A friend was a person who fed him; he did not judge any further than that.

A memory rose through the dark. Patrick was five or six, taking a rare outing with his mother, who usually left him in the care of his nanny. They were waiting to cross a busy street: Pennsylvania Avenue, he thought, near the Old Post Office Tower. A mother and son stood in front of them, hand in hand. The boy was bouncing up and down, pestering the woman with questions which she bent to answer with laughing eyes. 'Hold on tight,' she said as the light turned green. Patrick wanted what that little boy had. He wanted it so badly he reached up for his own mother's hand. It must have been one of her bad days. She shook him off at once. 'I've got packages,' she snapped.

Packages. He'd never reached for her again, nor had she asked him to. 'Patrick doesn't like me to fuss,' she always said, but the aversion wasn't his.

She'd abandoned him a long time before that cult leader lured her to Colorado.

He lifted his brandy and tipped a slow swallow down his throat. Until she'd left, his father hadn't been much different. He didn't have a temper like his wife, but he'd looked at his son without seeing; had listened to him without hearing. Perhaps it was time Patrick faced the truth. The senator's long-ago neglect was part of the reason he'd wanted to master Audrey. Even now, he didn't quite trust his father's affections. Thirty-eight years old and he still felt he had to buy them.

His upper lip curled. Lord, what a pitiful thing was a man who couldn't leave his childhood behind.

The sound of glass doors sliding open brought him around, but the intruder wasn't Audrey, it was Basil. Without waiting for an invitation, he joined him at the edge of the roof. 'Gazing at the moon without me, dearest?'

Patrick shook off the fingers that had crept up his neck. 'I'm not in the mood for your games tonight.'

'Tut-tut. Our watcher will think we've had a spat.'

'Let him.'

Patrick's blunt answer would have driven off anyone but Basil. He set a second snifter on the ledge and filled both from the brandy bottle he'd carried outside. 'I've got a question for you.' Patrick huffed the air from his lungs, but Basil's composure did not falter. The light from the living room illuminated his soft, sardonic smile. 'Do you respect your submissives?'

'What kind of question is that? Of course I do.'

'You say "of course" too easily. I don't think you realise how much you need Audrey.'

Patrick's hand clenched around the stem of his glass. 'I know she's special.'

'You say that too easily, too.'

Patrick shook his head. Basil had no idea how completely the balance of power had shifted from his hand. Audrey was the one who didn't know how special they were together. Audrey was the one who didn't even consider him a friend.

'She's not a person to you,' Basil said.

The urge to hit him was very strong. Not wanting the cat to sense his anger, he set Newton on the ground. 'You couldn't be more wrong.'

'I'd like to be wrong, but I don't think I am. I've yet to see you unscrew the clamp you've got on your emotions. Oh, I've no doubt you're fond of her, just as you're fond of that cat. But she's no more an equal to you than Newton is.'

'What do you want from me, Basil?'

The threat in Patrick's voice did not alarm the other man. Basil tilted the brandy glass, letting its contents swirl over the warmth of his palm. 'I want to see the heart beating under all that Irish charm. I want to see if you can bleed.'

'Believe me,' Patrick said, 'I can.'

'I believe you did, once upon a time. But I don't believe you've let anyone close enough to cut you, since. Where's your little submissive tonight, eh? Have you already started pushing her away?'

Patrick shoved him, one brief explosion of violence. Taken by surprise, Basil stumbled and dropped the brandy bottle. It shattered when it hit the bricks, showering glass and liquor around the singer's feet.

'Shit,' Patrick cursed, mostly at himself. He squatted to pick up the worst of it.

'Don't.' Basil pulled him up by the shoulder. 'It's too dark to see. You'll cut yourself.'

'Christ, you're not even wearing shoes. Don't move. I'll lift you out.' Patrick hoisted him up and gave him a shake. Tiny splinters rattled from the cuffs of his linen trousers. Wincing at the crunch of glass beneath his shoes, he curled an arm under Basil's knees and carried him towards the pool. The singer didn't weigh much more than Audrey did. To his credit, he didn't cling. Apparently, even Basil had some sense. Patrick lowered him on to one of the loungers. 'You all right?'

'Perfectly fine,' Basil assured him. 'If a little breathless at that display of masculine force.'

'Goddamn it.'

Basil laughed, which told Patrick he'd meant to get a rise out of him. Patrick's legs were shaking, and not entirely from exertion. He didn't often let his temper loose. He sat on the slightly raised edge of the pool, ignoring the small chlorinated puddle that seeped through his trousers. Even sitting didn't steady him. He braced his head on the tips of his fingers. He was too disturbed to flinch when Basil rubbed his shoulder.

'She's young and breakable,' he said. 'If you don't treat her right, you won't have her when you're old and grey.'

Until Basil said the words Patrick hadn't realised that was precisely what he wanted. He pressed his lids to burning eyes. 'I'm treating her as well as I know how.'

'You haven't let her see you bleed, Patrick. You haven't let her see you feel. She won't be yours until you do.'

'She's twenty-two years old. It's doubtful she'll be mine, as you put it, regardless of what I do.' He flung down his hands and lifted his head, feeling baleful and hot. Audrey had said 'I'm yours,' but she'd said it while she hung in chains, in the heat of her submissive moment. The minute she'd caught her breath she'd run back to Tommy. Her 'best friend'. Fuck, he thought, and glared at Basil. 'I didn't invite you here to be my therapist.'

Basil's smile would have done a Buddha proud. 'But maybe that's why I came.'

'Now that's a load of crap.' Patrick was pleased to see the Buddha flinch. 'I'm not the only one who isn't sharing what he feels. You had a reason for coming here, and it wasn't to do me a favour.' He pointed his finger at the singer, surer than ever that he was right. 'You're here because you're pissed off at me for something and you thought you'd get a chance to make me pay.'

'I am not pissed off at you,' Basil said with great affront.

'Like hell you're not. I let it ride because I thought you were annoyed with me for not wanting you –'

'– and when did you decide you didn't want me? When you were shoving your cock down my throat? Or out here at night when you threw a boner every time we kissed?'

'I could walk away from you without a second thought and you know it!'

Patrick had leapt to his feet, his hands fisted by his sides, his body once again shaken by rage. The light was brighter by the pool and the stiff hurt on Basil's face was very clear. Shit, he thought, swallowing to make room for his apology.

Basil spoke before he could get it out, his voice rough but dignified. 'You're quite right. You could walk away from me without a second thought. I've always known that. I suppose that's what made me so angry. I've known you for two years now. I've seen you every week, four nights a week. We've had untold meaningless conversations. You know my deepest, darkest secret. Nonetheless, never once have I felt I was a person to you, much less a friend.'

Patrick sat again, so shocked his breath wouldn't come. 'That is not true. Of course, you're a person to me.'

'Am I?' A tear rolled down Basil's cheek. He shook it angrily away. 'When Steven –' His voice faltered and he clenched his jaw to get it under control. 'When Steven died, you didn't come to the funeral. Everyone from the bar was there, even the busboy, who'd known me two fucking weeks. When he came up to me afterwards, he thought my name was Barry. You couldn't even send flowers. You couldn't even say "I'm sorry for your loss, Basil. Let me know if there's something I can do."'

'But I didn't –' know, he started to say. Except he had. It was coming back to him now. He'd heard the waitresses discussing the train wreck on break, talking about how devastated Basil was, and how sad they were because he and Steven had made such a sweet couple. He'd even met Steven a few times, a tall, quiet man with a boyish smile. But the knowledge had never sunk in. He must have thought, why go to

220

a funeral for a man he barely knew? He hated funerals, and Basil and he weren't close. Basil was just an employee, a man he joked with sometimes, an eccentric man who liked to dress in women's clothes ... Christ, Basil was right. He was a cold, closed-up bastard, and probably a bigot as well. Oh, he'd congratulated himself on how tolerant he was, hiring a transvestite to sing in his bar, forgetting how much business that transvestite brought in. He'd even congratulated himself on how well he respected Basil's privacy. He'd never pried into his personal life, never judged, never bloody said he was sorry his lover had died.

He covered his face, overwhelmed with self-disgust. 'I am so sorry, Basil. I have no excuse. Of all people, I should have known better, and you're absolutely right. I've been a bastard to you, to everyone. It's no wonder Audrey wouldn't have me for a friend.'

'Let's not lay it on that thick,' Basil said, with a shade of his old irony. 'Audrey would have you for a friend in a minute. So would I, for that matter, if I thought you meant it.'

Patrick lowered his hands and laced them between his knees. He wanted to promise he'd be different from now on, but the words wouldn't come. How could he promise to change when, until tonight, he hadn't known how much he needed to? A hard, furry head butted his shin. Newton had reappeared. Mewing plaintively, he wound himself around Patrick's ankles. Perhaps the fuzzball was growing sensitive to his keepers' moods. Patrick squeezed his arching spine. Delighted with the attention, the cat plopped over and bared his belly for a rub.

'Well,' Basil said drily. 'He's quick to forgive.'

Patrick heaved a little sigh. 'Basil?'

'Yes, dearest?'

221

'When this is over and it's time for you to go –'

'Eager to have me out of your hair?'

'No,' Patrick said, surprised that it was true. 'But I was wondering, when you do go, would you consider leaving Newton with me?'

For some reason Basil found this amusing. He wiped a mock tear from his eye. 'Ah, Patrick,' he said. 'There may be hope for you yet.'

Audrey thought Tommy would never give out. Twice he came and twice he rose harder than before. He seemed to have a dozen mouths, a dozen hands, and none could get enough of touching either one of them. Watching the two women together had inspired him. Working side-by-side with Audrey to bring Cynthia pleasure drove him to unprecedented erotic feats. Audrey knew he'd never been so potent before. She also knew Cynthia wasn't the reason.

Cynthia stood outside the bond that had formed between Tommy and her, as if he and Audrey were two male friends who could only fuck each other through a woman. When Tommy drove his cock between Cynthia's flailing legs, he knew Audrey watched its glistening thrust and draw. When Audrey rolled Cynthia's nipples between her fingers, he knew the caress was an offering to him. Between the two of them, they screwed Cynthia to exhaustion. When Tommy tired, Audrey would love Cynthia's pussy with her mouth. When he recovered, she'd lie behind Cynthia, smoothing her thigh over his hip, squeezing her breasts, tickling her anal bud until she cried out in titillated shock.

From time to time, Tommy's gaze would lock with Audrey's. Then his hand would stray to her face, fingertips glancing her mouth. If she touched him back, he'd tighten like a man being lashed.

Cynthia slept before he came the final time. He

pulled out, stripped off the condom and grabbed the half-empty box. 'You,' he said, his eyes glassy and wild.

They made it as far as the bathroom door. There they kissed like starving animals. He took her standing up, thumping her into the wall until their knees refused to hold them. They folded down beneath the lintel. Her back was on the floor, her calves around his neck. The soles of her feet braced against the door frame. Half-sitting, he rode high in her sheath, bumping her most sensitive flesh with every thrust. Her sex throbbed so strongly, so pleasurably, she thought she might be coming already. She longed for another spike, though, for the sharp demarcation between 'no' and 'yes'. Desperate to scale the next height, she clutched his shoulders. His knees were planted on either side of the threshold. He had one hand beneath her buttocks and the other wrapped protectively behind her head. When she groaned, the hand on her bottom tightened like a pincer.

'I want it, too,' he panted, low and rough. 'God, I can't stand it.'

His words made her groan again. He pumped even faster, cramped by the doorway, quieter than she but far from silent.

Cynthia would hear. Cynthia would – The spike she longed for pierced the root of her sex. Tommy moaned her name and ground in deep, deep, his whole body straining against her as he came.

They were drenched in sweat. Their skin slipped as they rearranged their contorted limbs. He kissed her softly and pulled her to her feet. 'Come,' he said.

Naked, they padded down the stairs to the living room. He spread his napping quilt over her favourite leather chair, then wrapped them both in its warmth. Audrey curled in his lap and rested her head on his shoulder.

'Now,' he said, 'tell me why you came here tonight, and don't even think of holding back. We both just screwed my girlfriend. As a bonding experience, that has to rate near the top.'

Audrey stroked his upper arm. 'Something happened with Patrick. Something so good it scared me.'

'Tell me,' he said, the way a brother would.

It was hard to explain without hurting him, but as well as she was able, she did. She told him about the power of the night and the power of iron chains. She described the rapture of surrender, and the magic of Patrick's phantom touch. She didn't know how well she succeeded, but Tommy listened to all she said. His only response was to kiss her cheek or to tighten his arms around her back.

'I'm just not sure it was as special to him as it was to me,' she said.

'Which was the really scary part.'

'Right.'

He pressed his lips to her brow. 'Do you love him?'

'I told him I did.'

'And he said . . .?'

'He said, "take care of yourself."' She grimaced, then tried to shrug off her misery. 'I was on my way to see you. I think I took him by surprise.'

'So you don't actually know he doesn't love you back.'

'No.'

The streetlamp in front of Tommy's house cast slivers of light through the vertical blinds. She and Tommy were striped, as if they belonged to the same exotic species of human. She lay her hand over his heart and felt its slow, steady thump. She loved him more than ever. She doubted anyone would ever mean to her what he did. She also knew that, whether Patrick had intended to or not, he'd opened her heart to this intensity of feeling. If she hadn't fallen in love with him, she couldn't have loved anyone else so deeply.

She'd thought submission would help her rise above her emotions. The truth was just the opposite.

Tommy stirred beneath her, breaking her reverie. He spoke with endearing hesitance. 'If you asked him how he felt, do you think he'd tell you the truth?'

She smiled against his shoulder. 'I know he would, which is the really, really scary part.'

'Hey, no guts, no glory. From what you've told me tonight, maybe he is worth the risk.'

She could guess what it cost him to say that. If Patrick were in love with someone else, she doubted she'd be so supportive. But Tommy was one in a million. She drew a circle on his chest and wished she never had to leave the safety of his arms. 'Tommy?'

'Yes, Aud?'

'I'm sorry you're not in love with Cynthia.'

His sigh riffled her hair. 'Me, too. For both our sakes. But you and I, we'll be friends forever.'

'Forever,' she agreed, snuggling closer. The peace of a child stole through her veins. She knew this serenity couldn't last but, for the moment, it was all she asked.


Eyes alert, tail twitching with interest, the cat watched Patrick from the top of the living room bar. Basil had taken himself off who knew where, leaving Patrick to contemplate his newly discovered sins. Only Newton had not defected. The glossy black marble threw back a reflection that was much less kittenish than before. Sitting still, the fuzzball almost looked dignified.

'It's you and me, buddy,' Patrick said as he opened a bottle of Tullamore Dew, a Christmas gift from his father. Brandy was fine for relaxing, but genuine heartache – one that had caught him flat-footed – that demanded the tears of the gods.

Or perhaps he wanted to remind himself the senator really did love him.

Maudlin bastard, he thought, and poured two fingers into a heavy tumbler. Fine Irish crystal, it was, for fine Irish whiskey. He sipped, savouring the bite of it going down, the warmth as it hit his belly.

Which was, naturally, nothing to the warmth Audrey could inspire.

He rested his elbows on the bar, closed his eyes and pressed the glass to the bridge of his nose. Bored by this, Newton batted a bottle cap on to the floor and leapt after it with a less than graceful thud.

'Fine. Go play,' Patrick said. He watched the cat skitter across the rugs as if the rolling cap were the cleverest mouse who'd ever lived. He smiled in spite of himself, then found tears starting in his eyes.

How had he failed to notice he'd fallen in love with Audrey? 'Mine,' he'd said, on more than one occasion. He'd never been particularly possessive of his subs. His care for their feelings had descended from lofty realms, its basis in principle rather than emotion. He'd never tried to surround them as he'd surrounded Audrey. He'd never wanted to share his life, the ordinary parts of it: the laundry and the shopping, the grumpy before-breakfast moods, the nights spent sleeping, nothing more, with his lover cradled in his arms.

I probably ought to marry her, he thought. Immediately, his chest was swamped by a wave of terror: of what he wanted, of the chance that Audrey would refuse him. When the wave passed, it left a taste like iron in his mouth. He downed the rest of the whiskey and prepared to pour another. The doorbell rang.

He prayed it was her, even as he told himself Basil had forgotten his key. He strode so quickly to the door Newton decided he'd be more fun to chase than the bottle cap. With infernal feline intelligence, he managed to be exactly where Patrick wanted to step. 'Watch it!' he said, barely catching himself as he tripped. With a muted yowl, Newton streaked behind the couch. Patrick's heart was pounding like a jackhammer. He took a deep, slow breath and opened the door.

She stood like a waif on the soft gold carpet of the hall, satchel in hand, mouth worried out of shape by the press of her teeth. Relief washed through him and, with it, heat. He feared it was flooding his cheeks and hoped she didn't notice. She shuffled her feet. 'I hope it's all right,' she said in a small, tight voice, 'my coming back so soon.'

How could she think it wouldn't be? Forgetting everything but her, he opened his arms. As she fell into them, she began to cry. Her tears were not a submissive's, but a hurt young woman's. Soothing her meant more to him than soothing anyone had. He held her trembling form, rocking her, stroking her smooth wavy hair. 'Of course it's all right,' he said, closing the door behind her. 'Never doubt it.'

He guided her to the couch, arm around her shoulders, lips pressed to her temple. She sat and sniffled her thanks. Her tears were drying, but he pulled her against him all the same. 'I'm glad you came back.'

He offered her a clean handkerchief. She laughed – because it was old-fashioned, he supposed – then blew noisily and wiped her eyes. 'There's just one thing I need to know,' she said.

'Yes, love?'

She lifted red-rimmed eyes and tear-dewed lashes. He brushed his thumb across the curve of her cheek, lost in her storm cloud gaze. Rather than drift with him, she straightened her shoulders, visibly girding herself. In her best grown-up voice, she said, 'Was it like this for all of them? Did you hold them while

227

they slept? Did you –' he heard a throaty swallow '– did you touch them without your hands? Did you make them fall in love with you?'

A hot, tingling shock crawled across his scalp. She'd said it again: that she loved him. This time she wasn't leaving; she was coming back. Could she really mean the words?

'No,' he said, shaking the joyful addlement from his head. 'Never. No one has been as close to me as you. No one ever made me want to be better than I am.'

She choked out a laugh. 'For God's sake, don't get any better. I'll never break free of you then.'

'Is that what you want?' He cupped her chin. 'To break free of me?'

Her lashes fell. 'I don't know,' she whispered. 'I have no idea what you feel about all this, about my . . . loving you.'

'I feel incredibly honoured.' Her lips pinched together and he knew he hadn't said the right thing. He patted her denim clad thigh, then left his hand above her knee. His heart beat faster. He had to do what Basil said. He had to let her close enough to cut him. 'There's something you should know about me. My mother ran away when I was fifteen.'

Audrey's head came up. 'Your mother ran away?'

'Yes. She went to join a commune in Colorado, to find her "spiritual centre". She's still there, as far as I know. She doesn't write and neither do I. I suppose losing a mother at that age isn't a big deal. I was old enough to take care of myself. The problem was, she wasn't really there for me before she left. For as long as I can remember, she was more concerned with herself than anyone else. She thought going off to join this guru was a change, but it was just more selfishness, the difference being this time she got to pat herself on the back for it.' His voice fell. 'Sometimes I think she's the reason I am the way I am.'

Audrey turned sideways on the couch, her brows drawn together. 'You mean you think you're dominant because your mother wasn't there for you? My mother was there for me. My father wasn't. Is that why I'm submissive? Now that I'm grown up, I can finally get spanked?'

'Don't be flippant about this.'

'Then don't talk as if who you are and what you enjoy is some sort of illness that has to be excused. If that's what you believe, I'd like to know why the hell you dragged me into it.'

Her huffy tone amused him. 'That isn't what I meant.'

'Then what did you mean?'

He sighed. 'Basil was kind enough to point out that I have a hard time getting close to people, trusting them, I guess.'

'Are you trying to warn me you'll never be close to me?' Her words sounded strange, not so much hurt as concerned. When he looked at her, he knew his eyes swam with tears. Hers were no less full. She touched her heart with the fingers of one hand. 'You've reached places inside me I didn't know another human being could.' She shook her head. 'If you could see the look on your face right now, you'd know what you feel for me isn't cold. It isn't distant. Maybe you don't trust me, but I can tell you want to.'

'I do,' he said, suddenly hoarse. He wanted to say the rest. He wanted to say he loved her, but, by God, she was twenty-two years old. He was only the second man who'd mastered her. How could she be sure she loved him? How could he be sure the next strong man she met wouldn't inspire the same response?

She squeezed his hands and smiled. It was a feminine smile, full of shy secrets. 'I don't need promises,' she said. 'I can wait to see what happens. If you want me to stick around.'

'I do,' he said, then blushed for sounding like a broken record.

She laughed and clasped his cheeks and kissed him. When their tongues stroked together, he forgot to be embarrassed.

# Chapter Thirteen

*A*udrey hummed as she put away the groceries, her bare feet shuffling out a dance on the shiny red linoleum. She'd found fresh mangoes today and a sinfully rich vanilla ice cream on which to serve them. Basil would be so surprised when she offered to make dessert, and even more surprised when he discovered it was edible.

She giggled and slid a bag of lettuce into the crisper. She'd miss Basil, his sense of humour, his easy conversation. The thought of being alone with Patrick made her nervous, though it also excited her. She had plans for him, plans which demanded total privacy, plans which included this kitchen floor, come to think of it.

Hope warmed her heart like sweet spring wine. Patrick wanted her to stay. 'We need time together,' he'd said, 'to explore what's happening between us.' He didn't specify what he thought that was, but she knew he wouldn't live with a girl who'd said she loved him unless he welcomed being loved. The knowledge went a long way towards appeasing her insecurity. True, he'd made no promises but, for the moment, the future seemed a beautifully wrapped present. Why rush to open it when anticipation was so sweet? If he loved her – and she was beginning to think he might – she could wait until he was ready to say the words.

She shut the refrigerator and stroked its stainless steel handle. Patrick had gone to visit his father this morning, to warn him he'd decided to confront Sterling Foster. She hoped the senator wouldn't be angry about the premature end of their ruse, and that he could weather whatever scandal Sterling chose to unleash. Patrick assured her his father was a tough old bear. Whether he was or not, Patrick's decision to put her well-being before anyone else's made her feel cherished, and determined to deserve his care.

The only sad development was that Basil was moving out. Audrey racked her brains for the best way to express her gratitude. Dessert, she decided, was just the beginning.

She stowed the ice cream and turned to fold her bags. Without warning, an explosion shook the dishes on the shelves. Her pulse jumped like oil on a hot griddle. The sound was very close. Had something blown up? Was the building on fire? After a moment's paralysis, she rushed towards the entry.

'Audrey!' roared an all-too-familiar voice.

Chills swept her skin as every hair on her body stood on end. Sterling stood in the doorway with two huge men behind him. A battering ram hung between their bulging arms. The boom she'd heard must have been the door slamming into the wall. Sterling obviously hadn't helped. True to form, he didn't have one silver hair out of place.

'Are you crazy?' she gasped, goggling at the splintered frame. This was breaking and entering and trespassing and – The words died, unspoken. Sterling was acting as if no one could stop him, as if he knew she was alone. Adrenaline poured so forcefully through her system she felt sick to her stomach. She wanted to run, but she knew he would catch her. Screaming, however, was still an option.

As if he had all the time in the world, Sterling shot his cuffs and stepped on to the patterned marble floor. The polished sunburst reflected back his pale, double-breasted suit. 'I'm not crazy,' he said in his coolest, mildest tone. 'But I have been wondering if you are.'

Audrey backed towards the living room. Once she reached the phone, she could summon help. Her knees were shaking like jelly. She didn't like that glitter in Sterling's eye, or the impassivity of the two musclebound goons he'd brought along. To her dismay, the more she retreated, the faster they advanced. In desperation, she lunged for the receiver. Before she could reach it, Sterling caught her wrist in a brutal grip. He held her arm high above her head. 'Ah-ah-ah, little Audrey. Let's not ruin the game before it starts.'

'I'm not playing,' she said, wishing she didn't sound like a twelve year old.

With a knowing smirk, Sterling grabbed her peach silk blouse and ripped it down the front of her chest. Beautiful mother-of-pearl buttons scattered across the carpet and rolled under the leather couch. The shirt hung open. She wore no bra. Patrick hadn't left one for her this morning. Sterling's face darkened when he saw the tiny gold leaves that dangled from her nipples. He didn't seem to appreciate the wonderful Indian craftsmanship or the showy hardness of her flesh. 'Where,' he said in a voice like frozen steel, 'are the rings I gave you?'

Ice slithered down Audrey's nape. 'I took them off.'

His hand flashed to her throat, not quite strangling her but forcing her to her toes. 'You took them off?'

Despite her terror, Audrey couldn't imagine why

this surprised him. 'Yes, I took them off. I left you, Sterling. Why would I want to keep your gifts?'

His eyes narrowed. The grey glare that had once made her melt now left her utterly cold. A bracing flare of anger surged through her veins. Ignoring the fist at her throat, she gave him a glare of her own. Unfortunately, it did not sway him an inch.

'It's time,' he said, 'to remind you of what you've been missing.'

'As if,' she scoffed, but her scorn failed to dent his ego. Evidently, Sterling could not conceive of being replaced. He nodded to the two silent hulks. They propped the door back in place, then advanced on her. Audrey tightened her jaw. 'If they touch me, I'll scream.'

Sterling chuckled. 'Scream all you want, little whore. This floor is remarkably well sound-proofed.'

She screamed anyway, though she felt foolish. She could have saved her breath. No one came. No one heard. Sterling's men carried her up to the second level, one on either side. Their huge ham-like hands dug into her armpits. She wished she'd worn shoes. Her frenzied kicks didn't have any more effect than her screams. 'You're acting like a crazy person,' she yelled back at Sterling. 'I do not want this. I'm not consenting. Do you hear me? I am not consenting!'

Sterling ignored her. 'Find the bartender's room,' he said. 'I want to take her in her lover's bed.'

An involuntary snort burst from Audrey's nose. She knew laughing was the last thing she should do, but she couldn't help it. Patrick always took her in her bed, never in his. As a territorial gesture, this one was a bust.

As she'd expected, Sterling did not appreciate her reaction. His hand clamped on the back of her neck. 'You find this amusing, little whore?'

Audrey shook her head and forced a hysterical

234

giggle back down her throat. 'Please,' she said, struggling to convey her sincerity. 'I'm really not interested in you any more. You ought to let me go.'

She might as well have been talking to the cat. Newton sometimes listened. At Sterling's direction, the goons wrangled her face down on the bed. They dug their knees into her legs so she couldn't kick. It was not an imprisonment she enjoyed – not that Sterling noticed. He was too busy yanking Patrick's key from her waist. Its loss made her cry out as nothing had before. He flung the chain into a corner.

'You're my creation,' he said. 'I'll always be the centre of your thoughts.' With the same mind-boggling assurance, he lashed her wrists to Patrick's ornate iron headboard. 'I know it's been hard on you, a woman of your nature being without your master for so long: but, rest assured, you won't be suffering much longer. I've forgiven you, you see, and I'm prepared to give you another chance.'

Audrey tugged at the coarse ropes that bound her to the bed. 'I don't want another chance. I don't want you.' To no avail, she tried to wriggle away from the meaty hands that were stripping her trousers down her legs. The goons were as oblivious to her protests as Sterling. In moments she was naked, wrists bound, belly propped on a pillow, chest tight with a laugh that would probably send this lunatic over the edge.

Sterling rubbed his hands together like a villain from a silent film. 'Remember,' he said. 'Your master knows what you want.'

It was too much. The laugh broke from her just as Sterling's palm struck her bottom. Once loosed, she could not get the outburst under control. The harder he hit her, the louder she laughed. The hired muscle must have thought she'd lost her mind. They gripped her ankles as they would a dangerous beast's. That struck her as funny, too. Tears of amusement rolled down her cheeks.

'I am your master,' Sterling insisted, infuriated by her response. 'I know what you want!'

Audrey wailed hilariously.

'Ahem,' said a laconic voice from the direction of the door. 'Am I interrupting something?'

'Basil,' Audrey gasped, craning around to see him, her body shaken by humorous aftershocks. 'Would you please, please tell this man I'm very happy with my current partner.'

'Deliriously,' Basil obliged. He crossed his arms over a tight black T-shirt. His white jeans were equally snug, clearly delineating his private assets. For the first time since she'd met him, he looked as gay as gay could be.

Sterling was not intimidated by his defence. 'Audrey,' he pronounced, 'will never be happy without an iron hand and a ready whip. Your lover is not equipped to give her what she needs.'

'Nonsense,' Basil said. 'There's nothing wrong with Patrick's whip hand. I gather it's a bit more sophisticated than yours, but quite potent, I assure you. Personally –' he inclined his head towards the reddened flesh of Audrey's bottom '– I always thought welts showed a lack of restraint. If you can't master a slave without bruising her, how effective can you be?'

This, at last, seemed to cut through Sterling's disdain. He took two threatening steps towards Basil's lounging post. 'You're saying Patrick Dugan is a dom? To both of you?'

'Now you're catching on.' Basil pursed his lips in disapproval. 'Honestly, you might have done a bit more research before you entrusted little Audrey to his care.'

'I did plenty of research,' Sterling spluttered. 'I'm

known for my research. I – You're lying. She put you up to this, didn't she? This is all a game.'

Basil examined his perfectly manicured nails. 'I can show you where he keeps his toys, if you like.'

'He's been mastering her?'

'Quite, and with a good deal more judgment than you ever showed. Patrick's iron hand is sheathed in a velvet glove. She's bound, but not broken, just as she should be. Face it, Mr Foster, it's time to retire from the field.'

Basil's awareness of his name stole some of the wind from Sterling's sails. He was not, however, prepared to give up without a fight. His eyes thinned down to arctic slits. 'I could make life very uncomfortable for you, Mr Arch. Or should I call you Basha?'

Basil's alter ego was his most precious possession. To hear it threatened with exposure, if only by implication, could not make him happy. Nonetheless, he shrugged off Sterling's salvo. 'Of course you could, and the three of us could make life equally uncomfortable for you. Our friends may not be as rich as yours but, believe me, they get around. Before you start slinging mud, you should ask yourself how many international bankers have your skeletons in their closets.'

Sterling glowered at him, visibly weighing his resolve. Basil responded with a slow Mona Lisa smile. Audrey wanted to clap, but feared it would ruin the effect. She was glad she'd restrained herself, because a moment later Sterling snapped his fingers for the goons to untie her.

'He won't keep you happy for long,' he said as she sat up and rubbed the rope burns on her wrists.

'Maybe not,' she agreed with a ghost of Basil's poise. 'But since you never made me happy at all, he's already leagues ahead of you.'

Miraculously, this left Sterling speechless. He gave

her one last hard look, then retreated with the shreds of his dignity. Audrey was so relieved her head almost floated off her shoulders. It was over. She was free. Whatever did or did not happen with Patrick, from now on, she knew she had limits beyond which she could not be pushed. She might be submissive, but she'd always belong to herself. Once again, thank God, she could trust her own judgment. The victory was sweeter than any she'd ever won.

'Whew,' said Basil as the outer door scraped shut behind the goons. 'Your ex-boyfriends are much more colourful than mine.'

'There,' Patrick said, his voice a balm to her recovering spirits. 'Isn't that better?'

His back was propped against the head of his bed and his long, trousered legs were stretched out. He'd laid Audrey crosswise over his lap and was smoothing tea tree oil into her buttocks. The last of her pain faded beneath his touch.

Humming with pleasure, she studied his room through heavy eyes. This was the first good look she'd taken since Sterling's men had dragged her up here. The decor was more dramatic than she'd expected. The walls were emerald, like the hills of Erin, she supposed. Black and gold tapestry draped the picture window, a good match for the Chinese bureau and the medieval-looking chairs. His bed's black iron frame was forged into heraldic figures, foremost of which were rampant lions. Looking strangely jaunty, her broken waist chain hung around one mane. Taken together, the room was as exotic as the concubine's nest he'd arranged for her downstairs. She was glad she hadn't noticed her surroundings earlier. They might have put her in a sensual mood and spoilt Sterling's rout. Egos like his didn't need much encouragement.

Focused on his task, Patrick worked his strong, warm hand into the curve between her thighs. The intimacy seemed casual, but not completely so. Heat rose from the basket of his groin, pressed now into her lower belly. He wasn't hard, but she thought he might be swollen. 'I'm sorry I wasn't here when you needed me,' he said. 'Your safety means more to me than I can say.'

His words were as soothing as his touch. Audrey wriggled and closed her eyes. 'I don't understand how he got here so quickly. You didn't even speak to your father until this morning.'

His oiled palm slid up the channel of her spine. 'Father's investigator has solved that mystery. I sent him the nipple ornaments Sterling gave you. I don't know why, but something about them struck me as odd: the weight, the choice of metal. It seems they were tiny transmitters. When you took them off, he must have realised he wouldn't be able to pinpoint your movements any more. I imagine he panicked.'

Audrey lifted her head. 'He was tracking me? Electronically?'

'Apparently, he didn't trust the watcher he'd hired not to lose you.'

'How bizarre.' She shivered and laid back down. 'You must think I'm an idiot to have got mixed up with a nutcase like that.'

'I don't know that he qualifies as a nutcase, though he's certainly controlling.'

'Not to mention delusional.'

Patrick's stroking hesitated, then continued in a figure of eight around her shoulder blades. 'Basil tells me you laughed him out of the flat.'

Audrey chuckled. 'I didn't plan to, but that part was kind of fun.'

'So you're certain you won't miss him?'

She twisted around to see his face. His expression

was guarded, but she thought she read a hint of unsureness in it. Her heart clenched. Of all people, Patrick was the last with any cause for insecurity. Of course, knowing she could inspire it was a kick. 'Patrick,' she said, very clearly. 'I will not miss Sterling Foster. I stopped missing him the day I met you and, having met you, I'll never miss him again. You, my dear, have forever raised the bar.'

Colour flooded his face. 'Well. That's . . . that's very nice to hear.'

'I am not being nice,' she said sternly, though his blush delighted her. She tugged his tie until his mouth covered hers.

The kiss was deep and sweet. He did not try to own it, but its progress was definitely more in his control than hers. One big hand pressed the plain of skin between her shoulder blades; the other circled her hip. The position tipped her breasts against the warm, smooth cotton of his shirt. She loved being naked when he was fully clothed. The contrast made her feel vulnerable, as did the slow stab and draw of his tongue. His cock grew rigid beneath her hip, but when moans rose from her throat, he drew away. 'What about Tommy?'

He was flinching, as if in anticipation of a blow. Audrey marshalled her will. If he intended to separate her and Tommy, this relationship was over. On that she would not bend. 'I won't have to miss Tommy,' she said, surprising herself with the firmness of the declaration. 'Tommy will always be my friend.'

He cupped her face, his eyes so sad she wanted to promise whatever he asked. 'I'd never try to keep you from your friends. That's not the way I operate. I'm glad you've worked things out between you. I know you'd miss Tommy if you couldn't see him. I suppose I should have said, do you think you could come to consider me your friend as well?'

Oh, that he could ask such a thing! She covered the hand that cupped her cheek and met his gaze head on. 'Tommy will never be to me what you are and, perhaps, you'll never be to me what he is. But, yes, I believe we could be friends. In fact, it would mean more to me than you can imagine.'

He smiled, a beatific, boyish grin. 'I wouldn't bet on that, lassie.'

A tingling warmth crept up her breasts. Despite her embarassment, she was utterly, ridiculously happy. Her entire body was buoyant with it. He wanted her friendship. It seemed more extraordinary, more precious, than if he'd said he wanted her love.

He'd unravelled the first few inches of her present's bow.

'Yes, well.' She rubbed the powerful tendon at his wrist, still squirming beneath his thousand-watt smile. 'Speaking of friends . . .'

'Yes, sweetheart?'

The endearment drew more heat to her cheeks. She slid her hand down his forearm. 'Speaking of friends, Basil was a good one today. I might have laughed Sterling out of the flat, but Basil barred the meta-phorical door behind him. He convinced Sterling you were such a good dom you'd mastered us both.'

'Is that so?'

Fighting amusement, Audrey patted his bicep. 'I'm sure you could have mastered us both if you wanted to. My point is, we owe him.'

'*We* owe him.' The glint in his eye had shifted towards suspicion.

Audrey set her grin free. 'What could mean more to Basil than a thank you gift from both of us?'

'Oh, Lord,' Patrick groaned. 'Tell me you're think-ing of a watch.'

\* \* \*

Basil's farewell dinner went well, mostly because Audrey bought everything prepared and Patrick supplied a delicious beaujolais. The microwave didn't ruin the shrimp or the saffron rice. Of course, Basil was so flattered to be feted, she could have served spaghetti from a can and he'd have enjoyed it.

As it was, he exclaimed over everything: Patrick's fancy place settings, the way they'd both dressed up, the gift certificate for the spa they'd chipped in to buy him. He looked happier than she could remember seeing him since they'd met. Basil, she decided, was a man who needed to be fussed over now and then.

She was deviously glad there was even more fussing to come.

At last, Basil dropped his dessert spoon into his bowl and collapsed in his chair. 'That was fabulous. Thank you very much, both of you.' He dabbed his mouth, employing the androgenous grace she'd grown so fond of. 'So tell me, Audrey, how did your meeting with Patrick's father go?'

'Terrifying. I was shaking in my shoes.'

Patrick flicked her shoulder with his napkin. 'Liar. You had the old reprobate eating out of your hand.'

Audrey giggled. 'I did, didn't I?' She fluffed her hair. 'I think he was taken by my youthful charms.'

'That's one euphemism for it,' Patrick grumbled. Audrey wasn't fooled. She knew his father's approval meant a lot to him, especially since Patrick thought he'd let him down by cutting their masquerade short. For his part, the senator had waved Patrick's worries away. 'Let the bastard do what he likes,' he'd said. 'Audrey is safe. That's all that matters now.' He didn't come out and say so, but Audrey got the distinct impression Sterling's threats had never concerned him.

The senator was a deep one, deeper perhaps than Patrick knew. He didn't seem to realise events had fallen out precisely as his father wished. On the one occasion when his son left the room, the senator had questioned her very closely. He'd wanted to know if she was interested in the S&M party scene the way Patrick had been before he met her. When she said she wasn't, he seemed relieved. Audrey deduced that, while he might not mind his son being a dom, he preferred that he settle down and play in private. She couldn't be sure, but she suspected he'd been match-making when he threw them together.

She hadn't decided yet whether to share her suspicions with Patrick. Lips curling with secret enjoyment, she turned her wine glass in a circle. Maybe she'd tell him when the outcome became clearer.

'So you got on,' Basil said, breaking into her thoughts.

Audrey chuckled. 'My, yes. When I told him I was applying to business schools, he practically threatened to bribe a trustee to get me in.'

'"Practically" being the operative word,' Patrick added.

'You'll be accepted,' Basil assured her, 'and when you graduate and open your shop, I hope you'll promise to carry my size.'

'Always.' She leapt up to hug him. 'You'll be my number one customer.' Basil hugged her back, then rose to clear the dishes. Audrey pressed him into his seat. 'No work for you. You're the guest of honour. You might want to freshen up, though. Patrick and I have one more present for you and it could take a little time.'

He turned a wide-eyed gaze from her to her lover. 'Another present?'

Audrey had to hand it to Patrick. He neither rolled his eyes nor winced. 'Yes, indeed,' he said. 'So fasten your seat belt, lad. It's going to be a bumpy night.'

\* \* \*

Patrick carried the toys to the second floor. Audrey had insisted Basil would find his bedroom the most exciting. Obviously, she was correct because their guest boasted a fine erection by the time he arrived in his distinguished burgundy smoking robe. Watching the silk bob and lift, Patrick realised he'd never seen Basil's cock without a covering. Their long pretence must have lessened his aversion. The knowledge that he finally would see his prick, and soon, sent blood rushing to his groin.

The singer paused at the door. He blinked at Audrey's leather corset. Patrick had chosen it, of course. Her beautiful breasts spilt over the top, glittering with gold, thrust up and out by the garment's custom frame. Her hair poured in glossy waves to her waist. Fishnet stockings stretched up her shapely legs. Her feet were slipped into shiny black heels just low enough to walk in. She was a baby dominatrix, thoroughly adorable, a mistress one would obey only from affection. Fortunately, Audrey inspired plenty of that.

'My, my,' Basil said, smoothing one lapel down the greyhound rise of his chest.

Audrey held a wooden paddle. She swept it to encompass the room. 'Welcome to our parlour, Mr Arch.'

'Already I like this present.' Basil stepped forward, then paused when Patrick's costume caught his eye. He wore black leather trousers, a loose shirt in blazing white silk, and a small black mask. In his hand he held the companion to Audrey's paddle, a worn leather quirt. Basil shuddered. 'You're not going to hurt me, are you?'

Patrick was pleased to hear a note of intrigue beneath his fear. 'If I'm going to fuck my first man,' he said, 'you're going to get your first spanking.'

'You're going to fuck me?' Basil's eyes were saucers. 'Good Lord.'

Patrick smiled, aware that the mask turned the expression sinister. He was surprised to be enjoying this so much, but Basil's shock was delicious. 'I know I'm a big man, Basil, but I think you can take me. I've been practising on Audrey. She says my technique is very sensitive.' Appealed to for agreement, Audrey nodded and wagged her brows. 'If you still have doubts, you can end this any time. Just say the word.'

'The word?'

'Your safe-word is "velvet".' Patrick began to circle their prey. 'Say it any time you want to stop. You can say it now, if you like.'

'No, no.' An involuntary shiver chattered Basil's teeth. 'By all means, bring on the big guns.'

His gaze slid to the bulge at Patrick's crotch, leaving no doubt as to which big gun he craved. Patrick should have been offended but he wasn't. He put his lips to Basil's ear. 'Since you're an S&M virgin, we'll let Audrey warm you up.'

At his signal, Audrey stalked to Basil's front. She pointed imperiously with her paddle. 'Remove that robe. We want to see what you've got, little man.'

Basil's compliance revealed a lean, pale body and a world-class set of buns. Patrick's palms itched to test them. Small and tightly muscled, each cheek was no more than a handful. In opposition to, but hardly lessening their charm, his cock jutted forward from a nest of trimmed brown curls. The strut and head were dramatically darker than the rest. An erection so emphatic could not fail to please his mistress. Basil's attitude, however, assuredly could.

Audrey was far too sharp-eyed to miss the crinkling of amusement around the singer's eyes. 'Smile all you want,' she warned, 'and we'll see who smiles the next time you try to sit down.'

She backed up her threat with four sharp thwacks of her paddle, two for each of his pristine cheeks. The blows were harder than Patrick expected. A pink glow suffused the virginal skin. The sight dried Patrick's mouth. He'd seen other doms work before, but something about watching his own submissive playing top made his nerves squirm under his skin.

Basil was squirming, too. 'Good Lord,' he exclaimed. He had just enough self-control not to reach back and rub his injured flesh.

Audrey dragged the edge of the paddle up his crack. 'Want more?' she purred. 'Or perhaps you'd prefer the flat of my hand.'

'Yes,' he said, gone somewhat breathy at the unexpected probing of his arse. 'I would prefer your hand.'

'Hah!' Audrey barked and gave him four more smacks with the paddle.

Basil spluttered in astonishment, his face pink, his erection lurching down and then up as he struggled to process this unusual stimulation. In the end, his cock remained up, even higher than before. Seeing this, Audrey tossed the paddle on the bed and moved to his side. Her arm swung down and clamped noisily on to his buttock.

'Nice and warm in back,' she said and gave his cheek a squeeze. Her other hand gripped the base of his shaft and dragged upward so forcefully Patrick saw veins stretch under the skin. 'And nice and hard in front. That's the way a man should be. Ready for anything with anyone.'

Basil's lips moved, but nothing intelligible came out, just high, garbled sounds. Audrey knelt before him to examine his cock at microscopic range. Patrick hadn't thought she could be so bold. He found himself leaning closer, his own cock shoving at the placket of his trousers, so heavy and so sensitised it felt like a separate being. He was sweating, he knew, but that

246

wasn't the only moisture running into the supple cloth.

'Ah,' she said, her nose an inch from Basil's glans. 'I see you're not circumcised. How convenient.' Her fingers toyed with the wrinkled skin, forcing it back over the head, using it to polish the reddened dome. Basil moaned as two sets of nerves played pleasurably off each other. Patrick wondered where she'd learnt the trick, then could think no more. Basil's shaft, already straining, stretched and thickened as she played. His glans swelled like some oily, carnal fruit. Clearly delighted, Audrey squeezed the flesh around his narrow eye. Basil gasped out a curse. Audrey laughed, dark and full of promise, then dug something shiny from the front of her corset. It was a clip-on earring, a silver hoop with a screwing back. She slipped it around the top of Basil's foreskin and began to fasten it down.

'You liked my piercings so much,' she said. 'I thought you'd enjoy seeing how you'd look with one of your own.'

Basil groaned and huffed as she completed the task. When she released the hoop, it clung tightly to his foreskin, sliding back over his glans as the skin retracted. The bauble came to a halt on his upper ridge. It was a slave's ring, a primitive mark of ownership. Basil couldn't seem to look away from it. The glitter of sweat joined the flush on his brow.

'So pretty,' she said. She drew one finger from the base of his balls to the flare at the bottom of his glans. A bead of pre-come welled in the mouth of his slit, clear and pearl-sized. 'I think you're ready for the master now.'

Patrick had been so engrossed in the drama she'd enacted, his heart jumped at the passing of the torch. 'Yes,' he said, pulling his composure into place. 'You do look ready to me.'

The quirt was not a sensation to be taken alone, not the first time it was administered. It required distraction, and preparation. Consequently, he began by caressing Basil's buttocks. As he'd expected, they were hard as steel and rose-petal smooth. He lingered over the curves; probed lightly between them. When his finger grazed the anal crease, Basil pressed his lips so tightly together they whitened. Presumably, he was afraid of seeming too enthusiastic. Experience had proven how easy Patrick was to spook.

But what sort of master would he be if he condoned this repression of response? Smiling to himself and more aroused than he would have thought possible, he knelt to kiss the small of Basil's back. His spine was knobby but beautiful. Patrick drew his hands up the front of Basil's legs. Their skin had been shaven smooth but their muscles were well-developed. Basil's breath hitched as he reached his inner thigh, almost, but not quite touching his balls.

'Don't hold back,' Patrick said. 'I want to hear what you're feeling. All the moans. All the sighs.' His fingers stroked the light hair that curled around Basil's scrotum. His testicles were plump and hot and hard to the touch. They twitched as Patrick rubbed, causing his own balls to pulse in sympathy. Growling, he set his teeth into the curve of Basil's buttock. 'Your pleasure belongs to me. It's as important as your pain.'

Basil sighed, a broken, lengthy sound. It held a surrender that fired Patrick's blood. He stood again and nudged Basil to the side of the bed. Audrey climbed up as they'd agreed. 'Bend over the mattress,' Patrick said, in his softest, darkest voice, 'and put your head in Audrey's lap. You're going to be the first to know how much she enjoys watching you sweat.'

From the gleam in Audrey's eye, she was enjoying

it already. Her skin glowed from breast to brow and she petted Basil's hair while he nuzzled her upper thighs. Red satin suspenders attached her corset to her stockings. Other than that, her lower torso was bare. Basil seemed to like the view. His buttocks, thrust out by his position, alternately clenched and relaxed. He was restless, taut. Patrick knew he'd never be readier than now.

His hand smacked down first, catching the meatiest part of Basil's arse. Then, before the sting could fade, Patrick lashed him with the quirt. Basil went up on his toes.

'Good Lord,' he gasped.

Patrick grinned. What he'd just created was, without question, a singular sensation. The diffuse pain of the spank prepared the recipient to bear the sharper pain of the whip. This allowed him to use the quirt very lightly while still evoking a strong response. Patrick loved strong responses. He hated leaving marks.

'Want another?' he offered, letting Audrey see the laughter in his eyes. Hers danced just as merrily, especially when Basil admitted that, er, well, of course he did.

Patrick gave him a good basting, pinkening his flesh from thighs to waist. His bottom began to dance, both begging more and trying to evade it. His hands fisted in the coverlet by Audrey's hips, crumpling the black and gold satin. Patrick used the quirt more intimately. He smacked it between his cheeks, warming the hairy crinkle of his anus, threatening the tender hang of his balls. As light as his strokes were, the pain would be slight. The vulnerability of the flesh he hit was what gave each lash its power.

Basil was sobbing out little cries, not of pain, but longing. The motions of his hips changed to those of a man humping an imaginary cunt, one he sincerely wished were real. He dragged his face across Audrey's thighs, inhaling her scent, begging silently for aid. Audrey seemed happy to give it.

'It's time,' she said in a husky voice. Basil shuddered from head to toe.

Patrick dropped the quirt. 'I'm taking off my clothes,' he said, 'but you mustn't turn to look.'

Basil whimpered a protest. Naturally, he wanted to see his tormentor's cock, to know his excitement was shared.

'Shall I give him the mirror?' Audrey asked. Patrick nodded and she slid a cloisonné compact from beneath one of the pillows. Basil fumbled it open and studied Patrick's reflection. Since the glass was magnified, his view was good. Even more importantly, the mirror enabled Basil to ogle whatever he chose without feeling as if Patrick were watching him, and perhaps taking offence.

Audrey had devised the method. Patrick had to admit it was a stroke of psychological genius. With the relish of a peeping Tom, Basil quivered as Patrick undid the buttons of his shirt. Bit by bit, he shrugged the silk over his shoulders. He did not hurry the striptease, though he was more self-conscious than he would have been with Audrey alone. Feeling half foolish, half vain, he ran his hands over his chest. He ruffled the thick hair; massaged the aching nipples. He tightened his muscles until each stood out in sharp relief. The pressure behind his zip grew heavy. It begged to be touched; demanded to be rubbed. Basil sighed as his hand cruised towards his crotch. Giving in to the irresistible urge, Patrick stroked himself with the heel of his palm, fingers spread to squeeze his balls at the bottom of the push.

This time the sigh he heard was Audrey's. 'Pull down your zip,' she said. 'Show him how beautiful you are.'

Careful not to catch his flesh, Patrick lowered the metal tab. His cock was too long to spring free so he lifted it out with both hands. He stroked his length, thumb and fingers sliding up either side. His erection hardly needed help, but he knew his audience would appreciate the further engorgement of his sex. Already Audrey was breathing through her mouth. As for Basil, the mirror flashed with his jerks of excitement. He was so beside himself he couldn't keep still. Suddenly Patrick felt immense, god-like. His penis throbbed in his hands, his pleasure doubled by the eyes that drank it in. Heat gathered in his balls. Knowing he had to slow down, he stopped rubbing himself and pushed his trousers down his legs. He stepped clear and kicked the leather away. Now all he wore was the mask. This, he suspected, Audrey had chosen for his benefit, to free him from the last of his inhibitions. It certainly seemed to. He wanted what was coming, wanted it so badly he hurt.

Audrey unwrapped a condom and handed it over on the tips of her fingers. It was thicker than his usual, and lubricated. He rolled it down and snapped the base into place. Anticipation cascaded along his nerves, a little fear, but more desire. He reached for the small blue pot Audrey held. 'This is Audrey's favourite,' he said, scooping out a dollop of cream. 'We've tested quite a few. She says this one stays nice and slippery, no matter how long and hard one thrusts.'

Beyond speech, Basil made a sound like kittens mewing. Patrick braced one arm on the mattress and spread the dollop around Basil's anus. His cry rose half an octave, then changed to a gasp as Patrick pushed the cream inside. 'Sensitive, are you? I like that.'

He worked his fingers deeper, getting a feel for Basil's size and conformation. His sphincter muscle was strong but agile. It gaped and clutched with each insertion. Patrick noticed he was holding Audrey's hands now rather than the covers. Both their knuckles were white. That was good, but he wanted Basil as aroused as he could be. Taking a breath for courage, he reached around and grasped the other man's cock.

Basil moaned like a dying man. 'Yes,' he said, his head falling back. 'Oh, yes.'

Patrick's greasy fingers slid easily up his shaft, as easily as if he'd been wanking himself. Basil, however, had one thing Patrick didn't. His foreskin was as soft as Audrey's hood, and as useful for rubbing sweet spots. The ring she'd clipped to it trembled with Basil's pulse. How wonderful, Patrick thought, surprising himself. He let the skin retract and continued to explore. His mind marked the differences between them: girth, length, the patterning of their veins. Basil was marvellously responsive. His shaft leapt with each pulling squeeze. His knob was satin smooth, swollen to the limits of its skin. The eye dripped pre-come over his fingers as he stroked, a rich, slippery flow. The response was familiar, but the fact that the cock wasn't his drove the sorcery home anew. He would have continued for some time if he hadn't feared Basil would come. His balls were very tight, his breathing ragged.

'Ready to take me?' he asked, his own voice rough.

In answer, Basil moaned and thrust his buttocks upward.

Patrick's blood pumped harder. He spread Basil's cheeks and braced his feet. He positioned his hips. Only the first bit was hard, when he pressed his broad tip against that male, hair-prickled star. His cock didn't care, though. His cock just wanted in.

'Push,' Basil urged, one hand fumbling back for his thigh. 'You're driving me insane.'

Patrick gritted his teeth and pushed. Resistance

stretched the skin of his glans. He worked half way in, then stopped, his hands clasped lightly at Basil's waist. His passage was hot and close. It throbbed around Patrick's cock, or perhaps Patrick's cock throbbed into it. A sense of comfort enveloped his groin, pleasure overlaid with a strong itch of impatience. But impatience would not pay, not here, not now. Forcing himself not to rush, he pressed carefully to his root. His sense of urgency increased. The swell of Basil's prostate was neatly lodged beneath his glans. The hard almond swell was unmistakeable, a prod to his most sensitive flesh.

Basil squirmed, rubbing the two surfaces together. 'You,' he sighed, 'are an absolute perfect fit.'

It was true on the outside as well. Patrick barely had to bend his knees to take him. He sighed himself, and it was only partly relief at clearing the hurdle of entry.

With a fond smile, Audrey stroked his hair. 'Shall I ask him now?'

'Ask me what?' Basil huffed.

'If you'd like to take me while Patrick is taking you.'

Basil's head was turned to the side on Audrey's thigh. His eyelids wrinkled as he closed them, forced from smoothness by the stress of too much need. 'Yes,' he said, barely able to get the words out. 'I'd like that very much.'

Patrick's bed was high, waist-level for Basil. Patrick bumped him forward as Audrey spread her thighs. Her musk rose from lush, rosy flesh. Her clit was plump and raised, her lips sticky with arousal. Patrick was almost as aroused as if he were going to thrust inside her himself.

'Let's get this off you first,' she said, and removed the ring she'd fastened to Basil's cock. 'We wouldn't want you to lose it.' Basil chuckled, then jerked. Her

253

hands had remained between them. Patrick suspected she was playing with his foreskin again, because Basil's anus clenched and his pulse abruptly spiked. The beat of his blood tapped Patrick's cock like summer rain, a delicious, hidden stimulation. Audrey reached for the packet she'd stowed beneath the pillow. With a grin, she tore it open and rolled a thin latex sheath down Basil's shaft.

'Thank you,' Basil said, breathy and playful. 'You know I like being dressed by a lady.'

He kissed her, then slid inside with a throaty moan. Audrey's fingers speared his hair. Wanting to get closer, Patrick spooned Basil's back. He could hear their mouths moving together, the wet click of their tongues. The effect was strange but not unpleasant. He was both voyeur and participant. Planting his elbows immediately outside Basil's, he blew in the other man's ear. Basil laughed and reached for his hip. 'My pace,' he said. 'You two have been in charge long enough.'

Patrick knew Basil wouldn't want to end this quickly, but his self-control astonished him nonetheless. Each time he neared completion, he slowed. Each time he caught his breath, he quickened. Audrey was soon pink in the face from trying to delay her orgasm.

'No, no, no,' Basil scolded. 'There's no need for you to wait.' He squeezed one hand between them, working it towards her mound. A moment later, she convulsed with a protracted cry. As she shook, Basil dropped kisses to her brow. 'That's the way. You feel lovely when you come. It's like a hand squeezing up and down my cock.'

Patrick could have said the same of Basil's anus. The man had amazing muscular control. Not sure he could hold off much longer, he focused the force of his thrusts against the swell of Basil's prostate. Basil stiffened.

'Demon,' he said, trembling under the erotic barrage. His thrusts strengthened and his head rolled on his neck. Then, when Patrick was sure he had him, he slowed.

Patrick tapped Audrey's cheek. 'Do something,' he ordered. 'I am not going over alone.'

Audrey laughed and set her mouth to Basil's nipples. Basil did not speed up, but he did push more forcefully with his hips. The fervent swivel massaged Patrick's cock. He groaned. He couldn't stand it. He was going to bust. Audrey's hands slipped up the singer's leanly muscled back, then squeezed Patrick's shoulder. 'Touch him with me,' she said. 'That will get him.'

In desperation, Patrick touched him. He stroked Basil's straining thighs. He squeezed Basil's clenching buttocks. He trailed his fingertips over his ribs and cupped his twitching groin. And all the while he drubbed his deepest pleasure point, strafing his own sweet spot over the tiny swell, over and over, until his cock screamed for release. Basil swore but Patrick could not understand the words, could barely hear them over the thunder of his blood. He was going to come. He felt the rising pressure, the heat, the upward squeeze of his balls. Audrey's legs rose, hugging them both. Sweat rolled down her calves. He forgot finesse and simply thrust into the body that held him. His belly slapped Basil's arse. His hands clamped his hips. He was jarring Basil into Audrey and Basil was churning like a madman. The sound was incredible: three sweaty bodies, two slippery cocks, sheets rustling, weight thumping the mattress in a rising panic of lust.

Images flashed through his mind. He saw Basil sucking him off in the kitchen, Audrey humping the purple dildo, the earring shining at the end of Basil's foreskin, all tightening his nerves like thumbscrews. He couldn't bear it. His cock stiffened; jabbed.

'Now,' Basil groaned.

Audrey cried out, falling over the brink with Basil. Abruptly, every muscle in Patrick's body seized, locking him deep inside Basil's arse. His consciousness blurred beneath the flaming gush of pleasure. On and on it went, hot pulses of relief. Wetness pooled at the head of the condom until his cock swam in its seed.

'Oh, my,' Basil sighed. 'Oh, my, my, my.'

The words repeated in Patrick's head. My, my, my. The world held more surprises than he'd known. Reluctantly, he pulled free and helped Basil stand.

'Uh-oh,' Audrey warned. 'Don't look now, but someone's been watching us.'

Alarmed, Patrick glanced behind him.

'Meow,' said Newton from the window ledge, as pert and proud as if he'd discovered the North Pole. Obviously, closed doors were no longer proof against him.

'Beast,' said Patrick.

With a show of nonchalance, Newton licked his front paw.

Basil snorted in amusement. 'You know, Patrick,' he said. 'I think I'd better leave that cat with you. He's far too pervy for me.'

The moon rose on their contentment. Barely dressed, Patrick and Audrey shared a lounger by the pool. He nursed a whiskey while Newton chased windblown rose petals across the bricks. Watching him, Audrey felt like a proud parent. She suspected Patrick did, too. He seemed as pleased by Basil giving them the cat as she was.

Weary, but too comfortable to suggest going to bed, she slid her hand down his muscular belly, wriggled it under his boxers, and cupped his flaccid sex. Patrick grunted and let his legs loll wider. She curled her fingers around the weighty shaft, his skin cool and silky smooth.

Mine, she thought, though she wasn't worried.

They'd made love again after Basil left, in the shower with her shoved up against the tiles. The upstairs bathroom was all black, as black as Patrick's hair, as shiny as Patrick's eyes. He'd taken her roughly, passionately; as reassurance, she thought, for both of them. He'd gone as deep as he could go, then struggled to shove deeper yet. 'This is the centre,' he'd said, thick and hard inside her, his fingers stretching around her bottom to touch the place they met. 'This comes first. Everything else has to circle outside.'

'Yes,' she'd said, clutching his shoulders, kissing his throat. 'This comes first.'

Which didn't mean he hadn't enjoyed his homo-erotic foray, or that he shouldn't, conceivably, enjoy another.

'Tonight was fun,' she said with all the innocence she could muster. 'We should have Basil over again.'

Patrick hummed his agreement into her hair, then stiffened. 'You mean have Basil over for dinner, right?'

'Whatever,' she said, and stifled her giggle against his chest.

'Maybe we ought to invite Tommy and his little friend Cynthia over, too.'

Audrey gave his cock a friendly squeeze. 'Been there, done that.'

'What!'

Patrick sounded so shocked her laugh came out whole. 'Had him. Had her. Then had them both together.'

'When did this happen? No. Don't tell me.' His

voice dropped to a threatening bass. 'I'll enjoy beating the story out of you more.'

I'm sure you will, she thought. Then again, she was bound to enjoy it, too.

As if he knew why she was squirming, he saluted her with his glass. '*Sláinte*, my love,' he said, and kissed her smiling mouth.

' "My love"?' she repeated, one brow raised.

'My love,' he insisted, as if expecting contradiction.

He wouldn't get it from her, not in this lifetime. She snuggled closer. His cock was swelling in her hand, stiffening as if it, too, were determined to press his case. She would let him press it, of course, until the words came easily, and the trust, and the faith that what they felt would last.

This, after all, was a master she could keep.

# BLACK LACE NEW BOOKS

*Published in October*

## THE TIES THAT BIND
### Tesni Morgan
### £5.99

Kim Buckley is a beautiful but shy young woman who is married to a wealthy business consultant. When a charismatic young stranger dressed as the devil turns up at their Halloween party, Kim's life is set to change for ever. Claiming to be her lost half-brother, he's got his eye on her money and a gameplan for revenge. Things are further complicated by their mutual sexual attraction and a sizzling combination of secret and guilty passions threatens to overwhelm them.

ISBN 0 352 33438 X

## IN THE DARK
### Zoe le Verdier
### £5.99

This second collection of Zoe's erotic short stories explores the most explicit female desires. There's something here for every reader who likes their erotica hot and a little bit rare. From anonymous sex to exhibitionism, phone sex and rubber fetishism, all these stories have great characterisation and a sting in the tail.

ISBN 0 352 33439 8

*Published in November*

## VELVET GLOVE
### Emma Holly
### £5.99

Audrey is an SM Goldilocks in search of the perfect master. Her first choice is far too cruel. Her second too tender. When she meets Patrick – a charismatic bar owner – he seems just right. But can she trust the man behind the charm, or will he drag her deeper into submission than she's prepared to go?

ISBN 0 352 33448 7

## BOUND BY CONTRACT
### Helena Ravenscroft
#### £5.99

Samantha Bentley and her cousin Ross have been an illicit item for
years. When Ross becomes involved with the submissive Dr Louisa,
Sam senses that Ross's true passions aren't compatible with her own
domineering ways. Then she reads the classic novel *Venus in Furs*,
which inspires her to experiment with being his slave for a month.
When Dr Louisa shows up at Ross's country hideaway, there are
surprising shifts in their ritual games of power and punishment.

ISBN 0 352 33447 9

*To be published in December*

## STRIPPED TO THE BONE
### Jasmine Stone
#### £5.99

Annie is a fun-loving free-thinking American woman who sets herself
the mission of changing everything in her life. The only snag is she
doesn't know when to stop changing things. Every man she meets is
determined to find out what makes her tick, but her wild personality
means no one can get a hold on her. Her sexual magnetism is
electrifying, and her capacity for unusual and experimental sex-play
has her loves in a spin of erotic confusion.

ISBN 0 352 33463 0

## THE BEST OF BLACK LACE
### Ed. Kerri Sharp
#### £5.99

This diverse collection of sizzling erotica is an 'editor's choice' of
extracts from Black Lace books with a contemporary theme. The accent
is on female characters who know what they want in bed – and in the
workplace – and who have a sense of adventure above and beyond
the heroines of romantic fiction. These girls kick ass!

ISBN 0 352 33452 5

If you would like a complete list of plot summaries of
Black Lace titles, or would like to receive information on
other publications available, please send a stamped
addressed envelope to:

Black Lace, Thames Wharf Studios,
Rainville Road, London W6 9HA

# BLACK LACE BOOKLIST

All books are priced £4.99 unless another price is given.

**Black Lace books with a contemporary setting**

| | | |
|---|---|---|
| PALAZZO | Jan Smith<br>ISBN 0 352 33156 9 | ☐ |
| THE GALLERY | Fredrica Alleyn<br>ISBN 0 352 33148 8 | ☐ |
| AVENGING ANGELS | Roxanne Carr<br>ISBN 0 352 33147 X | ☐ |
| COUNTRY MATTERS | Tesni Morgan<br>ISBN 0 352 33174 7 | ☐ |
| GINGER ROOT | Robyn Russell<br>ISBN 0 352 33152 6 | ☐ |
| DANGEROUS CONSEQUENCES | Pamela Rochford<br>ISBN 0 352 33185 2 | ☐ |
| THE NAME OF AN ANGEL<br>£6.99 | Laura Thornton<br>ISBN 0 352 33205 0 | ☐ |
| BONDED | Fleur Reynolds<br>ISBN 0 352 33192 5 | ☐ |
| CONTEST OF WILLS<br>£5.99 | Louisa Francis<br>ISBN 0 352 33223 9 | ☐ |
| THE SUCCUBUS<br>£5.99 | Zoe le Verdier<br>ISBN 0 352 33230 1 | ☐ |
| FEMININE WILES<br>£7.99 | Karina Moore<br>ISBN 0 352 33235 2 | ☐ |
| AN ACT OF LOVE<br>£5.99 | Ella Broussard<br>ISBN 0 352 33240 9 | ☐ |
| DRAMATIC AFFAIRS<br>£5.99 | Fredrica Alleyn<br>ISBN 0 352 33289 1 | ☐ |
| DARK OBSESSION<br>£7.99 | Fredrica Alleyn<br>ISBN 0 352 33281 6 | ☐ |
| COOKING UP A STORM<br>£7.99 | Emma Holly<br>ISBN 0 352 33258 1 | ☐ |
| SEARCHING FOR VENUS<br>£5.99 | Ella Broussard<br>ISBN 0 352 33284 0 | ☐ |
| A SECRET PLACE<br>£5.99 | Ella Broussard<br>ISBN 0 352 33307 3 | ☐ |

-------✂------------------------

Please send me the books I have ticked above.

Name        ...................................................................

Address     ...................................................................

            ...................................................................

            ...................................................................

            ........................ Post Code ........................

Send to: **Cash Sales, Black Lace Books, Thames Wharf Studios, Rainville Road, London W6 9HA.**

US customers: for prices and details of how to order books for delivery by mail, call 1-800-805-1083.

Please enclose a cheque or postal order, made payable to **Virgin Publishing Ltd**, to the value of the books you have ordered plus postage and packing costs as follows:
    UK and BFPO – £1.00 for the first book, 50p for each subsequent book.
    Overseas (including Republic of Ireland) – £2.00 for the first book, £1.00 for each subsequent book.

If you would prefer to pay by VISA, ACCESS/MASTER-CARD, DINERS CLUB, AMEX or SWITCH, please write your card number and expiry date here:

...................................................................................

Please allow up to 28 days for delivery.

**Signature** ...................................................................

-------✂------------------------